PREFACE

Contemporary philosopher and writer Alain de Botton attributed the root cause of most blighted human lives to the fact that one "is forced to live before one knows how." Such is the case in the life of Rosemary Duncan, orphaned at the age of five and forced to grow up with a debilitating stutter. Rosemary is the daughter of the legendary Australian flying ace and war hero, Charles Curnow Scherf, who having returned without a scratch after WW2, mysteriously dies three years later in a car crash near Emmaville, NSW.

The circumstances and scandal surrounding Scherf's death are hushed up, setting his young daughter up for a life-long search for answers. Raised fatherless on the margins of wealth but cruelly excluded from it, Rosemary is shunted off to live with relatives in another town and never sees her home again. Her mother, Hope, abandoned with four children, too readily accepts the rejection from her dominating in-laws who never considered her "good enough". In exposing the many forms of violence others casually inflict on the disenfranchised,

Rosemary paints a harsh picture of post-war country Australia.

At the centre of this gritty autobiography is the larger-than-life character of Charles Curnow Scherf, whose charismatic energy radiates off the page. Charles' early athletic accomplishments, instincts and confidence are emblematic of the Australian landed class and set him up for spectacular success as a Squadron Leader in the RAF where he mixes effortlessly with British aristocracy and military elite. Expecting to be admired on his return he is undone by the attitude of the small community who resent his status and sass. Scherf is of German origin as well, so must face his inner demons and a spiralling sense of disconnection. A Gatsbyesque collision of worlds ensues and an early tragic death shatters the family and community for years to come.

This is a novel so resonant of the grand Australian classical works,themes and archetypal characters who grapple with their changing fates in a harsh landscape. With scholarly research and an extraordinary ability to get under the skin of her characters, Duncan seeks to understand their contexts, their shortcomings and, more importantly, herself. Ultimately the reader is left with the same feeling one experiences at the end of a Greek or Shakespearean tragedy: that though great damage has been caused, one has learned so much.

— Maureen Bushell M.A. M.Litt. J.D.

**Maureen Bushell is a freelance writer for a range of publishers including Cengage: National Geographic, OUP (Asia), and a former academic, teacher and syllabus evaluator in the fields of Literature and English education.*

THE VIOLENCE OF OTHERS

ROSEMARY DUNCAN

Published in Australia by Sid Harta Books & Print Pty Ltd,
ABN: 34632585293
23 Stirling Crescent, Glen Waverley, Victoria 3150 Australia
Telephone: +61 3 9560 9920, Facsimile: +61 3 9545 1742
E-mail: author@sidharta.com.au

First published in Australia 2022
This edition published 2022
Copyright © Rosemary Duncan 2022
Cover design, typesetting: WorkingType (www.workingtype.com.au)

Rosemary Duncan
The Violence of Others
ISBN: 978-1-925707-94-6

Rosemary Duncan was born in Glen Innes NSW, the daughter of a widowed mother. Coming from a poor background, she saw the chance to better herself through education and, with the aid of a scholarship, entered university at the age of sixteen. After graduating with a B.A., Dip.Ed. in Modern Languages, she went on to complete a M.Litt. in French philosophy and literature. After gaining a scholarship to study in France, she spent her career as Head of Department in secondary schools throughout NSW, QLD and Hong Kong.

Rosemary's father was the highly decorated Squadron Leader Charles Curnow Scherf D.S.O., D.F.C. and bar, one of the six aces of WWII. Upon his return from the war, he was killed in a tragic car accident at the age of thirty-two.

Rosemary now lives on a large rural property on the Granite Belt of Queensland where she continues to write.

The events of the novel are based on the author's experience, research and the recollections of her family. The novel is, above all, a work of literature in which some of the events and conversations relating to real people have been recreated and adapted. By telling the story 'as it needed to be told', it is hoped that a deeper understanding and healing for everyone might be gained.

CONTENTS

PART ONE

THE DAUGHTER

'There will be time, there will be time
To prepare a face to meet the faces that you meet;
There will be time to murder and create,
And time for all the works and days of hands
That lift and drop a question on your plate;
Time for you and time for me...'

The Love Song of J. Alfred Prufrock – *T.S. Eliot*

CHAPTER 1

THE DARKNESS BEGINS

Glen Innes 1949

S oon it would be time for the dwarf to appear.

He was methodical and precise, always on time, and he came into my dreams every night after my grandmother had put me to bed. I don't know which nightmarish world he had come from or why he had decided to haunt a defenceless little girl.

'Goodnight,' my grandmother would say without bending over to kiss me. 'Don't forget to say your prayers and don't forget to pray for your dear mother.' I heard her shuffle away in her old slippers, and I cast a mournful look at the thin sleep-out walls of my makeshift bedroom.

There was a lattice partition along one side of the verandah, which screened off the space from the outside world, and a dark corner where a spare bed had been placed. The rest of the verandah was open to the elements and connected to the front garden by a wide staircase. Not much protection for a tiny girl of five. If anyone had wanted to get in, they simply had to open the front gate, walk up the steps and creep around the corner to my bed.

I wanted to call out to my grandmother, to ask her to stay with me until I fell asleep, but I was afraid of her and I knew instinctively that I was already a bother. So I lay there and waited, listening to the creepers growing in the night, scratching against the lattice. It is a frightening thing for a child to be alone at night in a bedroom without walls.

Then I froze in terror as I heard the dreaded footsteps in the night and caught sight of his squat face and fleshy nose, the bulbous warts erupting through the skin on his cheeks and the drooling mouth which mumbled something incoherent. He held a huge carving knife in his hands and he picked his way around the dark verandah towards me, the knife bobbing up and down as he edged closer and closer. He stopped at my bedside and I could see the incontrovertible intent of the predator in his glassy eyes.

He was worse than horrifying; there was something deliberate and inevitable in his demeanour, as if some primal force had summoned him. So I tried to stay awake and forestall his appearance. But every night, as I was drifting off to sleep, he would come obediently into my twilight world, mumbling curses under his breath as he moved in for the kill. I say 'his' and 'he' because although he resembled my grandmother with the warts on her face, he was decidedly masculine and could well have represented my other grandfather, the arrogant son of a German migrant with a moustache like Hitler's.

I prepared myself for the lunge of the knife, the pain and the blood, but just as the blade reached my throat, I woke up.

As a child of five, I did not understand why I was forced to leave my family home in Emmaville and live with my grandmother and grandfather in another town, Glen Innes. Adults were not accustomed to explaining things to children in those days, as they assumed that children were incapable of understanding and sensitivity. As long as you were clothed and fed, the idea of psychological damage was inconceivable. You were simply packed into the back seat of a car, driven to another house and expected to be grateful that you had a bed to sleep in.

Their house was a rambling weatherboard dwelling with no insulation against the bitterly cold New England winters. An open fire burned all day in the lounge room, the 'good' room, which was reserved for visitors and my grandfather's afternoon naps in his favourite chair near the smouldering coals. A cedar table covered with a white damask cloth for formal occasions stood in the centre of the room, a bleak reminder of the day I had spilled beetroot juice on the cloth, sealing my grandmother's disapproval of me forever.

Dividing the house in two was a long hallway adorned with stern family portraits, a photo of Queen Elizabeth as a young girl and an idealised picture of a guardian angel with a naked bosom and a sword in her hand. In the centre of the hallway stood a silky oak hallstand displaying two brass urns and the family bible.

My grandmother's bedroom was located at the end of the

hallway and, creeping along the corridor, I often dared myself to enter its musty, cloistered interior. It was shut off from the rest of the house as if it had been sealed with mothballs in a camphor chest. Once inside, you felt imprisoned because the room turned in on itself and suffocated you with its stifled cries and buried dreams. The pungent smell of urine from the jerry pot under the commode assaulted my nostrils, along with the glass of brandy which grandma took at night when she had bad cramps in her tired, veiny legs. The blinds were always drawn to guard against chills and the glaring Australian sunshine.

I was both repelled and fascinated by the room, fascinated by the bric-a-brac of an old woman's life and repelled by the secret odour of the marriage bed. Sometimes I would hesitate outside the room, not wanting to disturb the aura of privacy behind the closed door, and for the same reason, I never entered my mother's bedroom when she finally took me back.

Another favourite place, but quite the opposite to my grandma's bedroom, was my grandfather's study, divided from the dark pantry at the back of the house by a fringed curtain. A sense of importance and of connection to the outside world surrounded this sunny, outward-looking room. My grandfather, Samuel Thomas Herbert O'Hara, commonly known as Herb, had the distinction of being the local vet, even though he was self-taught. Charts of horses' teeth hung on the walls with diagrams of the anatomy and dissections of various domestic animals. His roll-top desk was littered with papers, half dried up bottles of ink and jars of various concoctions. It contained the paraphernalia, equally fascinating, of the serious world of male activities, of recent visits to outlying farms from which the smell of sick and suffering animals still lingered.

Outside there was a spare block with a vegetable garden and a small orchard. Poppa would let me pick my own peaches and nectarines when summer came and nothing ever tasted so good again. A tank turned on its side was used as a woodshed and provided a good hiding place when I wanted to escape from Grandma. The flower beds around the house were screened from the public footpath by an immaculate hedge, the pride of my grandfather who was said to have the straightest eye in town.

A family member once whispered to me that grandfather used to whip his sons. I see him now, walking with his arthritic legs towards a horse pen, like the Tin Man in *The Wizard of Oz*, easing his body onto the fence, balancing on the highest rail and smacking an agitated horse on its rump as it raced by. I see him inserting the cruel twitch in the horse's nose and lancing the abscess without anaesthetic while the poor beast whinnied and frothed at the mouth. Perhaps he did whip his sons.

Yet I see him creeping into my bedroom at daybreak, smiling tenderly as he coaxed me to sit up for the morning cup of tea, drowned in too much condensed milk. Years later, at my graduation, I see him sitting sideways on the ground with those same stiff legs flailing in the dirt as he struggled to descend the steps to the ceremony, indifferent to the rude stares of the crowd. I know that he would not have missed this graduation for his life, so proud was he to see 'his little girl' obtain the university diploma he had never been able to acquire himself.

My grandfather, my Poppa, I did not have you long enough.

You were the only man who ever loved me and now I cannot remember your face.

*   *   *

The solitary days passed and dissolved into months.

There are no defined times in the life of a lonely child – just vague patches of fog and sudden, brief storms which roll in and out of the landscape, dividing and separating the hours into meaningless frames. Unable to ask questions, unable to make sense of the inanition, I allowed myself to drift until I was scarcely able to tell the difference between what was real and what was fantasy. As I had no playmates, I spent my lonely childhood days wandering around the gardens and inventing games. The yard became a huge maze full of unexplored corners, traps and secret passageways. The back verandah became a ship, a castle or a ghostly ruin, images stolen from childhood fairytales, as delicious as save-for-Sunday patty cakes from Grandma's hidden cake tins.

In the gardens the shrubs slipped in and out of their shapes, changing into wispy beings or magical forests. My sister had read me stories from the famous children's book, *The Magic Faraway Tree*, and I imagined the gnarled and ageing nectarine tree to be my own 'faraway tree'. It was here that I invented lively conversations with Silky and the Saucepan Man and waited breathlessly for the next adventurous 'world' to arrive in the top branches.

Some of my pastimes were not as savoury as playing in the

garden. A dark spot on the sandy floor of the garage held a particular fascination for me, a spot where the oil from the car spilled onto the dirt in small, rainbow-coloured circles. I found the pungent smell intoxicating and it was there in the silent coolness of the garage, enclosed from the rest of the world by the dark walls, that I crouched down to sniff the spilt oil and place tiny pieces of the soaked grains of dirt into my mouth. Grandma found me eating the dirt one day, sent me outside with a sharp smack and I was barred from playing in the garage ever again.

Loneliness can also be described as the common ground of terror. With my constant nightmares, I felt as if I were running down one rabbit hole after the other, an easy prey to the good intentions of strangers who, like unrelenting foxes, blocked my escape with their bristling whiskers.

The ordeal of school was one of those rabbit holes and there were no fairy godmothers to rescue me or safe passageways in which to hide. My grandmother, anxious to do her duty as well as 'to get me off her hands', insisted that I be enrolled in the local primary school as soon as possible. A few weeks after my arrival, she made the following announcement:

'You'll be going to school tomorrow. I've been up to see the teachers and made all the arrangements. Margaret Gillies will take you. She lives about five houses up from us and she knows the way.'

I was terrified at the thought of more strange buildings and unfamiliar people but there was no escape. Grandmother had spoken and her arms were folded squarely across her chest.

On my first day, I waited outside on the footpath, trussed up like a lamb for the slaughter by the straps of the oversize haversack on my back. I felt nervous and miserable because my memories of school in my small village belonged to another world where the sun had shone. Even though I was only four years old when my mother first sent me to school, also 'to get me off her hands', I felt proud to be riding on the school bus with my older sister and the other big kids. I was happy when I became the first pupil in the class to learn the letters of the alphabet off by heart and I felt warm inside when my pretty young teacher beamed at me.

In this new town everything seemed to be out of step with my former life so I knew something was bound to go wrong. Margaret Gillies did not turn up. It was what I had dreaded as I waited, anxiously checking the empty path for a sign of my guide. There was no sympathy from Grandma; she simply pointed me in the right direction and ordered me to walk the five blocks by myself. I could actually see the school in the distance but the path seemed to stretch out forever, and the large, double-storey brick building loomed up like the castle walls of an evil giant. I thought tearfully of my little wooden bush school with its two friendly classrooms, a water tank at the side, toilet out the back and a hitching rail for horses. By the time I arrived, I was terrified and very late.

The Infants School was run by two spinsters, the Misses Mellings, who lived in a charming blue brick residence opposite the school. Female teachers were not supposed to marry in those days so nobody bothered to ask themselves if a romantic, girlish heart had ever beaten in their buttoned-up, virginal bosoms. Besides, there were many single women in the years following the war, whether through a shortage of men or through a general mood of uncertainty. Everybody seemed to take the social predicament of the Mellings for granted and were only too happy to lend their offspring to the two spinster sisters for the first years of their school lives.

Taking all these thoughts into consideration, I was still appalled when I found out that my grandmother had actually given away one of her sons to her sister, a maiden aunt without any prospects of marrying, who desperately wanted the company of a child. We always regarded this uncle with suspicion because he didn't seem to belong to the family yet was always organising watermelon parties in the park. The hapless boy grew up in a sunless house with the old spinster and remained a solitary child. As an adult, he found consolation with his comrades in the Communist Party, went to Russia and, on his return, suffered a complete nervous breakdown.

Nancy and Dorothy Mellings had invested their whole lives into the training and education of young minds. Most of the local people could remember their strict, authoritarian methods of teaching and there were certainly a few adult males in the town who remembered the sting of their cane. On the weekend, they played competition tennis at the local Tennis Club and the older sister was said to have had a surprisingly good backhand.

When I arrived at the school, I was taken to the classroom by an office lady. My heart sank as I entered the room and saw a large class of unfamiliar faces staring at me in a haughty manner and sniggering amongst themselves because they noticed I was wearing shabby clothes and carrying a rough, canvas haversack instead of a smart, little Globite school port like all the town children. The look in their eyes made me think of the hateful, beady eyes of the farm chickens who select a conspicuous outsider in the flock and ostracise her for life. This was obviously going to be my lot.

Miss Mellings announced my arrival in an imperious voice, sounding aloof and displeased like a priest who has examined me and pronounced me unclean.

'Class, this is the new pupil. Rosemary Scherf. She comes from Emmaville and her father has just passed away.'

I noticed that she pronounced the word 'Emmaville' in a very disdainful voice and I instantly felt that my father's death was a black mark against me.

'I am appointing one of you to look after her at recess and show her around. Hm... let me see.'

She scrutinised the group of reluctant faces, the pupils averting their eyes as soon as her gaze fell in their direction. Finally, Miss Mellings seemed satisfied.

'Ah, yes. Dorothy Linton, you will look after our new pupil at recess and show her around the school. Now, back to work, all of you.'

When the bell rang for recess, I waited for Dorothy Linton to fetch me but she ran away with a group of laughing girls. This continued for weeks and like the defective chicken I hid myself in the grey corners of the playground so that no one would notice that I was alone. The worst thing was that even though Dorothy was my tormentor I secretly pined after this girl and would have given anything to be part of her group. She bore all the marks of a well-loved child, pleasantly plumpish figure, rosy complexion, pretty but rather spiteful countenance and thick brown hair which fell in soft ringlets while mine was dead straight. To complete the picture, her doting mother had made Dorothy her own special school blouses, cut from a dimply Dimity fabric and finished off with a charming Peter Pan collar. For the rest of my primary school life, I wished that I had been born with curly hair and that I could have worn Peter Pan collars, but the regulation cotton blouse and peak collar were considered good enough for a girl from the boonies without a father.

It took me a while to develop any friendships. Everything about me seemed so wrong, as if I had been found guilty of something which would disqualify me forever from acceptance in their social club. It was humiliating and embarrassing to play by myself at recess, to sit alone every lunch hour, to suffer the stares and giggles. I had also started to feel very uncomfortable when the other girls talked about their daddies for it appeared that I was the only pupil in the class without a father. This was difficult to believe when so many countrymen had died in the war, yet there I was, forced to endure my father's death as if it had been my fault. Worse, whenever my classmates related snippets from so many happy family outings with daddy, I was obliged to smile cheerfully and swallow my envy like a spoon of caster oil.

The stigma, if that is the right word to describe it, seemed to follow me around for years like the smell of cat's urine which you can never get out of carpet. To make matters worse, at the beginning of each year, the new teacher would start by asking the students to introduce themselves around the class and say something about their families. Everyone would wait gleefully for my turn and turn a malicious gaze on me as I stared at the teacher in silence, then struggled to blurt out my story. That small moment as I hesitated to speak seemed to hang in the air for a long time as I tried desperately to think of something pleasant to say without mentioning my father but all I felt was depleted and detached as if a part of me had just got up and walked out of the room. It puzzled me that my school mates derived so much pleasure from my embarrassment but later, when I learnt German, I found the right word to describe their cruel behaviour. Schadenfreude.

*   *   *

The dwarf stayed with me for many months, even after I was promoted to a bed inside the house. It was a very large brass and iron bed with pink porcelain finials and a pink satin eiderdown. The bed became available when my sick uncle was finally able to return to his own home. For months he had lain in this darkened room, staring at the ceiling, the terrible demons of war held at bay by the shock treatment.

'Shh. Don't wake Uncle Ross,' my grandmother would hiss at me as I skipped up the corridor. My childish mind could not understand why a man could lie in bed with the blinds drawn for so long, a prisoner of some infernal world where mud and slush drag your feet into the earth and the blinding flash of an exploding shell erupts in your brain. My uncle had occupied the bed after the war in between his visits to Concord Repatriation Hospital in Sydney, and even though I longed to cheer him up, I was forbidden to disturb him.

When I grew older, I was relieved to see him, presumably alive and well, arriving at our house for a family party and winking at me as he came through the front door. After he had consumed several beers, my grandmother was able to coax him into performing for us one of the great classical arias of the day. Uncle Ross had a startlingly beautiful baritone voice which filled the room with wonder and brought tears to our eyes. He was completely untrained but each note was delivered with such refined diction and depth of passion that, for those few moments, my poor uncle seemed to be radiant, transformed, released from his dark prison. The whole room fell silent for, as his voice soared beyond the thin walls of my mother's modest house, we felt as if we had been transported to heaven itself.

My uncle Ross, you might have been a famous Opera singer but you sang for us like a fallen angel, keeping one arm in your coat pocket and a lighted cigarette in the other to stop your hands from shaking.

I hated the room with its smell of fear and suffering but my grandmother moved me into the enormous bed as soon as he had left. My tiny frame made a small indentation in the bedcovers and I had to be lifted onto the bed by my grandfather. There was a curtained recess in the corner where a jerry pot was kept and I suspected that the dwarf would soon take up residence there.

I was right. At night I hid under the pink eiderdown, peeping out to check for the slightest movement in the curtain, then bracing my tiny heart against his murderous nocturnal sprees.

While the war raged on in Europe, I had my own private war. My grandmother's house was never a home – it was a series of spaces with suggestions and overtones of safety and fear, an alien territory which had to be negotiated each day. I suppose my family in Emmaville may have visited me but I do not remember seeing them or my beloved brother. I waited for someone to come and take me home but nobody ever appeared, nobody ever explained what had happened to my family or why I had to leave my home. I never again saw the homestead where I once lived, the school where I was happy and I gradually forgot that I had a brother and two sisters.

I only felt the silent command from the adult world to be obedient and not cause trouble. Now I knew that the world was unsafe, that it contained dark rooms and monsters and sick uncles and cruel classmates. It was my first initiation into the dangerous game of life, the mysterious, seductive world of adults and the evil of the Urwald.

Thus I became a shadow, but a shadow which carried the best of the life I was never to live.

*   *   *

When I try to remember the events leading up to my separation from the family, they are somewhat blurred. Adults did not explain things to children in those days as they assumed that children were too young to understand and as long as you were clothed and fed, the idea of psychological damage was inconceivable.

The tragedy happened in Emmaville, a village near Glen Innes, on a very cold night in July, 1948. It was the sort of cold that made the old cottage lean into itself and the dogs on the chains whimper. In the morning, the dripping taps were frozen into immaculate suspended icicles, like glass daggers.

Winter in the New England Ranges is cruel. It can awaken terrible thoughts in your head and release the monsters from the underworld; it can turn healthy people into dying invalids, drive lonely people crazy and send faithful husbands off the rails.

I had slept restlessly that night because I had taken my weekly bath and gone to bed with wet hair. It was freezing cold and my sister had pulled all the blankets to her side of the bed so I had drifted off to sleep huddled up against my sister's back.

Then the dream had come … or perhaps it was a vision.

At about 2 am, a group of beautiful women with green dresses, grey cloaks and long, streaming hair appeared in my room. They were softly weeping and singing a mournful song, a haunting song full of dire premonitions and the pain of the prescient who weep for the ones who will die soon.

I felt an incomprehensible melancholy even though I had no idea why a child would have been capable of such feelings. The ladies seemed to have come from a world before my time yet I felt safe with them as they wrapped me in their green tenderness. In a strange way that I have never experienced again they belonged to me and I have referred to them as 'my ladies' ever since. I wanted them to stay with me forever but the dream was ending.

Suddenly my cat, Felix, leapt up off the bed, clawing my arm as he shot into the living room. I woke up abruptly, ran after him and was surprised to see that the light was on, and that my grandparents from Glen Innes were sitting in the living room, talking to my mother in very subdued voices. An awful adult seriousness filled the room.

'Grandma. Poppa. What are you doing here?' I exclaimed in happy surprise.

'Go back to bed,' my grandmother snapped at me and I crept back to my room, feeling the beginning of something ominous.

I don't remember much about that night or the days that followed. My mother had red, teary eyes but never spoke to me; we sensed that we should not bother her and stepped around her if we were in the same room. The cottage was filled with a deathly silence but I was surprised to see that some of our neighbours had started to appear at the front door with a basket of food and to speak to my mother and my grandparents in whispers. My grandparents remained in the house for several days, talking seriously with my mother but breaking off their conversation if the children came into the room. I still did not understand the reason for their visit.

Two days later, I was in the lounge room with my older sister, who was stuffing caramel lollies into her mouth in between great outbursts of tears. I didn't know what was happening, so I thought it was better to imitate her because she always knew what to do and I wanted some of those caramel lollies. I tried very hard to squeeze some tears out of my eyes but ended up begging her to tell me why she was crying.

'Don't be so stupid,' she yelled at me. 'Don't you know our father's dead!'

The news shocked me but did not really sink into my heart. The stranger who had turned up at my grandmother's house and brought us to his family's property in Emmaville had, apart from his escapades, remained a somewhat distant figure. I knew in my mind that he was my father but I could not recall ever sitting on his knee or receiving any special attention from him. I don't remember if I was allowed to attend the funeral or not and I was certainly not permitted to view the corpse.

The week passed in a mournful gloom and soon it was time for my grandparents to leave. On the eve of their departure, my grandfather put his arms around my mother's shoulders and spoke to her in a very serious tone.

'You'll have to pull yourself together now, dear. For the sake of the baby.'

It was true. We could hear our baby sister crying in her sharp, urgent little voice, and our mother rocking her, rocking her until both of them fell into an exhausted sleep. It was awful to hear that rocking start up, over and over during the night, and our mother looking more and more distraught every morning.

I was sitting in the living room when my grandfather outlined his plan to my mother, speaking out loud in front of me as if I were not there.

'This is what your mother and I have decided to do, Hope,' he declared solemnly. 'We've talked it over. You will have to stay here with the baby, of course, until everything is settled. Mal is still too weak to move, so we'll take Rosemary off your hands and leave Maureen. She's old enough to help you in the house.'

My mother agreed to the suggestion, too exhausted to think through the implications, too grateful that there was now one less child to care for. With a dead husband, a three-month-old baby and a child recovering from rheumatic fever, she was happy to accept any sort of relief.

The day of our departure dawned like any other wintery day. The frost was very heavy on the grass, painting every blade with gleaming silver. It could have been a beautiful day because after a frost, the skies were always a clean, sharp blue and the sun at midday was almost hot. It was the sort of day when my little brother and I couldn't wait to go outside and play on the rocks but he was still lying in his bed with a frame over his legs. Instead, I was dressed in my best dress and deposited in the back seat of my grandfather's car.

I don't remember asking any questions but I suppose somebody must have told me where I was going. It was like an event that belonged to the grownups and had nothing to do with me. I cannot remember my little suitcase being packed or my family waving me goodbye. The last thing I saw of my home in Emmaville was my cat dashing wildly around the side of the house as the car pulled away.

So began my new life with my grandparents in a strange house in a strange town. One may ask why I found everything so unfamiliar for it was actually not the first time I had ended up in my grandmother's house. Apparently, my mother had lived there with me and my older sister during the war years when families banded together like huddled survivors in a snowstorm.

In fact, I was born in Glen Innes on 19 May, 1943. The event was not a happy one and I was later inclined to agree with the old aphorism that all babies born in May should be drowned at birth. I consoled myself, however, by calculating that I must not have been the only unwanted child in the world for when you think of the millions of children born every day, there must have been hundreds of unfortunate babies like me who were not planned.

The thought stayed with me and always made me feel sad. When I grew older and could understand such things as copulation and conception, I began to think about all the unplanned pregnancies, especially in wartime or during some other horrible disaster. A jerking spasm among a pair of splayed legs, two bodies retreating to their own side of the bed and the tiny spark of life left to grow in an indifferent womb and, after the brutal act, what if the father was not married to the mother or what if he died or became paralysed or simply walked away, and what if the mother, a timid little girl, was left to raise a child on her own? So, in spite of the romantic platitudes describing the universal joys of motherhood, it is a fact that my birth was a mistake. There was certainly no need for another child in these, the worst of all possible circumstances.

In 1943, the world was beginning to spread leaks everywhere. Hitler had led the German nation into one of the most barbaric periods in human history. Huge slabs of oppression and enslavement fell across Europe and stamped the free world with fear and desolation. The whole consciousness of the world was darkened as humanity turned against itself and justified the most horrible acts of destruction.

In order to assist in the struggle for liberation and peace, my father enlisted in the RAAF, left his home in Australia before I was born and disappeared into the flaming skies of Europe. I was conceived in a hotel room in Sydney a few days before my father was due to sail when my mother, Hope, travelled from Emmaville to Sydney to say a last, tearful farewell to her husband. I am sure that a pregnancy was far from her thoughts.

She had been anxious about the journey but the ache in her heart to be reunited with her husband for a brief reprieve was overwhelming. For over a year, as he completed his training, she had tried to hold down the daily fear that he was going to leave Australia one day and might never return.

Like all the war wives she would be obliged to wait quietly at home while the incomprehensible drama of war raged in a landscape she would never see. Simple domestic tasks would fill her days and at night the family would gather around the radio, straining to hear the latest news. She would comfort herself by singing the sentimental songs written for the thousands of women compelled to surrender their loved ones to the brutal arena of war.

Red sails in the sunset, way out on the sea

Oh, carry my loved one, home safely to me
He sailed in the dawning, all day I've been blue
Red sails in the sunset I'm trusting in you.

The overnight train journey from Glen Innes was long and tedious. Travellers departed at 5 pm and arrived in Sydney the next morning around 11 am. There were four to a seat in the cramped compartments and you were obliged to sit shoulder to shoulder with your fellow passenger and try not to slump onto him in your sleep. It was lucky for those who managed to find a spot early because resourceful people sometimes put a suitcase on the bench in the hope of securing extra room for the night. They covered the suitcase with a coat and stuck a hat on the top, giving the impression of a sleeping body.

Hope had tried to sleep but the cold weather outside had begun to steal into the compartment and the sooty smell of the steam train made breathing difficult. She was conscious of the disruptive sound of doors being flung open at Werris Creek, of heavy iron foot-warmers being thrown into the compartments at Werris Creek, of the dull thud of metal hitting the floor contrasting with the station master's piercing whistle as the train took off again.

Her husband's young face, blurred now by their impending separation, swam in and out of her consciousness. There was so much she wanted to say to him but her old habit of shyness had returned and overcame any feelings of excitement.

As the train pulled into Central Station, her confidence waned at the sight of the seething mass of human activity outside and she was suddenly overwhelmed by a deep apprehension, conscious of the great gap which was growing between them. What could she give him now that he would not lose in the uncertain future? The smells and sounds of Sydney were all around her and she stumbled along the crowded footpaths, dragging her little port and feeling so out of place in her unfashionable suit.

Suddenly, he was before her, with his usual cocky grin, and they hugged fiercely. As they walked together towards the hotel, she glanced shyly at him and noticed that a brightness not just of excitement but of pure elation had begun to enliven the features of his face, and that there was something else which she could not quite explain, something in the new spring in his stride which made her heart sink.

After the farewell dinner, they hurried back to the hotel room and lay together in the darkness. He kissed her tenderly, his dear wife, his own little bunny, and lovingly thrust his organ inside her. In and out, firm and slippery, getting deeper and deeper inside her as he would imagine over and over during those lonely nights in England. Suddenly, he stopped and withdrew:

'What's the matter?' she whispered, trembling. 'I'm sick of poking into rubber,' he complained.

So she dutifully removed the diaphragm inserted by the local doctor to protect a woman who might never see her husband again.

The realisation that she was pregnant must have come as a great shock to Hope. She had moved into my grandmother's house in Glen Innes with my sister, Maureen, and was staying out the war in the comfort and security of her family but there was no denying the awful nausea in her stomach and the secret visits to the toilet in the morning.

'Oh, Hope. Couldn't you have been more careful? And Charles on his way to the war! What were you thinking?' My grandmother moaned.

'I'm sorry, mother. I suppose I missed him too much. He didn't like the rubber thing.'

My grandmother sighed and shrugged her shoulders. The weight of bearing eleven children had compressed her body into a squat, flabby shape so that all her conversations seemed to carry a complaint against the unhappy lot of women. Deep in her heart, however, she knew only too well that she could not accuse her daughter of the awful thing she herself had agreed to, month after month, year after year, baby after baby.

The cold stillness in the room enveloped the two women like the first frost of winter. There was nothing Hope could say to explain or to account for this apparent weakness in her character. Why hadn't she spoken up for herself that night? Hadn't she always been the one to give in? Charles had always dominated her from the very first moment they had met when he had suddenly appeared from nowhere without any prior explanation from her father. How could she ever forget that day? Not expecting anyone to turn up at their isolated farmhouse, she had been startled by his sudden appearance in the dark laundry doorway while she was plucking feathers from three dead chickens. 'G'day,' he had said with a cocky grin. 'I'm Charles Scherf from Emmaville and I've got three hundred sheep outside. Where do you want me to put them?'

Then he burst out laughing, expecting her to join in the joke. She turned sharply from bending over the old stone tubs but could barely make him out in the dim light. Realising he had startled her, he moved back into the sunlight of the doorway and the radiance of his young man's vitality made her blush. She was suddenly alone with a man she had never seen or been introduced to and the sight of her bare arms and chest covered with feathers and smelling of mouldy dampness filled her with embarrassment.

He was a strong young man, not as tall as her brothers, but with the body of a natural athlete. She noticed that his facial features were more refined than those of a common grazier with his high cheekbones and arched eyebrows. Even through the dirt and sweat she could feel him scrutinising her in a bemused, slightly patronising way.

'I've brought three hundred sheep here,' he explained, 'because we're running out of feed back home. Your father said we could let them graze in your fields for a while.'

He smiled at her with that confident, roguish grin which would always melt her heart in the future.

'Look. We've come a long way. You couldn't find your father for me, could you, and rustle up a cup of tea? I'm dying of thirst.'

Then he burst out laughing because he had surprised her in the middle of such an uncomplimentary activity. She had blushed, pushed past him and scampered away in search of her father. The bucolic charm of this shy woman, caught off-guard and cornered in the old washhouse like a frightened rabbit, stirred something very tender in his heart, and he called her 'Bunny' from that day onwards. Yes, he had stormed into her life and had always had his way with her; it was no wonder that their first child was born just seven months after the wedding.

Hope had always been bewildered by her own passivity, her stupid willingness to go along with everyone else's desires while her older sister had left the fold and opened up a business in Sydney. In her whole life she had never argued, never raised her voice to assert herself; it seemed as if her every individual dream had been surrendered to a stronger masculine will, beginning with her father who would not let her become a nurse because he didn't want his daughter washing the cocks of dirty, old men. He had ordered her to leave school at the age of fourteen to help look after her brothers and she had obeyed him without question, even following the family to a remote farm 50 miles from the nearest town.

Always the same easy acquiescence, as if it was her second nature to be ruled.

A nostalgic memory came to her of a carefree young girl galloping her favourite horse through the paddocks to collect the mail, of the hectic frivolity of those country dances when, at the end of a cold, starry evening, she would brush the ice off the saddle and let the horse find his own way home as she dozed peacefully. It seemed so long ago, her happy-go-lucky childhood with games of hide-and-seek with her older brothers, moonlight picnics near the creek and mad dashes through the fields to find the first blackberries of the season. And, like a hidden seam of gold in an abandoned mine, the cherished memory of the other man, the quieter, more reticent boy she had secretly loved, the one, true sweetheart she had abandoned to marry Charles.

But now, as she took in the features of her mother's careworn face, she felt ashamed, ashamed of her submissive nature, ashamed of what her husband made her do under the blankets and ashamed of the child growing within her.

'I'm going to peel the vegetables,' she mumbled and turned towards the kitchen.

She did not see my grandmother's eyes following her and the expression of universal sadness on her tired face. Watching the uneasy gait of her daughter, she recalled the doubtful joy of her own marriage many years ago, having been hauled from Sydney over the New England Range on a bullock dray and almost freezing to death when she reached the snow-covered hills of Ben Lomond. Her new husband, a blue-eyed Irishman from County Clare, had jumped on her like a bull, jamming eleven babies into her until the change of life had lifted her woman's curse.

She had washed nappies for twenty-five years and now there was to be another baby in the house. And how many more for her hapless daughter? Poor Grandma, ground down by childbearing to a pulp of herself, like an old tree stump. In every conversation about the miserable lot of women, Grandma, who always had the last word on everything, would suddenly grow quiet. She was vaguely conscious that there were other words, clever words with which she could have started a deeper discussion on the nature and role of women or on what was referred to in earlier times as 'The Woman Question'. Time and lack of education were against her and her ignorance had piled up inside her like the endless loads of washing which she never had time to fold away.

She sighed helplessly as she watched her daughter walk awkwardly towards the kitchen, then she uttered the same words which she always used to sum up every conversation about the fate of women, words borrowed from the title of her favourite radio serial:

'When a girl marries …'

*   *   *

On 18 May, 1943, a day after my father's birthday, Hope sensed the first dreaded signs of the onset of labour. She waited in the house, resting on her bed, hoping to forestall the ordeal, but at 11 pm that night, my grandfather had driven the car out of the garage and had placed her small suitcase in the boot.

When grandfather was at the wheel with the engine running, you were compelled to get in the car immediately or he would take off before you had time to even slam the door but my mother cried that night and refused to budge. She thought of Charles, lost once more in the darkened skies of France, and wondered if he would ever return alive to see this baby. To face the ordeal of labour alone was too daunting.

'Hurry up, dear,' my grandmother urged, not wanting to

29

irritate her impatient husband any further.

My mother struggled into the front seat but when the car began to slowly reverse out of the driveway, she opened the door and tried to get out. Vivid memories of the oncoming labour had been steadily assembling in her brain, memories of the torture rack, where intolerable bolts of pain had to be endured over and over, and for how long this time? The rising contractions, the short relief before another rumble of agony, then finally that great, hissing, clanging steam engine inside her, charging down her body to her pelvis, its centrifugal force locked for a moment inside her throat.

'There's no use pushing from your throat,' the midwife had said with her practised air of calm efficiency.

Finally, to feel oneself rent in two as the flesh, forced to stretch into jagged tears to allow the head to pass through, expelled its human burden.

'Oh, Charles. I just can't go through this again,' Hope gasped, straining to heave her huge, pulsating stomach out of the passenger seat.

She did not realise that she was holding back my life.

'What in heaven's name are you up to, Hope?' My grandfather cried out in consternation, grabbing onto her arm, trying to restrain her and hang onto the steering wheel at the same time. My grandmother, speaking sharply to her daughter now, pushed her back into the car and slammed the door but as the car drove off toward the maternity home, her face crumpled and she closed her eyes in prayer.

'Oh, Hope. My poor girl. Oh, God be with you, my dear.'

I was born at 6 am the next day. There was nothing distinctive about me. Another girl, soft and pink and rosy. My father telegrammed and sent a card with the inscription: 'Call the baby Rose after its father's nose,' so they called me Rosemary but the name had nothing to do with my father's physiognomy. It was the name of the daughter of his commanding officer in England.

I hardly knew my mother's touch. It was stolen from me at birth when she almost died. I knew that my mother almost died because all my life she reminded me in an accusatory tone that, 'I almost died when I had you.'

Only two weeks after I was born, Hope woke up with chills and a fever.

'It's only your milk coming in,' the nurse explained brusquely.

This was followed by a dose of diarrhoea. My mother's stomach began to swell and became so noticeable that a passing nurse commented, 'Oh, Mrs Scherf. Haven't you had your baby yet?'

Soon the nurses noticed that the baby also appeared to be distressed. When placed on the breast, she now refused to suck, dark patches had appeared around her eyes and she seemed to be shivering with intense cold. Her throat had swollen, her skin had become mottled and the soft spot on her head was bulging. Soon her breathing became more and more rapid and she lay motionless in the crib.

The greyly whispered word 'septicaemia' was pronounced and hung in the corridors like cobwebs. Infection was feared then because there was no known treatment. Death was imminent and unavoidable.

I was removed quickly from my mother and isolated in a humidity crib.

As we struggled against our own death, thousands of men were killing each other in Europe. Women, children, newborn babies – we could do nothing against the male force of militancy which ruled the world at that time. Huge slabs of annihilation fell across us and stamped us with their terrifying darkness. Human life was cheap and there were tales of unbelievable atrocities; everything we had called civilisation had returned to barbarism. A woman and a child dying in some remote corner of the earth were of little significance, a pathetic addition to the millions of women and children obliterated by the machine of war.

I did not blame my mother or the hospital staff for our predicament. People were so out of their routine that they had become careless. Nobody knew who they were anymore and women no longer knew how to have babies. The war had interrupted our continuity, making us play roles in which we no longer recognised ourselves, forcing us to betray our own substance. My mother's gentle nature was no match for the brutality of the times and I suspect that, unwittingly, she had allowed the dark cruelty of the times to seep into our souls, for the aggression of men had sealed our spirits in helpless quiescence.

*   *   *

I am a baby dying. My mother has fed me her poisoned milk. How can I describe my death when I do not yet have language? The poison in my blood has caused my throat to swell and my skin is turning blue. I can hardly breathe for there is not enough oxygen to reach my lungs. I bleat like a lamb.

No one touches me and I touch no one. For the first months of my life, I lie motionless in a hospital humidity crib, growing weaker and weaker. An eternal loneliness is registered in my brain and I begin to record a sensation of isolation. Forever there will be a glass barrier between me and the world and I will remain on the inside looking out. I will long for the company of other humans and I will not understand why I am alone.

Nerve centres in my brain are beginning to close down. A terrible coldness is seeping through my whole body. My blood pressure is sinking and I cannot feel the extremity of my toes and fingers. I am pinned to a block of ice. Is this what death is like?

They have sent for the minister to give my mother and me the last rites. My grandmother has spent the day walking around the garden outside the hospital dormitory, weeping and praying continuously. She was sorry she had spoken so sharply for it was too much to lose a daughter this way, a gentle girl who would hurt no one and a baby girl who would never see the sun. Oh, Father! Why? Why? In all her babies this disease had never taken hold.

The old town doctor who delivered Hope sought the refuge of his office. There was talk of unwashed hands and dirty instruments. Yes, he had been a little too hasty to break her waters, but some women do insist on going into labour at the worst times and he desperately needed sleep. Besides, hadn't he cautioned her about getting pregnant while Charles was away? Why hadn't she done what he had told her and used the preventative device he had given her?

'Damn women,' he muttered to himself in disgust. 'They all want the same thing, then end up here and expect me to help them out. You'd think they'd have more sense with the war on.'

He ran his fingers through his thinning hair and closed his eyes in defeat. No. No. No. Hope was no town tramp. He knew only too well that old Herb was one of the most respected men in the town and that Hope's husband, an enlisted man, was fighting for their freedom in England. Now it looked as if she and the baby would die and there might be rumours.

'Not the kind of news a fellow wants to hear when he's on the battlefield.' He sighed and began to rifle through his weary mind for some way to save them.

He had been reading lately in his medical journals about the use of a drug called penicillin which was supposed to have undreamt-of, life-saving possibilities for people with blood poisoning. It had been discovered by accident in 1928 when a Scottish professor noticed a mould growing on his Petri dishes but it was not until 1939 that an Australian scientist had begun purifying and developing it as a medicine. Wartime conditions had made production of the medicine very difficult in England but it was now being produced in quantities by the Americans and, as fate would have it, by the Commonwealth Serum Laboratories in Australia.

He'd read about the miraculous cure of the man in England who, in 1941, had scratched the inside of his mouth while pruning roses and had developed a life-threatening illness. The unfortunate man's face and skull had become swollen with huge abscesses, making it necessary for one eye to be removed and the other lanced. When he was injected with penicillin he'd made a remarkable recovery in just two days, but because the drug was easily lost through urine, there was not enough available at the time to save his life, not even when they extracted it from his urine. So they continued the trial on children, with better results.

'On children,' he spoke aloud to himself, dragged his weary body out of his chair and went off to find Mrs O'Hara. Of course, he'd have to get their permission first and work out where to locate the drug. It was a long shot but time was running out and it was their only hope.

The main problem was the availability of the stuff, especially for people in a remote country town in Australia. What had been produced had been sent to the battlefields in North Africa where it was hailed as a miracle, even saving soldiers' legs from being amputated. Now they were hoarding up the supplies for the invasion of Europe.

'Damn it,' he thought. 'It's worth a try. And I know exactly where I might be able to get some of the stuff.'

In the town of Tenterfield, just 56 miles away from Glen Innes, there were many large army camps. Troops that had returned from the Middle East were stationed in the London Bridge area of the town before being sent to New Guinea. Not even the locals knew how many men were involved but it was reported that ten thousand soldiers had been garrisoned there by Douglas MacArthur, the American general who was allegedly spearheading the formation of the infamous Brisbane Line.

'They're sure to have some of the stuff,' he told the waiting O'Haras before driving off.

The next day, the minister arrived to deliver the last rites for the mother and child. A sickly silence had descended over the ward and the grief-stricken parents were waiting, heads bowed, near the bed of their dying daughter and her tiny, disfigured baby. Suddenly, the doctor appeared and hastily injected the precious serum into the large muscle of their pallid buttocks.

It was the first time the small white drug had ever been used on civilians in the country. It was indeed a miracle. As early as two days later, it was obvious that the patients would live.

Suddenly, I awake and feel the life force spring back into me. I burst through the darkness and the lethargy of death. A hand reaches through the little door in my humidity crib and touches my fingers. Whereas before there had only been an empty vacuum, now I can sense the promise of something about to happen. So strong, so sure is this sensation that it has stayed with me all my life. Even as an adult, when I unexpectedly fall asleep in the day, I am jolted into waking with this same resurgence, like a computer being re-booted. I am ready, life is beginning anew and the seasons are just starting. It is the dearest, freshest feeling of hope.

We returned to my grandmother's house where we lived until the war ended. One would have imagined that having escaped death by the skin of our teeth, the bond between my mother and me would have been very close, but the larger spectre of war hung over us. Every day my mother waited anxiously for the post, her eyes constantly on the skies, dispirited, fulfilling the daily maternal routines begrudgingly like a hired servant. It seemed so long ago that she had accompanied her husband to Adelaide for his training with their first born, Maureen, who had been such a healthy, bonny child and a favourite with the wives and their husbands. Now, with the war rationing, there were two children to look after and she was living in a house where too many babies had been born already.

The grief piled up like stones in a funeral pyre. My grandmother was inconsolable at the news that her eighteen-year-old son, the most gentle and spiritual of her wild boys, had been killed in action. As a gunner in a fighter plane, he had occupied the most vulnerable position during an attack and had been the first to die. His agony over God's 6th commandment revealed later in the long, soul-searching letters he wrote home to his minister, had ended in a cruel and unresolved conundrum.

A spirit of profound sorrow and hopelessness pervaded the house and I became ill again. My temperature soared and red punctuate lesions appeared all over my body, fine but rough-textured like sandpaper. I was fighting for my life again not on a block of ice but in a blazing fire. Scarlet Fever was a dangerous illness in those times and a leading cause of death. There was no vaccine this time and I was left to struggle on my own, fighting against a raging thirst and an inferno of unbearable heat.

Somehow the May baby survived.

Two fatal illnesses and I was only two years old.

*　　*　　*

Suddenly, the war came to an end.

In the distant land of blue-eyed, fair-haired people, the wild men lay down their arms and everybody went home.

For a while there would be a father in the house once more.

One day, in May 1945, a man in uniform arrived out of the blue at my grandmother's home. My mother and my older sister had been waiting for him all morning on my grandmother's verandah because it had a good, long view down the street. I did not know where the man had come from or why he suddenly appeared and laid some sort of claim to us. Nothing had prepared me for his arrival, no explanations, no lightness in my mother's voice, nothing startling about the way in which the leaves in my Faraway Tree rustled as they did when a new world was approaching.

It was a day of reconciliation. Lots of other men came to our town that day, like immigrants eager to start life anew, a ticket in their pocket from London to Glen Innes. All day long the appointed officials were driving them from the airport, all day long families stood on verandahs and scanned the horizon, all day long couples who had been separated for years ran weeping into each other's arms, estranged and mangled hearts, beating against each other, lost in the ecstasy of their reunion.

A car pulled up outside my grandfather's house and a man in uniform leapt out. It was my grandfather who stepped forward first.

'Welcome home, son. We're so proud of you.'

My grandfather beamed at the stranger and shook his hand vigorously. Then my grandmother came up to him, arms outstretched, eyes filling up with tears.

'Oh, God bless you, Charles. God bless you. We've prayed so long for this day, prayed that God would bring you home safe. And here you are.'

My mother, who had been waiting timidly behind her parents, could not contain herself any longer and half-coyly at first because it had been such a long time, rushed into his arms. The stranger swooped her up in an exuberant hug and I could see that she was laughing and crying at the same time. My older sister ran boldly towards him and let him lift her right up into the air where she dangled like a circus acrobat.

I was the only one who did not move for I had been watching the man from afar, half-hidden behind my grandfather's legs. Then my mother pulled me out of my hiding place, pushed me towards him and urged me to say hello.

'Rosemary, this is your daddy. Say hello and give him a big kiss, now.'

The man held out his arms to me, ready to seal my birthright and claim the daughter he had never seen. A wave of shyness and fear came over me and when the man bent down and beckoned me to come to him, I screamed and ran to my grandfather. No amount of coaxing was able to extricate me from the hold I had on his legs.

It was a sinful thing to do, and now I see that it was the mistake of my life. Surely something in the way the same blood rushed through our hearts should have stirred me, an ancient thread of kinship, a flicker of recognition, but I was a stupid little girl, a two-year-old child without any knowledge in my heart.

There he was at last, extending his arm towards me like an

ancient monarch, searching for some family resemblance in my features, trying at the same time to close the two-year gap between us, to take in the enormity of this new life spawned unintentionally in that dingy room in Sydney. There was a second when the possibility of love and reconciliation stood in the gap between us but I clung desperately to my grandfather's legs and no coaxing could entice me to let go.

This small second meant that I would no longer come under the true protection of my father. Oh, he provided food and shelter for me but he never truly owned me from that moment. So great was his disappointment that he never called me to him again and accepted too easily that this would be the way between us.

It is said that in ancient times daughters would inherit their father's features so that they would not be attacked by male aggressors. My mother said that of all the children I looked the most like him. I had the same faraway look in my eyes, the same troubled and questing spirit but the time-honoured rule of kinship had been broken.

Oh, father, forgive me.

I might have been your favourite.

*   *   *

So the man returned and began to shape our new lives. He was full of ideas and eager to get started.

'Look, Hope, we've got to get back to Big Ben. My father's sick and needs help with the farm. I don't want to stay in the air force anyway – not as a test pilot. And they wouldn't dare tie me down to a desk job. Let's pack and leave as soon as possible.'

Something had shifted. We belonged to a new order now, to the strange man who wanted to take us away with him to a strange place called Emmaville. My mother was excited to leave and resume the life that had been promised to her in marriage. She knew that she had been a burden on her parents and she saw the chance for Charles and her to be together, to build their own world as they had planned, so she agreed without hesitation to leave within the week.

Packing up our things, she paused and took a last look at the familiar surroundings, a true haven in a world gone mad. The mellow ebb and flow of life in her mother's house, the sense of the old Irish family ties, the clinging together of women and children with the old men who could not go to war, the image of her congenial father beaming at us from his favourite chair, all these things still warmed her heart.

Oh, the tender communion of the ones who had stayed behind, the comfort of the family bible on the hallstand, the sharing of rations, the humble assembling of the faithful, heads bowed in church or straining together around the radio for the latest news of the war – all the unrecognised sacrifices in the monumental but sweet drudgery of 'keeping the home fires burning'.

*   *   *

It was not just a new awakening for our family – the whole nation began to turn itself over as the work force began to edge out the peacekeepers and make way for the soldiers who returned. Government departments were replenished, new offices were built, new businesses thrived, cities reached for the sky and there was employment for everybody. In rural Australia, towns threw off their torpor, pastures were replanted, stock replenished and modern machinery began to replace the old methods of farming. Wives could afford to buy new, fashionable clothes, children who had never gone to university suddenly became eligible and the energy which created the post-war prosperity was released.

I left my grandmother's house not knowing that I would be sent back in three years. Our farewell was sad and brief.

'Goodbye, Hope. Goodbye, Maureen,' my grandfather called after us. 'Goodbye, my darling little girl. Charles, mind that you look after my girls, now.'

Grandmother was stoical, wiping her hands on her apron and looking disapprovingly at the two girls bouncing around in the back seat of the new car.

'Drive carefully, Charles. For goodness sake, sit down, girls, and behave yourselves. You kids had better help your mother when you get there and don't be a nuisance. Goodbye, Hope. We'll come and visit you as soon as we can.'

Then she turned away quickly so they could not see her tears. There were times when she had struggled with the extra burden but the family had lived together for two years, sharing rations, news of the war and the never-ending battle to stay on top of things. As she walked unsteadily back to the empty house her small, bulky frame seemed to be even more compressed, but it was not the burden of duty which had reduced her vitality.

It was love ... after all.

THE STRANGER

Emmaville 1946

My father drove us to his family home, a large sheep farm about 56 miles from Glen Innes. The name of the closest village was Emmaville, named after Emma, the wife of the richest tin-mining magnate in the district. It remains forever in the edges of my mind.

Emmaville, a dreary, god-forsaken place, is a small village in the New England tablelands which knew a brief period of prosperity in the tin-mining days. There is nothing to distinguish it from other small towns in the region; it is stagnant, seemingly lost in the past and, like many former mining towns, decaying in its inability to re-invent itself. You would need a long time to discover its singularity but by then you would have acquired its soulless habits and you would have ceased to search.

It is spawned in a rather unique landscape. On the eastern

side, there is an impenetrable escarpment of rugged timber slopes and huge granite boulders which completely block out the horizon and the rising sun. On the western side, where the plains begin, there is too much altitude to benefit from the added warmth and the landscape abruptly turns its back on the fertile wheat fields of the McIntyre Valley. To the north, there is enough cleared land to support the prosperous sheep farms, the main livelihood of my father and his relatives.

There is a single road that leads into the town, one way in and one way out. It rises sharply over a large hill which the locals, for lack of imagination, called the Big Hill. About 10 miles out of town, it passes through a swamp of low-lying marshland which some lark had jokingly named Hollywood. There is a big dip in the road which flooded on many occasions and was always slippery and dangerous.

It is no wonder that the main reason for pioneering the region came from under the ground. Tin. Stannum. This discovery resulted in a rapid settlement by German mining families – the Garths, Starks, Gurks, Schumachers and Scherfs. Their heavy German names resounded in the remote, uncivilised bushland like the clang of an iron gate. When the mines closed down, they retreated into their bullnecks and, with typical German practicality, became storekeepers and graziers. They drank heavily at one of the eleven pubs which once existed in the town, fornicated and retreated from the world.

The town itself consisted of two streets only but boasted an elaborate courthouse and police station, a general store, shops, a haberdashery store decorated with lead-light windows, a

School of Arts hall, a public school and a hospital. As is typical of Australian country towns, a major piece of the best real estate had been acquired by the Catholic Church which had erected a beautiful two-storey convent and an imposing church. The other denominations and the strange squat building of the Masonic Lodge were represented in less impressive blocks of real estate and, as was also typical of small towns before the advent of television, there was a Roxy cinema and a community dance hall.

The road out of town eventually led to the vast land holdings of the Scherfs. Their properties stretched on both sides of the road for about 20 miles. 'Big Ben', the name given to the country estate of my grandfather, consisted of ten thousand acres and a grand country mansion. The house had wide verandahs overlooking a beautiful country garden, a formal dining room which would seat thirty people, an elegant lounge room which was only opened on special occasions and numerous bedrooms with bay windows. Outside, there was a tennis court and a six-hole golf course.

Visiting dignitaries were always expected to spend the weekend at Big Ben, the most prestigious property in the district. My grandfather, like most well-dressed men of that era, wore spats and carried calling cards in the pocket of his frock coat. My grandmother, an accomplished linguist, wrote articles for the Sydney Morning Herald and was one of the founding women of the Country Women's Association of Australia. She was assisted in the running of the house by two Irish girls who lived in the maids' quarters at the back of the house; rumours of grandfather chasing them through the house and exercising his *droit de seigneur* hung in the dark corridors. Two Chinese men tended the gardens and kept the family in vegetables.

Memories of civilised life persisted in the region. There were formal balls in winter, cricket matches against the neighbouring towns in summer, church fetes, tennis parties and formal dinners. Afternoon teas were very popular and every country woman owned a bow-fronted China cabinet with an English tea set, dainty silver cake forks, Toby jugs and crystal wine glasses.

When the children of wealthy landowners reached high school age, they were sent away to fashionable boarding schools, the girls to The New England Grammar School or the Presbyterian Ladies College in the provincial city of Armidale and the boys to Farrer Agricultural College, Tamworth or to The King's College or The Scots College in Sydney. Daughters were supposed to marry a local farmer of substantial means and sons were expected to take up their place on the land and play polo.

Adult males were the centre of all activities. They organised the running of the farms according to the seasons, rode around the paddocks, checked fences and livestock, ploughed fields, went on business trips to Sydney, argued boisterously in the pubs and squinted at the horizon for the hope of rain.

The town itself had no particular boundaries but just straggled haphazardly here and there. You could never really sense that anything was taking shape for very long. Everything seemed to proceed at its own mundane pace but the underbelly of the town was darkness. Gaping mining shafts, now full of rusty tools and thistles, pitted the countryside, crude, corrugated iron shanties lined with newspaper huddled together on the wrong side of town, sad children with snotty noses waited hungrily outside the pubs where too many men had squandered their last pay checks. Rumours of alcoholism, incest and suicide persisted.

The taking hold of the land had been tenuous, the winters bitterly cold, the families secretive, tired women standing behind tired, brutish men. The cemetery was one of the largest reserved blocks on the edge of the town, full of imposing Victorian headstones which contrasted with the tiny graves, simple mounds of dirt marked out by rusty, wrought iron railings revealing the all too frequent cost of pioneering life. You could read the history of the town in the elaborate messages engraved on the gravestones and trace the ancestral lines through the groupings of family graves where deceased relatives from other lands far, far away now lay together in their imposed exile.

*   *   *

We followed the stranger to this blighted town, like doubtful and displaced refugees, obliged to join our souls to a strange man and to a future of immense uncertainty.

We did not inhabit the homestead belonging to my grandparents but were installed in a tiny wooden cottage previously used by labourers. It must have been a come-down for my father, but he held fixed in his mind the memory of the solemn handshake with his father, ensuring that the property of Big Ben would belong to him one day. He had brought back some new ideas about changing the stock and growing new pastures, but his father, a dyed-in-the-wool sheep man, would not allow the innovations of his impertinent son. Like all men of his generation, unassailable in their entrenched patriarchy, he was determined to hang on to the property until he died. He relished his position in the highest ranks of the district's squattocracy and would not hand over to a whipper snipper, hero or no hero.

'Anyway, we can't leave this house, Charles,' his mother explained to him in her wheedling voice. 'Nobody knows us in Glen Innes.'

I cannot remember our arrival nor my first impressions of my paternal grandparents. I suppose they may have visited us in Glen Innes but for some reason they held themselves aloof and never seemed to approve of us.

Soon the days in our little cottage began to stretch into months and yield themselves to the flow of country life in Australia. My mother planted a beautiful cottage garden of dahlias and gladiolas in front of the house and was soon pregnant with her third child. I suppose she thought she had come home at last to that little world Charles and she had envisioned before the war. She was the ideal farmer's wife and her gentle heart began to beat to the rhythm of Monday Washing Day, Tuesday Ironing, Wednesday Mending, Thursday Cleaning, Friday Baking. Country women, like my mother, were strong, sensible girls, sharing the load of farm work, milking cows, making their own butter and soap, growing vegetables, laughing at the men's jokes, sharing a shandy (beer mixed with lemonade) and jumping on a horse in a muster if needed.

My father was absent again from time to time but we had the daily care of our mother and a thousand secrets of the Australian bush to discover. Even though we were still very young, we were sent outside to play all day and no one worried about our safety. Left to our own devices and inquisitive natures, my sister and I wandered as far from the house as we dared, re-forming the wild landscape according to our childish imaginations. Our favourite pastime was building a cubby house and furnishing it with discarded saucepans, an old straw broom, raggedy towels and bits of pretty, broken Depression glass which we discovered in a rubbish tip.

The new baby, a little brother, was born and started to follow us around as soon as he learnt to walk. I loved his gentle spirit and his little hand in mine as we explored our back yard together. He was named Mallory after my father's best war-time friend, Sir Trafford Leigh-Mallory, commander of the Battle of Britain. We teamed up together, sneaking off on our own at times to avoid our bossy sister. One day as we were fossicking in the tip, we discovered some beautiful pieces of broken glass which we hid in the trunk of a tree. Our favourite ritual was to take out the glass when our sister wasn't watching, stare at it, wash it and hide it back in the tree.

We were shabby bush kids and wore the clean but utilitarian clothes of post-war Australia. Everything was handed down, patched or darned. If you were given a new outfit or even a pair of shoes, they were always a size too big so you 'could grow into them'. Our mother knitted all our winter jumpers with a thick, coarse wool which prickled our skin. Our hair was crudely cut into a short, square shape with a piece pulled across to the side because we had the sort of hair which could not be curled or combed into a more flattering shape. My mother used to tie it up in rags overnight for special occasions but it never retained its curls for long. An aunt said that we were cursed with the Scherf straight hair – the straightest hair in the district.

*　　*　　*

The ebb and flow of country life began to create a sense of regrowth in our family. My mother rose early to fetch chips for the wood stove and start the breakfast preparation: lamb chops, bacon, fried eggs and toast for our father, porridge for the children. The old black kettle was always boiling on the stove in readiness for the numerous cups of tea served throughout the day or if unexpected visitors arrived. In the evening, we sat by the kerosene lamp, listening to the radio. If our father was in a good mood, he would sometimes play a record on the old gramophone and twirl our mother around the floor. On Saturday night the chip heater was stoked into action and we took our weekly bath, one child after the other in the same tub of grey water.

A pattern had begun to form in our lives as we learnt to move according to the seasons and the vagaries of nature, bound together in the dream-like torpor of bush life, like the misty figures in a Millet painting.

As for me, I was alive and my days were filled with wonder. I began to sense the harmony of the world around me, the land stretching out as far as the eye could see, the secret movements of the bush animals and the pleasant carolling of the magpies in the morning. My place in the world was becoming secure:

51

my mother boiling sheets in the old copper wash tub, my father out riding in some remote paddock but due home for lunch any minute, my sister standing guard at the cubby house door, my little brother trotting along beside me. At night, I would fall asleep peacefully with my cat, Felix, on the bed, my dreams full of stringy saplings, glistening granite rocks and the unexplored hill behind our house.

The sense of a birthright had started to form in our minds for we finally belonged to a man. As Charles' children we would eventually live in the big manor house, attend private schools in Armidale and take up our place as leaders of the small but selective rural community. I would grow up to be brave and clever and my father would be proud of me and learn to love me in time.

There was something else and I do not know how or when it happened. To talk about it is difficult and embarrassing because most people would not believe it possible for a child of five to have experienced such things and with such intensity.

I was generally shy and reserved but gradually the world around me started to open up as if a velvet curtain was being drawn back from the waiting stage, inviting me to turn myself over to a more instinctive and mythological power.

Let me just say that I had been waiting, waiting for the world to reveal itself to me, to wake up that old ancestor knowledge, that strange connection between inner and outer landscape developed through a steady accretion of sentiments. For I was learning to acclimatise the yearning of my soul to this wild countryside, my passion to the scorching summers and freezing winters, and my unfolding intelligence to the beckoning stars. In the lazy summers, I would lie on my back in the shade of a tree and absorb the clanging drama of the insects in the midday heat. In autumn, I would bask in the melancholy of golden leaves, overblown roses, orange sunsets and long, long shadows. In the winter, I would become intoxicated with the smoke of the open fires, damp, frost-bitten earth and the smell of mouldy leaves. Then one clear night, as I looked up at the brilliant stars, the universe suddenly opened up like a giant dome in an observatory and I knew that God existed.

None of my siblings or cousins experienced this connection but it appears that the old, old call of the shepherd was already lodged in my heart. In an extract from 'The Creek', a document published to celebrate the centenary of the Vegetable Creek/ Emmaville area, it was recorded that Big Ben was named after the well-known clock as it indicated to the shepherds the time to bring in the sheep for the night. A local vet also found an old shepherd's crook thought to have been brought from Germany by the Scherfs and there were other records of the Scherfs as shepherds.

This somewhat explained the strange and lovely thing that was happening to me. Like the shepherds of old, I felt summoned to watch over the fields and the hills, to learn how to keep them 'in life' simply by looking after and loving them, and to understand how my 'becoming' needed them.

So, even as a very young child, this land, the land of my father, the arena of my playing and my dreaming, had begun to build the most ineffable aspects of my identity. I would have been content to stay in this place forever, for never would I find a landscape more akin to my very being. There would have been no reason for me to see the rest of the world for it seemed to me as if the whole endeavour of human history could be played out here in this remote corner of New South Wales.

Big Ben. You were my one true home. I existed because you saw and loved me.

But when you came toward me to 'meet' me and be 'met', I had already disappeared.

*   *   *

Shall I speak now of my father? Gradually, his presence and personality began to imprint itself on our lives and we began, shyly and respectfully, to adjust to his demands and habits. On special occasions, we accompanied him to social events and sometimes drove in his car to town. In the evening, he would sit in the house smoking or drinking beer and in the morning, we would hear his tractor starting up. I don't remember him nursing me on his knee, reading me stories or putting me to bed, special intimate moments that might have narrowed the gap between us.

Sometimes, however, he liked to play very funny games. There was a standing joke which he liked to play at lunch time when we were all seated at the table in a rather formal manner. Our father insisted on good table manners and he himself never came to the table in his shirt sleeves; we children had to sit up straight, eat our meal in silence and never rest our elbows on the table. That is why it was so surprising when half-way through the meal, he would suddenly sit back on his chair as if surprised and cast a sharp glance at the front door.

'Come in,' he would shout, forcing us all to turn around to see who was at the door. There was never anyone there! Then he would laugh at us and we would gently chide him: 'Oh, Dad.' He would repeat this game over and over and we would grow more and more determined to hold out, to not let him fool us again, yet his fresh surprise and greeting were always so convincing that we would end up looking around at the door, see that there was really no one there and collapse into laughter one more time.

We loved this game because we were playing with our father but we didn't like it when he would suddenly faint into his soup and a trickle of blood would run out of his ears.

Sometimes his jokes went too far and the game became more sinister. After a drinking bout in town, he would drive us out to the old tin mines and run his car at top speed across the field pitted with deep shafts. The edges of the deepest pits were soft and crumbling and we were always afraid that the car would tip over backwards if it slipped into one of the holes.

'Let's give it a go today, eh kids? See if your ol' dad's still got his magic touch.'

'No, Daddy, no,' we protested, feeling the familiar rise of panic and nausea in our stomachs. As he took off, we lurched against each other, trying to steady ourselves by grabbing hold of the seat and the door handles. The wheels of the Oldsmobile spun fast as he skidded dangerously close to the gaping mouth of the mine and red dust splayed over the top and sides of the car.

Ignoring our screams and the frightened look on his wife's face, he seemed lost in another world as he accelerated, braked and reversed, darting around the mineshaft like a soldier ant whose nest has been attacked.

At one fast curve, the car went into a slide sending the back wheels over the edge of a very deep mine. The car tilted backwards, rocked a little and then seemed to hang in mid-air. We stared out of the back window, sick with terror as we saw the dark hole opening up beneath us. Charles just laughed, almost contemptuously, gave the accelerator a mighty thrust and the car shot clear of the pit.

'Told you I could do it. There, what are you crying about?' he said with a cocky grin.

'Oh, Charles,' my mother cried. 'I don't know what's the matter with you. I don't know why you do these things. You'd think you would be more careful with the children in …'

Then she would break off, cowered by the scornful, impatient look he gave her.

On the ride back home, we snivelled in the back of the car, glancing up ruefully at his dark outline in the front seat. Like all children of that time, we knew our place in the constant humiliation of the young and said nothing. The excitement had made us tired and, feeling the calm of another reprieve, we fell into an uneasy sleep.

* * *

We were soon to learn that our father was prepared to expose us to enormous risks. I suppose you could say that he was irresponsible, for speed, restlessness and alcohol were beginning to form some of our memories.

'Can we go to the movies?' my sister implored one snowy Saturday afternoon.

'Please, Daddy. We want to go!'

Maureen had more of a way with our father than any of the other children and she did not hesitate to pester him until she got what she wanted. She had the most wilful personality of all the children and Charles seemed to favour her for her strong determination.

'It's too slippery,' he replied. 'I don't really want to take the car out in this weather. You can wait till next week.'

'No,' Maureen insisted, doubling up her pleas. 'I want to go now. You promised last week and we can't go outside and play because it's too cold.'

She began to cry and increased her wailing until I joined in. I always followed my older sister and copied her way of responding to adults because she knew what to do. I did not understand the movies but I loved the flashing images in colour and the bright music.

This was too much for Charles who was already feeling tense, cooped up inside the house, so he grabbed the two girls by the arms, marched them out to the car and flung them into the backseat.

'Damn kids,' he yelled, ignoring our mother's pale face and urgent pleas. 'I'll take you to the bloody movies alright!'

Our father paid no attention to the dangerous condition of

the road, jamming his foot on the accelerator in the hope of releasing all his pent-up tension and impatience. We screamed as we were thrown all over the back seat of the car which revved and skidded over the icy roads. When we realised that the dangerous causeway was coming up, we doubled up our screams.

'No, Daddy! No!'

But his face was grim and fearless and he hit the causeway, took off into the air, soared over the dip and landed with a shuddering crash on the other side, the engine spluttering and stalling. Cursing and shouting at us to be quiet, he stumbled out of the car and cranked the engine to life once more.

We crouched, frozen with fear, in the backseat for the impact of the crash had reverberated through our small bodies, causing a terrible pressure in the back of our necks as if our heads were going to snap off. When we arrived at the theatre, shaken and sore, we crept gratefully into the empty seats at the back of the cinema and sat there in the dark, watching the movie in stunned silence. Our father drank at the pub while he waited for us.

The journey home was much slower, a sullen, drunk driver staring with bleary eyes at the road opening and closing in front of him and two sniffling children huddled in the backseat of the car. We did not dare to speak for the man at the wheel no longer looked like our father and the whole world seemed to have forgotten us as we drove along, an uncertain blot on an isolated road in the middle of nowhere.

Like blinded creatures who had lost all their bearings, we moved through the night, silently, aimlessly towards a spot which kept receding further and further into the darkness.

'Oh, goodness me, Charles.' My mother was waiting at the door and rushed out at the sight of the car. 'I've been worried sick. The kids … the slippery road. Oh, God, I'm so glad you're safe.'

He almost fell up the front steps and she felt him push past her and stagger into the bedroom. There was something in him that had begun to frighten her but she was afraid to confront him, especially when he had had too much to drink. It was better to put the trembling children to bed, to lock the front door, close all the curtains and leave the horror of the dark night outside.

*　*　*

Years later, recalling these incidents, I asked my mother if our father ever loved us. She thought about it and then she simply said:

'Oh, yes. He liked you kids well enough.'

I had this niggling feeling, however, that despite the terrors he inflicted on us that it was we who had somehow failed to measure up to his expectations. Childhood in my father's time was definitely not marked off as a protected period of dependence and development. We were expected to do physical work on the farm and grow up the best way we could. Accidents, childhood illnesses and fatalities were commonplace. If you had a toothache or an earache you had to endure the pain and the dreadful spoonful of castor oil was given as a cure-all for any complaint. Mostly we were left to our own devices as long as we observed the general rule of good manners and obedience to elders.

I knew there was one thing, however, that my father earnestly desired to see in his children, and that was courage. Apparently, our lack of fortitude during his daredevil stunts had disappointed him greatly and he was always looking for a glint of his own fearlessness in our temperament. He didn't know then what he came to learn later, that courage takes many forms, that for some people getting out of bed in the morning and facing the day requires inordinate strength and for others it might be performing a song in public with half your brain missing.

*   *   *

One day, he called us over to inspect four dead snakes which he had carefully laid out, side by side, on a flat rock near our house. The snakes had been discovered in an old wood heap near the chook house and we thought at first that he was going to give us a lesson on their habits and the best way to kill them. Our hearts sank, however, as our father started to explain his purpose and the horrifying realisation hit us that this was not going to be a lecture after all, but a test. A test to jump over the snakes without landing on their scaly backs!

We stood there, scarcely able to breathe, transfixed by the dreadful nearness of the creatures we had been taught to avoid at all costs. Although our father insisted that they were dead, we were not convinced as their gleaming, black bodies seemed to writhe and quiver in the midday sun. There was nothing in the world which would have impelled us to take the test; we screamed and ran for the safety of our house with our father chasing after us. Our mother had rushed out of the house to see what the commotion was all about and as we sought refuge in her kitchen, our father had to accept the fact that none of his children had inherited his fighting spirit.

'Bloody gutless kids I've got,' he muttered in disgust and went back to his work.

*   *   *

My father's idea of manhood was not an individual one. Extreme daring, hard drinking, love of speed and sheer bloody-mindedness were accepted and approved marks of manhood in country towns. Another stunt in which my father liked to engage was driving down the Big Hill as fast as he could on a starless night with the headlights off. There were no seatbelts in those days and no particular regard for the safety of children. We simply piled into the back seat or rode along, perched precariously on our mother's knee, too terrified to complain as he accelerated into the tunnel of darkness.

My grandfather suffered from the same sense of self-aggrandisement and obstinacy which almost cost me my life. Returning one night from Glen Innes with my mother, my brother and myself, and with too much Scotch under the belt, he insisted belligerently on driving home even though he could scarcely control the steering wheel. The car swayed as he careened all over the road and barely made it around the sharp corners, stones from the dirt road splattering against the sides of the car. Bushes scraped and tore at the car windows as we were tossed back and forward in the back seat and grabbed wildly for something to hold onto. Our mother tried to plead with him to stop but her cries were muffled by my grandfather laughing and cursing in his slurred speech. At a sharp bend in the road, my grandfather decided to accelerate and we peered mournfully into the darkness to see if he would make the turn. The sinking feeling of not being able to protest, of having to place our lives in the hands of a man too drunk to drive, meant that we were at the mercy of fate. When the headlights of another car suddenly came into view, it was too late to do anything but subject ourselves to the full force of a head-on collision. Suddenly, everything went black. I was thrown forward, hitting the front seat with a forceful thud and losing consciousness. Somehow, we must have been rescued and miraculously, the passengers in the front seat escaped with only cuts and bruises but, on noticing my limp body, everyone thought I had broken my neck or been killed. I was unconscious for days and when I awoke, I was wearing a bandage on my head and my eyes had swollen into tiny slits.

Very little fuss was made of the accident and there were no police reports. I felt no anger towards my grandfather and just accepted that I had had a lucky escape. What did bother me most was that, as a result of my disfigured appearance, I was considered too ugly to attend the upcoming Christmas party as a fairy. I had to swap my beautiful, blue tulle dress, my sparkly crown and wand with my cousin's Chinese costume. Her hair was curled into golden ringlets for the night while I suffered the humiliation of having to wear coarse, black Chinese pants and allow my mother to attach a horrible, woollen pigtail to the back of my head.

It was considered the perfect outfit for a girl with a swollen forehead and slanting, almond-shaped eyes.

*   *   *

Besides our fearless relatives there were plenty of things to be afraid of in the world of nature, like the sharp, painful tugs of the leeches in the river, the swooping of the magpies at nesting season, the snakes in the long grass and blackberry bushes, and the poisonous redback spiders which loved to nest in our outback toilet.

Our old black bull was a particularly cantankerous beast and known to charge anyone on sight. We never knew which paddock he would be grazing in at any time of the year but always felt that a black eye was watching us. One day, when we forgot to check, we decided to meet our cousins in the field with the biggest dam for amongst the reeds we had noticed the unmistakable holes of the tasty, blue-black craybobs that inhabited the slimy waters. Laughing and teasing each other as we dangled the unlucky creatures from our make-shift fishing rods, we suddenly caught sight of his unmistakable silhouette in the corner of a paddock. Someone must have opened the gate and let him in!

'What are we going to do?' my sister whispered, almost too scared to talk out loud in case he heard us. We could not avoid him as he was blocking our way to the cottage and suddenly, he turned and stared in our direction.

'Look,' my cousin called out. 'See? There's old Gilbert heading up to the dam for a drink. Let's grab him and climb up on his back. The bull won't attack a horse.'

It was a desperate idea but we all started creeping towards the old gelding, calling him in our soft but urgent voices. He was a rather clumsy, unintelligent but likeable beast who had known nothing in his life but humble obedience and, upon hearing his name, trotted towards us in his simple desire to be useful one more time.

'Get up quickly,' my cousin called out. There were five of us but we all had to fit on his back and unfortunately, as I was the last to get on, I ended up hanging onto his tail. As his huge haunches swayed through the grass, I almost fell off but fear of the bull – who was now regarding us curiously – caused me to clamp my legs and arms more tightly around his buttocks. Balancing precariously and trying not to slip, we urged old Gilbert through the paddock and managed to get past the bull without harm.

My sister was not so lucky in her fatal encounter with a dangerous beast. Mikey, the old farmyard ram belonging to our aunt, could always be spotted lurking behind some fence or corner of the house, fixing us with his heavy-lidded, doe-shaped eyes. He was Aunt Rose's favourite pet and she refused to think ill of him, deliberately ignoring the significance of the warning step he would take backwards when he spotted one of the children.

'Oh, Mikey. You naughty old boy,' she would coo at him as he backed slyly away. When she saw our frightened faces, she would hastily add, 'You don't have to worry about him. He's a lovely old boy and he only wants to play with you.'

The older Mikey grew, the more cantankerous he became and because he had the run of the place, he would sometimes slip across the road to our property. Somehow, he had worked out the time the school bus arrived and would set up his ambush behind the pine trees in our avenue. Every afternoon upon our arrival from school, we would alight hesitantly from the bus, look around and steal our way cautiously up the avenue as if we were walking the gauntlet. The worst part was that we never knew whether he would be there or not; it was just a question of luck. Some days he was too lazy to cross the road, but on other days he would suddenly appear from behind the trees and chase us gleefully up the avenue. There was no escape but to run for our lives up the driveway, the old ram's horns grazing our backsides as we flung ourselves over the garden fence.

None of the adults ever took these incidents seriously and Aunt Rose continued to pamper him until the fateful day.

'Come inside, you kids,' Mum yelled at us one afternoon, 'we have to be at Aunt Rose's for afternoon tea, so you had better wash your face and hands.'

I loved Aunt Rose's afternoon teas on Sunday as she always opened up her best room, that sealed-off room with the velvet drapes and the English China plates arranged on a decorative rail running around the walls. I loved to observe her as she laid the table, to stare at her beautiful, expensive ornaments and to linger for a moment in the unsullied room rather than join in the rough games of my brother and sister outside.

There was this other side of Aunt Rose which drew me to her, something which country life had failed to efface. In her rambling country home on a Sunday afternoon, I caught a sense of another world beyond Emmaville, a world beyond my mother's humble domain, a world that spoke of trips to Venice with her elegant sister to buy Venetian glass, of glamorous fashions like the glossy fur coat she had purchased in London for wintry 'town' days in Glen Innes and the sequinned evening gowns bought in Sydney for the gala balls they attended at the Royal Easter Show. I watched her spread out her best hand-embroidered tablecloth and set out a place for each visitor. The table was adorned with beautiful Irish linen napkins, pretty Royal Doulton teacups, polished silver cake forks and dainty cakes set out on doilies. There was a beautiful calm about the ritual of Sunday afternoon tea, a sense of things slowing down to mark time, a quietening of tired hearts grateful for the reprieve which Sunday afforded and an opportunity for the lady of the house to take off her gumboots and gardening clothes, don a pretty frock and demonstrate her finesse.

Suddenly, a scream of terror broke the silence, followed by another and another. We could hear a man's voice shouting and it sounded like Aunt Rose's son, Colin. My mother was the first to rush outside because somehow, among the din, she recognised the cry of her oldest child. She screamed in horror at the sight which awaited her. Old Mikey had bailed up my sister in a corner of one of the sheep pens and was butting her mercilessly, pinning her against the fence as he continued to attack her, digging his horns into her thighs and her stomach, the old 'ground and pound' instinct unleashed at full force.

Aunt Rose's desperate commands failed to bring him to heel for this time nothing was going to stop the old ram from venting his bovine fury on the humans he secretly misprised all along. He had slyly gone along with his domestication but the girl had been poking at him with a stick when she arrived and the commands from the old lady were not going to deprive him of this one chance to show his guardians the true nature of the beast.

My father arrived in time to help Colin pull the animal back and lift my sister out of the corner where she was wedged. Struggling to free himself from the stranglehold my father had on his horns, Mickey allowed his body to go slack and lay panting on his side between the two men. My mother rushed to my sister's aid, picking her up out of the dust, looking aghast at the bruises and gaping wounds all over her body.

'Oh, Rosie, he could have killed her!' she yelled accusingly at her sister-in-law.

Aunt Rose stood there in shock, glancing helplessly from her mangled niece to her deceitful pet. Everyone was fussing around my badly injured sister but there was something else that bothered me. Recalling the incident years later, I realised that my true sympathy had rested with my aunt. My poor aunt, my poor, genteel Aunt Rosie who should have married a gentleman but who, for lack of choice, had settled for a churlish husband and one male child, the uncouth Colin. Seeing the look of dismay on her face that day, I had somehow sensed the misery of her life as she tried to be a woman in a world of coarse, rough men, squandering her daily life in the kitchen and the gardens as a farmer's wife, singing and talking to her cats in a baby voice, her sensibility finding an outlet in the affinity she thought she had with all her animals. Now the special bond she had shared with the old ram had proven false and she was left with nothing but the full bitterness of his betrayal.

As the women struggled inside with my bleeding sister, the sound of a gunshot put an end to the afternoon tea and the flies swarmed deliriously on the dried-out delicacies.

Three years passed.

Three short but sumptuous years of country life, of happy days in the little cottage, games in the bush, cubby houses, trips to town, weekend parties at my grandmother's home, quiet evenings in the cottage playing Chinese Checkers by the light of a kerosene lamp. Three years with my daredevil father and Big Ben and the fields and the contrary animals. These dreamy days seemed to stretch out before me and in the evening, Felix would jump on my bed and I would sleep with the angels.

Three short years but enough time for my consciousness to align itself with the landscape and to believe that my happiness would last forever.

I did not know that it was already over.

All of a sudden, the luxurious years became narrow and the good things started to slip away. Like pearls on a broken necklace, the beads began to slide off, one by one.

At first, there was the drought, the worst in one hundred years, and my father had to slaughter a lot of his sheep. In the same year, my brother contracted rheumatic fever and was bed-ridden for months so I lost my best playmate. Then, quite unexpectedly, my beloved teacher, a beautiful young lady with laughing, blue eyes and wavy, red hair like Rita Hayworth, was found dead in a lonely, back paddock on her husband's property. Her shocked and heart-broken relatives were left to deal with their agonising questions for she had died as a result of the delirium tremors and nobody had thought to ask about the pile of empty metho bottles in the garbage.

These catastrophes were like omens pointing to a final decree. It arrived swiftly and with such finality as if someone were ticking off the last name on a list or turning the last page of a novel and closing the book.

Overnight, the news came that my father had been killed in a fatal car accident.

At first, I did not understand what had happened for everyone had started to talk in hushed whispers and tiptoe around each other. Nobody explained horrific events to children in those days and it was considered kinder to protect them from disturbing news. My sister, however, was only too pleased to blurt out the truth.

'Don't be such a ninny,' she retorted when I asked her why she was crying. 'Don't you know that our father's dead?'

I tried to cry but I did not feel sad and I did not understand the significance of the event and how it would change everything. It was only later that the full force of the tragedy began to surge into every aspect of my existence and I would spend the rest of my life treading water in the flood of my grief.

Death separated us all.

My father and I left our home at the same time but we did

not go to the same destination. 'We'll take Rosemary,' my grandfather had said. I was removed from my home and never returned. My father was laid in the cold, cold earth and the seasons piled up on his grave. All the gates were closed and the sun set on my life.

Big Ben. Oh, my home, did I remember you? When I outgrew the narrow, small-town life, when wider doors opened up for me and the lights of other worlds beckoned me, did I forget to love you? After so many years of absence and change it seemed impossible for a child to have hung on to such a distant past.

But I did. I did.

For when I was taken away from you, there was a part of me that did not move when I moved.

A split occurred in my psyche, the harmony of my life was disrupted and I became a stranger to myself. Never again would I inhabit a safe place where I knew what was happening around me, the patterns of territory marked out, the memories enshrined in rocks and hills. From that moment onwards, I would be homesick, anxious, restive, incompatible with my surroundings and the immense loneliness would begin.

Big Ben.

Home of my brief, enchanted childhood.

Forever I would harbour this acute longing, and in the end, it was more than a longing for a home or even for Big Ben but for a *place* where I had discovered joy, a *place* where I had lived and loved but could never go back to.

As the images faded over time and the memories blurred, it became my lament, not just for the actual object of loss but for the bittersweet *sense* of loss, the sense of something extraordinary which can never be retrieved but for which the yearning never dies.

My *hiraeth*.

*   *   *

My father's funeral was the largest ever recorded in Emmaville. I do not remember the service or even if we children were allowed to attend. All I remember are the sad faces of people I had never seen before.

It was my mother who had to face the aftermath as she moved anxiously, fearfully into the empty gap Charles had left. The shock of his sudden death had been explosive, her grief profound. She had busied herself replying to the hundreds of sympathy cards but her mind was in turmoil. What was her future in a place she could no longer call home and, without Charles to work the land, what use were the widow and her four children? Maureen was a lively nine-year-old capable of helping out but Colleen was only three months old and Mallory was sick. Thank goodness her parents had taken Rosemary off her hands; one less mouth to feed.

She suspected that there was little money in their bank account for he had spent all his war savings on the sheep. Like a lot of women of her time, she had no idea of her husband's financial situation and could not even write a cheque. It was true that the sacred handshake sealed her right to the land as Charles' widow, but there was no legal proof.

When I grew older, I was deeply angry about the loss of our inheritance but I understood my mother's predicament. Who can fight when you are forced to leave school at fourteen and shape your female will to the authority of men? Women like my mother were docile and compliant, no match for the haughty Scherfs.

Mr and Mrs Scherf appeared to be more distant, presumably lost in their own grief. Mrs Scherf had not replied personally to the sympathy cards but had merely placed a brief notice of thanks in the newspaper. She was worried about her husband because the usual number of shearers had not turned up for the shearing season and she feared that her obstreperous husband would try to make up the deficit himself. The life and livelihood of the old couple were in complete disarray but at least they had the decency to assist Hope in practical matters. My mother could not drive so it was a great relief to see a large box of groceries appear at her doorstep every week, presumably from her in-laws.

Hope also received help from her kindly neighbours and from a very unlikely source, a poor labourer called Aubrey who lived in a filthy caravan on Aunt Rose's property with his five skinny, snotty-nosed children and his wife, Mavis, a simple-minded woman who was always pregnant. The annex of the caravan was falling to pieces and inside, the benches were littered with dirty dishes, old cans and scraps of food, yet there was always a cup of tea for Hope who had begun wandering across the road more and more frequently.

'You don't want to be mixing with those people,' her mother-in-law declared disapprovingly.

'You're still Charles' wife and they're just common labourers. Surely, you've seen the state of their caravan and the way they live.'

Yet there was something in their manner which appealed to Hope, something about the way in which they lived out their distressed lives with such simplicity of heart. Their grief over her predicament was genuine and she was touched to find that, out of their meagre rations, they often deposited small parcels of food at her back door, wrapped up in old newspaper.

*   *   *

The rest of the aftermath of Charles' death passed like a nasty dream. The baby was always crying and often refused the comfort of the breast. Hope would rock the cot until she was exhausted in a desperate attempt to pacify the poor, little thing. After a frantic session, she would fall onto her lonely bed and stare out the dark window into an unfamiliar world. Everything was slipping away. A terrible feeling of displacement had begun to form in her mind. To make matters worse, her in-laws had started to make it obvious that her position in regard to the promised inheritance was tenuous and that she was becoming a burden.

It was time to take matters into her own hands. With constant worries about money, Hope decided that she should start to sell off the few things that Charles had bought without his father's help. She would begin with the sheep for the drought had broken and she could now expect that they would fetch a good price. Naturally, she would have to gain the assistance of her male relatives because there was no one else to help her and she had no idea how to go about selling stock at auction.

There are things that happen in the night and men who move stealthily through the darkness with secret intentions in their heart. These are the men who will always snatch an opportunity, brutish men who have struggled to tame this land and who have become insolent and greedy and feral as dingoes. They cross barriers of decency as easily as snipping a piece of barbed wire in a brother's fence and letting a few stray animals run through.

It was easy pickings after all. The unsuspecting widow did not have a clue how many sheep were remaining after the drought and later, when they took the remainder of the flock to the sale yards for auction, it was even easier to keep back a few bob for themselves.

'I'm really disappointed,' she confided to her neighbour. 'Of course I have no idea what a sheep is worth but I did expect to get a bit more from the sale. I really didn't know how to go about selling them myself anyway so I just had to let the men handle it.'

Hope could not disguise her disappointment when they brought the cash to her. It was clear that she was very upset but they simply shrugged their shoulders and walked away. When she was finally able to talk it over with her father, a man who certainly knew all about the cost of animals, she discovered to her horror that the men had cheated her.

'Well, I'll be darned!' Herb retorted. 'The dirty blighters! I never trusted those Scherfs anyway. Running around Emmaville in their fancy ways, expecting everyone to bow down to them as if they were bloody royalty. But when it comes to helping out a poor widow, they grease their own hands first.'

Herb's blue eyes flashed with anger and frustration because their duplicity would be difficult to prove. Besides, he knew his station in life would hold him back from a sufficient reprisal. They were powerful landowners and he was just the local vet, well-loved in the town admittedly, but everyone knew that he didn't have a proper degree from a university and was mainly self-taught. This lack of a piece of paper had come against him many times, especially when a university-trained man turned up in the town and stole half his customers. It took the sting out of his pride and Irish temper and introduced a certain tension into his dealings with his countrymen even though many farmers remained loyal to ol' Herb.

In this case, there was no way he could gain justice for his daughter and it stuck in his craw like a fishbone in his neck.

'The bastards,' he muttered to himself in bitter defeat.

There was still the new tractor, Charles' pride and joy. If Hope could get a good price for the machine, it would see them through the winter. As soon as she made her intention known, there was an urgent visit from Charles' older brother, Granville, and his tall, elegant wife.

Hope was very surprised to see them at her front door early one morning as they were not in the habit of visiting her in the cottage and usually only talked to her on social occasions at the manor house. She invited them in for a cup of tea, hastily retrieving from the back of her pantry cupboard her one good Shelley tea set with the hand-painted buttercups.

Granville sat stiffly in his chair, coughed several times and proceeded to explain the reason for their visit. He pointed out very carefully and deliberately that she was not entitled to sell the tractor because of a prior agreement.

'You see, Hope, Charles promised the tractor to me. I need it to plant my spring crop of wheat and lucerne and I really can't manage without it. Of course, I can't afford to pay for it but it was already agreed between us that I was to have the tractor if anything happened to Charles.'

Hope stared at her brother-in-law in dismay. He was stocky and over-bearing like her father-in-law and moved into a room as if he owned it. After all, he was the older brother with a property of his own whereas Charles' prospects had rested solely on a handshake. Besides, he lived in a mansion and had a beautiful wife from Northern Italy who was often asked to model for the local fashion parades in Glen Innes.

Hope was suddenly ashamed of her snub nose and mousey brown hair pulled back with a faded ribbon. She listened to her brother-in-law's case with growing despair, overwhelmed by his Teutonic sense of entitlement but hoping that they would be sympathetic when she explained her financial plight. In spite of her pleas, they remained adamant; the tractor belonged to them.

'Take it,' she almost spat the words at them as they stood up abruptly to leave. Then, with her last ounce of pride, she hurled a final curse at the departing couple as they trounced off down the garden path.

'Take the bloody thing!'

It was the first time my gentle mother had ever sworn at anyone.

*　　*　　*

Spring was turning into summer and life was supposed to begin again. On the neighbours' land, the merinos had dropped their spring lambs and it was delightful to see the babies running after their mothers on their gangling legs. The gnarled, grey fruit trees suddenly came to life with their fragile blossoms and the jonquils under the water tank had forced their delicate blooms through the hard ground. Normally it would have been the time to check the fences, the dams and the sheds.

Everything was waiting, waiting for the man to come and set things into motion.

But death hung over the land like a giant moth.

Susan Jane Scherf had grown more and more anxious over the past months and now felt that it was the right moment to speak to her husband. At 4 pm, she called him inside and set out the afternoon tea things with his favourite biscuits. Charles Senior enjoyed his afternoon cup of tea so she knew he would be in a good mood to listen to what she had to say.

'It's gone on too long,' she began. 'We'll have to make some other arrangements for Hope and the children. We can't keep providing for them like this.'

Her mouth had hardened into a determined shape, making her thin lips look even thinner. Of course she had grieved for the loss of the son she loved the most, her last baby when she was well past the age of child-bearing, but she could not allow her true feelings regarding her daughter-in-law to remain unvoiced any longer.

'I'm afraid I have to say something about Hope which I have tried to keep to myself for the past months. Deep down I think you feel the same. Let's face it, Charles. We can't let things go on like this any longer.'

Catching the look of growing interest on her husband's face, she continued to press her case with growing confidence.

'She can't expect to stay here forever. Charles is dead and a woman can't work the property on her own. We accepted her in the first place because she was Charles' wife but I couldn't imagine her ever becoming the mistress of Big Ben. The O'Haras are simple folk and they didn't believe in educating their daughters. Hope has no … well, culture and frankly he could have done a lot better, especially after his success in the war. And all those medals.'

There was an incident which had stuck in her mind for several years. She had never forgotten the stylish, sophisticated woman who, after the war, had followed Charles all the way to Emmaville from the United States of America. Enid had worked for the famous airline company, Pan Am, and had met Charles through the company's offer to fly with their first transatlantic aeroplanes. Charles had declined the offer but Enid had continued to pursue him in spite of the fact that he was married. It was indeed regrettable because this woman would have made a much more suitable partner for her dashing son and there was no doubt about the crush she had on Charles.

Australians were obsessed with America at this time, the nation of such promise and glamour. Susan had been delighted when her own nineteen-year-old daughter, Beryl, had married an American millionaire and was now living the high life in San Francisco; never mind that he was twenty-five years older. Then suddenly this sophisticated woman from America had turned up out of the blue and was a guest in her house.

Susan recalled the golden days when, after the Sunday tennis matches, Charles and Enid would sit together on the green lawn, sipping beer and gin. Dinner was followed by recitals of classical music on the violin and Charles would finish off the evening with a rowdy singalong around the piano. Ah, those long, languorous summer nights when everything around her seemed attuned to life.

'A real pity,' Susan sighed, pouring another cup of tea for her husband and sitting back in her chair. She stared glumly at the unused crystal and China in the mahogany cabinets, remembering how much Enid had loved a good party, how she had dazzled everyone with her fashionable wardrobe, those knee-length, A-line dresses with the fitted waists and tiny boleros, those pencil skirts which showed off her slim figure and oh! those high-waisted, silky, wide-legged pants she wore for the evening cocktails. She could still see Enid flitting around the lounge room, waving her long cigarette holder and capturing everyone with her adorable accent and those witty anecdotes about San Francisco.

It was a deplorable fact that Hope had no dress sense and could not have managed to properly present herself at the ball in Charles' honour if Beryl hadn't stepped in. She was completely out of place in sophisticated society and Susan wondered if Hope had ever noticed the growing intimacy between Enid and her husband. Before dinner, it was their habit to enjoy a cocktail on the verandah, sitting with their heads close together and bursting out laughing over some casual innuendo or private joke. After dinner, they would dance to old gramophone records, holding each other too closely, and some nights they disappeared for several hours while Hope dutifully went back to the cottage to put the children to bed.

They were a perfect match, this elegant, poised woman and her famous, handsome son. Admittedly she had to turn a blind eye when they disappeared for hours on end to the back of the woodshed, but she was fascinated by the American, an honoured guest in her house and she was determined to offer her the best of Australian country hospitality.

The affair came to an abrupt end one summer's evening after a prolonged bout of drinking. There was a terrible fight on the front lawn, accompanied by shouts, threats and a woman's screams. Someone said Charles had his hands around the American's throat, threatening to kill her. Hope couldn't believe the rage she saw on her husband's face and that strange, murderous look which wasn't there before the war. It took two burly relatives to restrain Charles and end the debacle.

The American left the property the next morning and was never seen again.

'A real pity,' Susan repeated as if the words alone could fully express her regret. She could not imagine what had caused the rift when everyone seemed to be having such a fine time. Yes, the post-war era had been a riotous and perhaps a reckless time with everyone wanting to kick up their heels but nobody could blame them for wanting to celebrate the outstanding achievement of their beloved son.

Well, the party was well and truly over now. Enid was gone, Charles was dead and their aspirations for the land and their social standing had declined.

'There's nothing more we can do for Hope,' she started up again, returning from her reverie like a traveller who has dozed off but suddenly realises she has arrived at her bus stop. 'I've been thinking it over for a while and I believe we have a solution.'

She hesitated for a moment, testing her husband's reaction, then continued in her wheedling voice.

'You know that old Teddy Robinson who lives in town? He's been looking for a housekeeper for a long time. We can ask him to take Hope.'

She spoke calmly and deliberately as if she had put a great deal of thought into the proposition and was now presenting an infallible case.

'He's years older than her, but he has a nice home,' she added. 'She could do much worse. Don't think he will relish the idea of young children in the house but Hope will have to keep the baby for a while, I suppose.'

Charles Senior was suddenly very interested in his wife's proposal but she would never have guessed his exact reason. Women can certainly mess up a man's life, he thought, recalling that embarrassing day last year when Charles was away at the wool sales and he had sneaked up to the cottage. Finding Hope alone in the kitchen, he'd enquired after her well-being, then, aroused by her timidity and polite deference, he had suddenly pressed himself against her. She was a pretty, small-boned woman but he was surprised at the fullness of her breasts and her firm rump. Mistaking his caress for solicitude, she had at first allowed him to kiss her and to press his rough, fleshy lips into her neck.

The old lust of the *seigneur* was awakened, his shaking hands began to grope her breast and he thrust his hard erection into her thigh.

'Come on. Come on,' he whispered hoarsely, urging her towards the bedroom. 'Don't be afraid. If you're worried about getting pregnant, I'll pull out.'

The terrible enormity of his intention broke over Hope like sudden hail on a tin roof and she struggled to push him away. She fought him like a cornered beast, responding with the only defence she knew would restrain his passion.

'If you don't stop, I'll tell Charles. I will. I'll tell him,' she spluttered and, with a final effort to disentangle herself, pushed past him into the kitchen, leaving him standing there with the fly of his pants undone.

Remembering the incident, Charles Senior looked contemptuously at his thin-lipped, bony wife, feeling a sudden stirring in his groin as he recalled how Hope had struggled in his arms, like a soft, terrified rabbit.

Silly little hussy, he thought. Who did she think she was anyway? She had obviously let Charles have his way with her before the marriage and he wasn't fooled by her prim and proper ways.

Suddenly the thought of getting rid of her was a great relief. He had been worried about his daughter-in-law's position on the land now that his son was gone, even though he didn't think she had a leg to stand on. It irked him to think that he might have to go cap in hand to her after she had made such a fool of him.

'I think you're right, my dear,' he replied, sitting back in his chair and taking out his pipe. Sensing her husband's approval, Susan Jane leaned forward, pressing home her advantage. Looking directly into her husband's eyes, she concluded her appeal with the following statement, as if she had tallied up the monthly accounts and presented him with the final balance.

'As for Hope's girls, they will have to go to an orphanage. I've already made enquiries. It's obvious that she can't support them and old Teddy will have enough problems with the baby. We'll keep Mallory, of course. He's Charles' son after all.'

Hope was summoned to a family conference at Big Ben where she listened to her in-laws with a sinking heart. With each colossal proposal she could feel the weight of layers of stones falling on her. Her heart was beating rapidly, the room had begun to spin around her and the faces of her in-laws swam before her like those distorted images in circus mirrors: her arrogant father-in-law with his bristling moustache, her mother-in-law with her sharp, prying eyes and the joking face of her husband with his cocky grin. They were all laughing at her.

It is usually the innocent who suffer in any conflict.

When I grew older, it made me angry to think that my mother had been treated so unjustly but I couldn't stop asking myself why she had not tried to stand up to them.

I could not have understood that the assault sprang not only from the cold hearts of my in-laws but had touched something on a deeper level within my poor mother herself. Feeling that her role in life was to fit in with others, my mother had no conception of fighting back. It was her device for concealing her ignorance, for always accepting the way things were, her ultimate protection for changelessness. All she knew to do was to endure the pain and hope to survive just as she did years later when she was dying in hospital and whispered to the hovering nurse:

'Don't fuss, dear. I'll be alright. Just let me lie here for a while.'

When the Scherfs stopped speaking, Hope left the room without saying anything. Outside, a wind had blown up and the pines were creaking. The old, familiar world was spinning away from her and she couldn't seem to find the path back to her cottage. In a daze she stumbled across the paddocks towards her neighbour's fence and scuttled under the barbed wire.

She had seen this sort of thing happen many times on the farm, a bewildered animal separated from the herd in readiness for the slaughter; now it was her turn.

Hazel made a cup of tea and promptly advised her to ring her father in Glen Innes.

Hope did not bargain for the fierce love and loyalty of an Irish heart. With the sheep and the tractor still sticking in his craw, the blue-eyed Irishman did not hesitate this time. There was no way those Scherfs were going to split up the children and shunt off his dear girl to the first available old codger.

'I can't believe it,' he retorted. 'I just can't believe it. Oh, my dear. Well, they won't get away with it this time. I'll work something out.'

'What can we do?' she implored her father. 'I haven't got any money. They've taken everything and they want to get rid of me. They want to kick me and the girls out!'

Now she was sobbing her heart out, great anguished sobs which interrupted the staticky conversation as she tried to explain her circumstances.

'They've explained it all to me. They want to send the girls away. They don't want us here. Only Mallory ... they want to keep Charles' son. And I'm supposed to go and live with that old Mr Robinson. Oh, why did Charles have to d—? Look at the mess he's left us in. I can't ... I just can't do it.'

In spite of the shock, a firm decision was forming in the old man's brain and he began to shout urgently down the phone.

'Now you listen to me, my dear. You'll come back to Glen Innes as soon as you can. Yes, that's it. I'll find a place for you and the kids and you can take Rosemary back. You must get out of there, get away from them as fast as you can. Hope, can you hear me? Hope?'

The phone line began to static and Herb struggled to get his last message across. 'Pack up your things and I'll come for you. Do you hear me, dear? I'll come for you soon as I can. I'll let Hazel know. Hope? Do you hear me ...?'

The line went dead.

Herb moved swiftly to find a house to rent in Glen Innes. He was lucky enough to find one just two doors up from his own house in Glen Innes and paid for the rent himself. That will make up for the sheep and tractor, he thought, feeling at peace with himself at last for he had recovered his pride and nobody could change his mind.

*   *   *

The day of departure arrived and Herb couldn't wait to make the trip to Emmaville. One can only imagine what my mother must have felt as she prepared to pack up her life and turn her back on Big Ben. When she timidly announced her decision to her surprised in-laws, she did not know whether they were relieved or annoyed. They muttered something about the land and Mallory and it sounded like a caution; or could it have been a threat? There was no turning back, however, but the thought must have occurred to her that her children would never return to their rightful home and that once the children had left, the inheritance was lost forever.

The sound of Herb's truck chugging up the driveway cancelled any further doubts she might have had and she stumbled onto the verandah with the last remaining boxes. With all her belongings removed, the cottage appeared weathered, empty and desolate and she wondered how she had ever turned this shabby labourer's hut into a home.

No one came to assist the old man but just as he was deciding whether he would have to make two trips, he saw Aubrey's old Ute bumping up the driveway with all the kids piled in the back. Mavis was sitting uncomfortably in the front seat, pregnant again, balancing a bag of Anzac biscuits on her swollen stomach. She lumbered over to Hope, tears welling up in her eyes, and hugged her fiercely. Then, as she could see Mr and Mrs Scherf walking towards them with a disapproving look on their faces, she bid the children say a quick goodbye and waddled off down the driveway with the five kids trailing after her.

Herb O'Hara stood impatiently by the loaded vehicles, anxious to leave Big Ben as soon as possible and to avoid the niceties of having to greet the Scherfs. Aubrey was instructed to follow him in the Ute. Goodbyes were very brief and for the first time Hope felt a surge of relief to be leaving the life she had never been meant to live. She farewelled her in-laws in a polite voice and made the children kiss them goodbye.

Something like steel was forming in her heart.

As she was about to get into the car, her mother-in-law came towards her and, without explaining, pushed a heap of crumpled papers into her hand and walked briskly back to her house. Hope glanced curiously at the writing and was shocked to realise that the papers were old receipts for meat and groceries, all made out to her name. She stood frozen to the spot, transfixed in the moment of her limit, all the events of the last year multiplying around her and the bitter realisation forming in her faltering mind.

My mother, my mother. A small, solitary figure standing in the ruins of her life like a witless pauper with a wad of unpaid bills in her hand.

Hope steadied herself because the children were eager to begin the exciting ride they had been promised and ordered

Mallory and Maureen to climb into the truck next to their grandfather. Shoving the bills into her handbag, she gave a last, longing glance towards her garden with the proud, blood-red dahlias at their peak. The cicadas had begun their shrill midday recital, the sky was unusually blue but storm clouds were gathering on the horizon. Her mind wandered distractedly for a few moments as she gazed at the dry paddocks, sizing up the possibility of rain towards evening, then she corrected herself. What did it matter to her anymore?

Suddenly, out of the corner of her eye, she glimpsed a flash of orange on the ridge of the big hill behind the cottage. A mournful wail startled her from her thoughts, the wail of the outcast beast, like a lost soul in purgatory. She recognised this cry instantly, the cry of the dingo, for the feral beast would sometimes pass by their land early in the morning when she was hanging out the washing. It would remain at a distance for several minutes, gazing at her intently with its yellow eyes before it uttered its mournful howl and trotted off into the bush.

She stood there, transfixed, staring at the hills. The dingo had been watching her stealthily and as she turned away, it lifted its head and uttered a long, farewell cry. She felt the hot jab in her stomach. Hope climbed into the Ute with the baby and left Big Ben without a tear, glad to be leaving this cursed place, relieved to be returning to Glen Innes, to her hometown and her own people. A new life awaited her there for she still had the kids to look after and she would make sure that they all survived. Her practical mind had begun to tick over and she was already planning her new home. It would be a lonely struggle but, with her parents nearby, she would find the strength to live out the widow's life.

My mother would never marry again.

Once the growl of the dingo enters a woman's belly, no man will ever touch her and she will live alone for the rest of her life.

CHAPTER 3

BREAKING AWAY

Glen Innes 1949

Glen Innes is a picturesque town situated on the Northern Highlands in the New England region of New South Wales. It was named after a Scottish settler, Major Innes, and became the centre of a tin mining bonanza in the late 19th century. The arrival of a rail service, the Main North railway from Sydney, brought a new prosperity to the town which resulted in the construction of many beautiful federation buildings. In later years, a circle of Standing Stones similar to Stonehenge and a group of stones representing the Southern Cross were erected on the hill overlooking the town, a monument to the Celtic people of Australia.

Glen Innes is situated only 35 miles from Emmaville but does not have the hillbilly appearance of the latter. It is more bourgeois with its impressive number of imposing blue-brick churches, two high schools, a show ground, banks, department stores, a main street full of heritage-listed buildings and an outstandingly beautiful town hall. The hierarchy of the town consisted not solely of landowners but of bank managers, merchants, local government officials and professional people.

The ordinary people in the town lived, worked and died there with the same air of mellow mediocrity. They worked hard with the sole purpose of 'making good' and, very sensibly, reserved their pastimes for Saturday afternoon and Sundays. Admittedly, life in Glen Innes was not very exciting but you could exist there quite happily once you had formed its habits, for that is what the town encouraged. Friday afternoon was 'town day' when well-dressed ladies ambled up and down the main street in hats and gloves and enquired politely after each other's health. Saturday was sports day; Sunday was church followed by afternoon tea with a favourite aunt.

You would be right in thinking that the amiable, industrious townsfolk could have suffered from intense ennui and you can only imagine the considerable effort they would have had to have made to suppress their Celtic yearnings.

One of my aunts from Emmaville, unimpressed by the bourgeois pretensions of the town, summed it up in the following words:

'The town is cold, the people are unfriendly and the meat is tough.'

* * *

My mother set about establishing a home for her children in the rented house in Glen Innes and I was re-united with my family. I don't remember the day they arrived or the excitement of moving into our new home. Traumatised people have memories that are very disorganised. They remember some things all too clearly and but cannot remember the sequence of events or other vital details. I simply complied with the new arrangements, moving helplessly from one space to the next, always harbouring a deep sense that something was missing.

The grief that lay frozen in my heart had somehow worked its way to the surface of my life and my health had deteriorated. By the time my mother 'got me back', I was suffering from severe malnutrition, my hair was falling out and I had started biting my nails to the quick. The doctor prescribed a strong tonic.

Our mother resumed the weekly routine of washing, ironing, cooking, cleaning. There was barely enough money for the family of five to exist on a widow's pension, all that a grateful government could spare for the family of one of its WWII aces, so she managed to obtain a part-time job at the post office.

It took legal action from service friends as far as the High Court to eventually gain a War Widow's pension for her. A letter written to the mayor of Glen Innes and signed by members of Charles' 418 Squadron assisted in this appeal:

'We somehow feel that, however he died, he was a casualty of war as we realise how he overloaded himself and how his health suffered flying. A man can only take so much and he took enough for twenty. The fact that he was ordered to do test flying in Australia when he returned home was the final straw.'

Hope never remarried. I don't think there would have been many suitors willing to take on the pretty, young widow with her brood of four, so it was surprising one night to hear the doorbell ring and to find a strange man standing on the front steps. Mum had answered the door first and was standing there shyly when we appeared. We rarely had visitors so we tried to race each other to the door to be the first to inspect the stranger, a tangle of wide-eyed faces, arms and legs pushing against each other like footballers in a scrum. The man took several steps back in shock, made his apologies and was never seen again.

We never wondered about her loneliness because she was just our mother. For a while she dutifully attended the formal country balls with her relatives but in the end, she preferred to be relegated to kitchen duties, peeping behind the curtains on the town hall stage to watch the wives dancing in their husband's arms.

'There were times,' she explained wistfully, 'when I told them I didn't want to go the balls anymore but they kicked up such a fuss that I gave in. Sometimes one of your kind uncles would ask me for a dance, but mostly I would just sit there staring at the happy couples. I felt so embarrassed because everyone else had a partner and I was all alone.'

My mother did not appear to be unhappy for she filled her life with her children but there was a degree of self-imposed isolation in her life. She kept herself apart from many community activities and would only socialise with her close relatives. Her bedroom always seemed to be cold and bare and we rarely entered the room, not just out of respect, but because it felt unpleasantly sacred, like a nun's cell.

One night she told us a story which disturbed us profoundly.

'Sometimes I used to go to the movies alone when you kids were older. I wasn't afraid to walk home by myself because the town was so safe but one night as I was hurrying along, I suddenly felt as if someone was watching me. I looked up and got a terrible shock to see Charles' face staring down at me. He was laughing at me in that joking way of his but the look on his face frightened me.'

We sat there, barely able to speak because, as country children left to our own imaginations and obliged to take ourselves to the outside toilet in the dark, we believed in ghosts.

'He had a terrible smirk on his face,' our mother continued, 'and I think he was laughing because he'd put one over me again.'

This story awakened an old anxiety in me, not just because of the ghostly element but because I felt that something fundamental had been disturbed. My mother was a widow now but hadn't my father loved her? I had grown up believing that marriage was sacred because there was no divorce in the O'Hara family. If there were any signs of a rift between the married couples, grandfather would get the car out, make a visit and nothing was ever said again.

What had been the true nature of my parents' marriage?

Why did my mother tell us such a terrible tale about our father? Did she make it up just to scare us? Or was it some sort of terrible warning?

I believed my mother's story, however, for I had already come to suspect that men could not be trusted.

*   *   *

Gradually I began to fit in with my brother and sisters even though the thoughts and sensations of my displacement remained in my brain as separate, frozen fragments. A sort of life began to overlay my existence like the lamination on a picture, the plastic coating covering the real image beneath but affording a satisfactory protection. Thanks to our mother and her practical nature, our days became peaceful and predictable and this allowed us to eventually develop a close sense of family in spite of our difficult past.

My little sister, Colleen, slept in a small bed in my mother's room for many years. She continued to cry for a long time and screamed hysterically if our mother ever left the house. We would tease her, like all siblings do, if our mother ever went three houses down to visit her parents.

'Where's Mum?' she would blubber, her face collapsing into a paroxysm of anxiety and terror.

'She's gone,' we would flatly announce, just to see her cry.

Then Colleen's face would crumple, she would set up a wail from hell and run on her little two-year-old legs to our grandfather's house, her shrill voice trailing along the footpath.

'You didn't wa-a-a-it for me-e-e-e!'

My little sister, who could make up a doll's game out of a pair of spoons, why did I not remember you growing up behind me? It was only when we developed into young women that age diminished the gap between us and we looked so much alike that people would confuse us. I left you when I was sixteen and you were only ten years old, but later you were to become my closest ally, friend and confidante.

You were the only one to fulfil our mother's dreams, for you became a nurse. You lived just around the corner from her all your life and looked after her in her old age. You were so busy trying to keep one eye on our mother and tabs on your older sisters that you never got to fully live your own life. Nobody knew that you could have been an accomplished pianist or an outstanding athlete if things had been different.

Maureen continued to dominate all our games and to keep us all on track. My grandmother attributed my older sister's strength and self-assurance to the fact that she could reach the fruit bowl on the top of the cupboard and we couldn't. Like a strong, young Brunhilda, she excelled in all sports, leading her House to victory on Sports Day and cutting an impressive figure on the tennis court with her solid, tanned legs and short, pleated skirt. She was constantly surrounded by a group of admiring suitors but kept them all guessing. When she finally married and moved overseas, she continued to 'mother' us from a distance and never forgot her little Aussie family.

My brother remained my closest companion for we shared games and sport. There were new cubby houses to build, forbidden places to explore, secret clubs with passwords nobody else knew, midnight feasts and dares. Every afternoon we would also play high jump with two rough, upright poles which our grandfather made for us and a bamboo stick that canned your legs if you knocked it with your bare feet. Mallory was a natural sportsman in spite of his bout of rheumatic fever, executing a perfect backhand on the tennis court, flying down the football field with his famous schoolboy team or straining to win the hundred-metre dash on Sports Day, the veins in his neck bulging, his eyes wild with determination, his damaged heart pumping frantically.

We never owned a car or dined in a restaurant but there was always a birthday treat of bacon or roast chicken and lots of presents at the end of the bed at Christmas time. I believed in Santa Claus for a long time simply because I knew that my mother could not afford so many presents, unaware that she put aside part of her pension every month in a secret chocolate box at the back of her wardrobe.

'Gee, Rosemary! Don't tell me you still believe in Santa Claus,' my cousin chortled one day, entering the bedroom with a group of smug friends as if they were some sort of delegation.

'Even Mal knows Santa's not real, and he's just a baby. Well, we've just come to tell you the truth. There's no such thing as Santa Claus.'

The words broke my heart because I loved Santa Claus. I felt as if something strong, gallant and protective had disappeared from my life and, without truly understanding the reason, I cried for this loss as I did the day the radio announced the death of our King George.

*　*　*

Growing up in a country town after the war was almost idyllic. There were delicious home-baked cakes awaiting us when we arrived from school, then we were sent outside to amuse ourselves anywhere, everywhere, in complete safety, until dusk. We raced each other through the parks, went for a swim at the local pool, played tennis or rode our bikes gleefully through the lanes which ran behind our house. In the evening, we would gather around the radio, listening to our favourite spooky stories or detective serials.

Once a year we were able to enjoy a holiday at the beach with one of our kind uncles who lived near Coffs Harbour. It was the most marvellous experience for, as inland children, the sea, that great expanse of the Pacific Ocean, represented something mysterious, alluring and, if we dared to admit it, madly frightening. We liked the excitement of plunging into the deep, green waters and our mother did not worry about us for we had taught ourselves to swim in the local pool and we soon learnt how to surf, thrashing, floundering and diving among the foaming breakers.

Every year as we wound down the torturous, dusty descent from the high tablelands, we would start to breathe in the green flood plains of the Macleay River, the lush tropical vegetation of the Northern Rivers and the biting smell of salty air. As we drew nearer and nearer to the coastline, it was always the same thing, the same time-honoured ritual. The anticipation would grip us, our bodies would tense up, our eyes glued to the car window, our attention focussed on the tree-covered coastline as each child strained with his whole being to be the first to call out:

'I can see the sea!'

Friday afternoon was our favourite day of the week. All the country people drove into town and my grandfather's car would be parked in the same spot, reserved unofficially for ol' Herb. As he waited with endless patience for grandmother to finish her shopping, the locals would file by the car for an obligatory chat, paying a sort of homage to him as he resided over the happy shoppers like a benevolent country squire.

We couldn't wait to rush up to his car for we knew the treat that awaited us. Like greedy little blighters we would wait on the footpath, trying to hide our impatience, and watch hypnotically as he slowly slipped his hand into his pocket and drew out a florin for each of us. Then we would skip gleefully over to the local fish shop and order a battered saveloy on a stick. There was nothing better than this treat on a cold, wintry day and as the sizzling batter burned our throats and the fatty sausage exploded with hot grease into our mouths, we thought we were in heaven.

One Friday another figure, thin and rather frail, stood impatiently beside our grandfather's car. We recognised our Emmaville grandmother, Nana Scherf, greeted her stiffly then stared in bewilderment as she thrust a package into Mallory's hands. There was no gift for us so we watched begrudgingly as he tore open the parcel wrapping. Inside the packet the small red and white globules of beef lying in a pinkish slime almost spilled over onto the pavement and Mallory, trying to hide his dismay at the bizarre gift, didn't know whether to laugh or cry.

'I thought you needed fattening up,' Nana declared haughtily. 'Your mother doesn't feed you enough.'

The incident seemed even more ridiculous because we were

not accustomed to receiving visits from Nana Scherf. However, after our grandfather died, my mother, ironically, was obliged to 'take her in'. Becoming more and more eccentric as she aged, she married again in her eighties, became Susan Jane Broughton but was constantly heard muttering to herself that, 'Broughtie was a silly old thing.' The marriage didn't last. There seemed to be some sort of poetic justice in her demise for she became quite demented. I actually have rather fond memories of her in our home, floating from room to room, reciting French irregular verbs, then disappearing into her bedroom before dinner and emerging in a very happy mood with a strong taste of brandy on her breath.

None of us ever forgot her preposterous gift to our brother. It was a standing joke from that day onwards, the day my father's mother gave her grandson a pound of minced meat for his birthday.

*   *   *

We grew up into typical country children of the fifties, carefree, innocent, unhampered by safety rules and regulations, our lives dominated by school, sport and the new influences arriving from overseas. It is difficult to estimate the extent to which American popular culture mined our souls in this era but we were entranced by Hollywood and by American movie stars. Every weekend we would join the queue at the local Roxy cinema to watch the latest offering from Hollywood. It was the era of musicals, swashbuckling sagas and old-fashioned westerns. The heroes were brash, handsome daredevils, the heroines pert, plucky little women who always succeeded in 'getting their man'. After the movie we would rush home, dress up in our mother's old clothes, fight over the most glamorous roles and re-enact the stories.

As we grew older, we discovered rock'n'roll music and our afternoons were spent jiving in a friend's lounge room to the beat of *Be Bop A Lula* or *See You Later Alligator*. Our starched petticoats hung on the clothesline every week, a painful task for our poor mother, for full, puffed-out skirts and tight waists were the fashion of the day. We also enjoyed the monthly Presbyterian dances where the boys twirled us through the Gypsy Tap and the Pride of Erin, and we wondered why they always carried a torch in their pockets when they thrust their thigh into our groin.

The times were innocent, there were no drugs or alcohol and no petting beyond holding hands in the back row of the cinema. We did allow the boys to kiss us during a game of Spin the Bottle but we hated it when they stuck their tongue into our mouth. Like all respectable girls, we 'saved' ourselves for our wedding day and dreamed of living happily ever after … like Doris, Jane and Debbie.

So, against the calm background of our mother's home and without the chaos caused by a restless and disappointed man, we reached adolescence, completed our schooling and prepared to enter the wider world. The ties woven between us in those years were rich, intricate, indissoluble and strong enough to mitigate our feelings of inferiority and difference.

As adults, when we left home to establish our own lives, we

continued to seek each other out, no matter where or how far away from each other we lived. Our reunions were joyful, filled with raucous laughter, exaggerated stories and private anecdotes. Ecstatic to be reunited whenever the opportunity arrived, we remained complete in each other's company, bound together by deep and desperate familial ties, in love with each other to the envy of the people we would eventually marry. We were the Scherf kids, who, like castaways thrown overboard, searched for each other under the murky waters and finding each other, clung together, tremulously, holding our breath and clasping each other's hands.

*   *   *

My personal salvation came to me through my brother, the little hand in mine. It was chiefly through his companionship and the games we played that I regained the world of wonder I had lost. These games, so richly concocted, so freely lived, enabled me to survive for, in spite of my new home, the nightmares and the feelings of insecurity had not left me. It was only in the realm of the imagination that I could romp freely, safe, unhampered and unlimited by the worst burden I was soon forced to endure. Without these games my spirit would have been broken and I would have shrivelled.

The streets around our house were the limit of our games but in our imagination they were the playground of a hundred possibilities. No space was considered inviolable: every street, every building, every home held a secret that could be unlocked, and we navigated the map of the town like ancient explorers. There were new hideaways, new clubs and new passwords which only my brother and I knew.

The old lady who lived in complete seclusion next door to us filled us with the greatest curiosity. She never ventured outside the house but occasionally we would see her ghastly, white face peeping out at us from behind a thick curtain. She paid a man to tend to her garden and each week a lady would arrive with her groceries. We decided that she had either been jilted by her fiancé like poor Miss Haversham or that she had an incurable disease like leprosy. In our restless sleep, her tomb-like face hovered above our beds and her deformed hands reached towards our throats.

I had been eyeing off the dense thicket at the back of her yard and had been estimating its potential for a while.

'We'll build a secret passageway from our house into her backyard,' I announced to my brother one day. 'It will be our best tunnel yet. We'll be the spies and the old lady will be the witch with evil plans to destroy all the children in the town.'

We discovered two loose boards in our neighbour's fence, leaving a space big enough for a small child to creep through. Every night after dinner we would sneak out, crawl through the gap and start hacking away the undergrowth. Soon we had hollowed out a perfect tunnel which we lined with old sugar bags.

One day, after two weeks of secret missions, midnight feasts and glorious moments of just sitting in the forbidden space devising our tactics, we discovered that all our work had been undone. The bushes were untied, the loose boards were repaired and the sugar bags were returned to our yard, not just thrown into a heap, but neatly folded. It made us feel slightly ashamed of ourselves especially since she had not reported us. We were sorry we had made her into the witch for she obviously liked children after all. Something was broken, however, for we had thoughtlessly intruded into her privacy and anonymity and we never saw her face again.

Our next great adventure took place in the Church of England, a very imposing stone building set among dark oak trees one block from our house. The most exciting dare for any child was to climb the bell tower at midnight. This time we were glad to have the company of our oldest sister. As the clock struck midnight, we crept outside into the cold New England air and hurried down the lane to the back gate leading to the church.

The side door was open and we slipped inside. Standing in the sacred stillness, we were suddenly overcome with the terrible fear that God would strike us down, simply for violating His holy place, just as He had destroyed the poor wretch who accidentally touched the ark. The church organ in the balcony hung over us like a giant bird of prey, shrouded figures seemed to lurk in the dark recesses and a thousand prayers whirled in ghostly whispers around the lofty arches. We were both terrified and elated but tried to calm ourselves with the knowledge that this was our church after all, that we had all been safely confirmed and belonged to Jesus. It was the custom on Sunday mornings for our mother to dutifully drag us out of bed and force us to walk without breakfast through the morning fog to church. Sitting in the hard pews with an empty feeling in our stomach, we would wait respectfully for our turn to go forward and taste the communion wine. The sherry burnt our throats but fortified our hungry bodies with its sharp, mellifluous taste.

Now, as we approached the communion rail, we hesitated, fearing that the minister would discover us, rebuke us severely and revoke our salvation.

'Hurry up,' my sister commanded, pushing me ahead of her. 'If you don't get a move on, I'm going home. It's freezing in here.'

I knew that this was just an excuse. She was just as scared as I and wanted me to face the consequences first. Mortified at the thought of being left alone in this doomed environment, I tiptoed across the nave and started up the narrow spiral staircase leading to the belfry. Suddenly I froze. A shimmery figure had appeared before me, blocking the way.

'What's the matter?' my sister hissed.

'It's the Holy G-g-g-ghost!' I screamed, almost toppling down the stairs, running for my life out of the church, up the lane to my house and diving under the bedcovers. Nothing in the world could have made me climb those stairs and I decided to never trespass into God's sanctuary again.

There was one last dare which was the supreme test of our childhood ventures. We cherished it as our final challenge and it was always there, resting in the back of our minds, cool and velvety like a mossy stone.

On the block of land opposite our house stood an old, abandoned hospital, which was later converted into the local museum. It had originally been a grand, colonial mansion with its wide verandahs, bay windows and coloured glass windows and it was there that my mother and I had almost lost our lives.

My brother and I found a loose window which we told no one else about as it allowed us to slip inside and wander through the long corridors. We liked to imagine the nurses walking up and down in their crisp uniforms and the patients sitting up in their crocheted bed jackets, waiting for their afternoon cup of tea. It was thrilling to think that we were the only children who knew how to break into this building and it soon became our favourite hiding place.

We would play around for a while, whispering to each other in the dark and trying not to think about the moment when the true test of courage would arrive. We knew this dreaded moment was waiting for us but we tried to ignore it for as long as possible and play in the safe, well-lit spaces. Suddenly one of us would stop and turn solemnly to the other. With a half-teasing, half-malicious glint in our eyes, we would then pronounce the fatal words:

'I dare you.'

The sacred words once uttered could not be contested, so we would grope our way through the winding corridors until we found it – a long, grey passageway leading to a set of plain double doors.

The operating theatre.

Standing outside, we imagined the horrors that the walls inside had witnessed: masked doctors with sadistic eyes and gleaming scalpels, helpless bodies being sliced open, blood oozing from cruel gashes, intestines hanging out, amputated limbs bleeding in a bucket, half-anaesthetised patients screaming in agony and the overpowering smell of death.

The theatre of madmen and butchers.

Nothing could bring us to open the doors yet we felt compelled to come to this room every visit. There was something irresistible about it and I suppose it had something to do with the basic human fascination with horror. Subdued and afraid, we always left this part of the hospital in a kind of stunned silence, deeply aware of our own mortality and grateful to be alive. We had to live with the fact, however, that the sacred code of 'the dare' had been broken and we would return home ashamed and disconsolate, determined to do better next time.

These games became my biological planner. They enabled me to negotiate the physical and social world in which I lived when I would have preferred to withdraw and live inside my head. They kept me curious about life. When the suffering began anew, they preserved me against detachment and oblivion.

Glen Innes. You were the closest thing I ever found to experiencing a sense of home but you were only the home of my mother.

How sad it was to return as an adult and to find that the town, with all its intricate spaces, was so much smaller than I had remembered and all the enchantment had disappeared.

* * *

STUTTERING:

Disordered breathing, including antagonism between abdominal and thoracic respiratory muscles; complete cessation of breathing, and interrupting exhalation with inhalation. Disordered vocal folds; including high levels of muscle activity or muscle tension; poor laryngeal too late or holding tension too long; poor coordination of laryngeal muscles e.g., incompatible contractions of opposing muscles. Disordered articulation, including dysfunctions of the lips, jaw and tongue in stuttering. These interruptions often include tension, unusual movements of the body and face and struggling behaviours such as facial tics, lip tremors, excessive eye blinking.

I was not aware as I began to heal and thrive, that this new ordeal was waiting just around the corner. The confusion, stress and humiliation of the impediment were so disturbing that they sabotaged the last hope I ever had of integrating the already fragmented thoughts, emotions and sensations in my brain. From then on, my mind would become a war zone.

I cannot remember a definite period of time when the stuttering commenced but it was early in the primary school. Perhaps the first signs appeared at home but my mother ignored them. As far as school was concerned, pupils in those days were rarely allowed to speak in class so it did not show up immediately in public.

It was around Year 4 when my teacher, a sophisticated, theatrical lady who loved classical literature and public speaking, would assemble us at the front of the class every morning and make us rehearse a variety of her favourite texts. As we waited in our rows, a respectful, expectant silence would fill the classroom, then she would lift her arms in the air like a conductor, raise her chin in readiness and instruct us to begin the recitation.

'Quinquireme of Nineveh from distant Ophir,
Rowing home to haven in sunny Palestine
With a cargo of ivory,
And apes and peacocks,
Sandalwood ...'

'No, no, no, students,' she would interrupt insistently. 'Softly, smoothly. Can't you hear the oars dipping into the water? Now, repeat after me ...'

Afterwards, we would recite lines from the 23rd Psalm, the Sermon on the Mount, Portia's 'Mercy Speech' from the Merchant of Venice or Paul's Epistle to the Corinthians. I never forgot the thing of beauty that language could be, even though I could not understand the meaning of all the words. In these recitations I would allow my mind to unfold and reach beyond the plain world of the classroom to a magical place.

Then one day, a horrible thing happened.

Language betrayed me.

It was the custom during the reading lessons for our teacher to ask the pupils to read aloud around the class. We were expected to read clearly and fluently with correct pronunciation and vibrant expression. As my turn approached,

I suddenly became very conscious of myself, my heart began to pound, my chest tightened and a curious tension began to creep over my whole being. When I opened my mouth and moved my jaw to speak, the words seemed to be stuck in my throat. I felt as if my brain had become addled and someone had jammed a steel bar into the speech circuits. I simply could not get the words out and the lines on the page swam before my eyes.

'Rosemary Scherf,' my teacher commanded, addressing me by my full name as if I were in serious trouble. 'We're waiting for you. Can't you see it's your turn?'

I tried again to read but my body seemed to have shut down. Then the words in the first sentence came back into focus and, as I opened my mouth to speak, the sound unexpectedly came out in sporadic, fragmented bursts. The hard 'D' at the beginning of the sentence had somehow become stuck in my throat, my breathing had become disordered and I could not get past the first letter. Doubling up my efforts to move off the consonant and slide into the vowel, I increased the volume of my stutter so that the sound ricocheted like a machine gun around the classroom.

'D-d-d-d-d-d-d—'

Sniggers began to sound behind my back and the pupil who shared my desk stared at me in disbelief. Somehow, I struggled through the rest of the paragraph and the reading turn passed to someone else.

In the following days, I noticed that a subtle shift had occurred between me and my classmates. As my turn approached in the reading lessons, the classroom would grow abnormally quiet and I couldn't tell whether this was out of fear of being told off by the teacher or out of some cruel, childish fascination with my humiliation. In fact, all my friends had started to avoid me, even outside of school. Sinister images of drooling village idiots and bedevilled children disturbed the edges of their minds and, although my classmates did not shun me completely, they never quite recovered from my weekly antics in the reading lessons.

To make matters worse, the teacher persisted in making me read aloud each week, possibly believing that I would eventually overcome my nerves or that I would grow out of my stuttering with practice. I became like a soldier on a special reconnaissance mission, spying out every scrap of information and any minor detail which could help me in my war on speaking. I would work out exactly which paragraph and which word I would have to read by counting the number of students ahead of me. Then I would mentally practise all the sounds I would have to make, going over and over them in my mind, imagining various pronunciations and trying to rehearse the sounds I knew would be a problem. Particular consonants filled me with fear and if I spied a 'd', 't', 'b' or 'c', the game was up even before my turn came.

There were no speech pathologists in those days so I was prepared to try any tricks and strategies to make the words less threatening, smooth and readable. Someone told me that if I stretched my tongue out for a while before reading, the stuttering would be alleviated. It wasn't easy to do this in the classroom, but I would put my hand over my mouth and strain every muscle in my throat and mouth to distend my tongue while the pupils had their attention on their reading books. Another sympathetic soul told me about the great orator, Demosthenes, who would fill his mouth with pebbles before he gave a speech. On reading days, I would go into the garden before school, stuff a handful of small stones into my mouth and practise speaking aloud to the plants, trying not to swallow the cold, gritty pieces.

In the classroom, however, none of these remedies ever worked. It was always the same horrible ordeal. As my turn to read drew closer, my body would prepare itself for the weekly ambush, my heart would beat wildly, adrenalin would flood my system, my mouth would go dry and I would stutter and stammer through the whole paragraph. What made it worse was that in my desperate attempts to produce the words, I began adding awful animal noises and facial distortions to my grotesque repertoire.

From that time onwards, I knew I had severely disturbed the uneasy peace of my school days and that a new monster had found its way into my disordered life. Even at home I could not talk to my siblings without stuttering and I couldn't even communicate with my mother.

'Mum ... mum ... mum ... mum. C-c-c-can I have a g-g-g-glass of water?'

It is difficult to describe the extent of my silent suffering for I did not know how to complain or ask for help.

'You need to speak more slowly,' everybody would lecture me. 'Take a breath before you speak.'

Then, becoming exasperated with my delays and repetitions,

they would jump in and finish the sentence for me or lose their patience. 'Oh, for goodness sake! Can't you just say it? Just get the word out!'

My older sister, in her imperious way, decided to take me in hand, ordering me to stand on a chair and read to her every afternoon. Finally, my plight reached the ears of the school headmistress and she invited me into her office to read to her on Friday afternoon before school ended. She was disappointed that I did not improve, but I mistrusted the genuineness of her intervention. Obviously, she had forgotten that one day, during our formal open-air assembly, when I had been caught daring to whisper to another pupil and she had slapped my legs severely.

There may have been speech pathologists in those days but they were unheard of in my small town. As with everything, I simply had to endure my affliction. Desperate to avoid exposing myself, I tried to develop my own strategies for surviving, like putting my hand over my mouth when I spoke, looking away or changing the word if I quickly perceived an anticipated stuttering sound coming up. This was not always possible as when shopping for a specific item, answering the phone or relaying a message.

Shopping became one of my worst nightmares; a simple pleasure like buying an ice cream was turned into a monstrous test of nerves.

'What would you like?' said the shopkeeper casually, leaning towards me, reinforcing the horrible intimacy of speaker and listener and the ghastly moment of expectation.

The answer was very simple, just three syllables, but I felt as if I were on the stage and a whole audience was waiting in suspense for my lines. Savouring the cool, flavoursome taste, I quickly scanned the word, thought I could get away with 'ice' but felt a rush of fear at the sight of the hard 'c' in 'cream'. With time running out, I abruptly changed my order to something I could manage to say, paid quickly and left the shop.

Something I could not avoid, however, was being asked by my new teacher at the beginning of the year to say our names around the class. I dreaded this introduction because I knew my stuttering would create a poor impression from the outset and I dearly wanted the teacher to like me. The other students would gleefully wait for my turn and relish the shocked look which appeared on the teacher's face when I tried to speak. That small second when everyone waited for me to introduce myself was like an eternity and the more I tried to push myself through the barrier of fluency, the more I choked and spluttered. In the end I had to admit that I could not even say my name.

I could not even say my name.

The daily humiliation together with the impatience and disapproval of my friends and teachers piled up against me and I began to think I was a freak. In the end, I had to accept that my exclusion from the world was final and irredeemable because people who would normally accept a child with a broken leg or a blind child never accepted a stutterer.

There were no clues to read my impediment because I didn't come with a wheelchair or a deformed body and on the outside, I looked like a normal, bright, well-behaved child. It was only when I opened my mouth that the flaming sword came out. Faces would crumple in shock, eyes stared too long then turned away, voices cut me off, stole my thoughts and finished off my words for me, children laughed, adults corrected and advised.

What puzzled me was the intensity of their indignation but I came to understand that every time I tried to speak, I violated their sacred belief in a fundamental and natural human right. Didn't everyone have the power of speech? For them to imagine such an aberration and still call me human was too difficult. All my energy then was directed towards protecting them from their nightmares, hiding my disfigurement by not speaking at all, making my existence easier for them.

But they never made it easier for me.

I lived in two worlds but belonged in neither. Isolation in one, shame in the other. There was no way of reconciling the two extremes for the only bridge was language and the gift of communication had been stolen from me. My heart longed to be with them, those carefree, callous chatterboxes, their love, anger, sorrow and joy exploding from the void of thought into sparkling showers of dialogues as they navigated their little worlds. Speechless, I watched as the whole drama of life passed me by.

If you cannot speak, you cannot express yourself. Every spontaneous thought I had in those days had to be scanned for the sound blocks. If I felt happy, I could not freely express my happiness; if I felt hurt, I could not say my pain; if I had a sudden idea or comment, it had to simmer inside my head.

I had become an apology for myself.

So disfigured was I by all the hesitations, revisions and substitutions that I realised I would never be truly heard by other people again.

I had created my own isolation.

I stuttered all through primary school and part of secondary school. It was always the same monumental struggle, bobbing, weaving and ducking through all the oral exchanges that lay in wait for me every day. My existence was entirely bizarre as, when I wasn't speaking, I appeared to be living a relatively normal life on the surface. It was like playing an endless game of charades, pretending I was someone else until I was exposed, until somebody guessed the real person behind the act in which I tried to hide.

How do children like me survive? There must have been some inner conviction, some flickering hope that made me believe that I could not give up on life. As I was always taught to do, I accepted my fate and grew up as best as I could although every time I had to face a new situation, I was filled with more than the usual degree of anxiety and always expected the worst.

My confident sister, on the other hand, was the most outstanding actress in the school and had won awards at the local Eisteddfod. She had even been invited to perform with the teachers in the local Arts Council productions and this meant that, after she graduated and went to college in another town, I was plagued by eager teachers who would bail me up as a possible candidate for their dramatic enterprises as soon as they found out my name.

'Oh, you're Maureen Scherf's sister,' they positively glowed at me. 'You must be a great actress. We'll get you to come and read for us. Now, don't be shy.'

Obviously I never accepted their invitation.

Miraculously, in my adolescent years, I 'grew out of' stuttering when speaking to my peers and my family but I could never escape the fear of public speaking. The damage was done and for the rest of my life I baulked before all such events. If I had to address a crowd of people, it would mean weeks of diarrhoea, of panic attacks in the night, of constant re-enactment in my mind of every aspect of the event leading up to the fatal moment. This meant that I lived through my working life in a state of anxiety because as a teacher and Head of Department, I was often called upon to address assemblies and staff meetings. No one could ever have imagined my distress because, as I was the Head of English, everybody expected me to be more than usually articulate and eloquent. However, once the first words were spoken, I seemed to be able to get through the rest of the speech.

Years later, when I had to present a paper at a conference of teachers in Sydney, I remember locking my collapsing self in a toilet, my brain reeling at the thought of the dreadful moment ahead of me, my heart pounding, my stomach turning over, my breathing strangulated, my whole system in shut down.

'Come on, Rosemary. Hurry up. They're waiting for you.'

My colleague was worried, dragged me out of the bathroom and almost pushed me onto the stage. The audience fixed a concentrated gaze on me, reinforcing that terrible moment.

I picked up the mic and opened my mouth …

At the peak of my stuttering, I found myself sitting alone again at recess and lunchtime. Schools are made up of the in-crowd and the out-crowd, and there are so many opportunities to discriminate and exclude. Watching the girls laugh and tease each other in the playground, I wanted desperately to be like them, carefree and cruel.

It is so hard to be different for difference and some kind of death always seem to go together.

There was only one friend who stayed with me during those dark days, Lynnette Winters, a big-boned, ugly, red-haired girl with freckles who lived on the wrong side of town. A genuine outcast in all respects. We did not play together at school, that would have been too much, but in the afternoon, we would wait for each other outside the school gates and walk home together in a kind of conspiracy of exclusion.

Lynnette lived in an area outside the town called the Common, populated by tin shacks, caravans and canvas hovels. Her house was dimly lit inside and the walls were lined with old newspapers.

'You shouldn't be seen with those gypsies,' my grandmother warned me. 'I've even heard people say that there are aborigines camped up there.'

My grandmother never liked my friends and only approved when, years later, I became friends with the daughter of an important man in the town. When I explained that Helen Bridge was just like any other girl and that her father was a silly man, she very quickly corrected me.

'You shouldn't talk about Mr Bridge like that, Rosemary. He's a Bank Manager.'

She corrected me with such genuine respect and propriety in her voice that I wondered if I might have been wrong after all. Bank managers were highly regarded in those days and my friendship with one of their daughters ensured my acceptance into the higher ranks of Glen Innes society. I suppose I secretly thought that I belonged there anyway because hadn't my father once been an important man?

Lynette Winters taught me a hard lesson about snobbery for I am ashamed to say that I was the one who discarded her later on. In the meantime, she was my friend. Everybody laughed at me but they did not know that my loneliness was unbearable and Lynette was the only girl who would accept me.

*   *   *

In my last year of primary school another life-changing event singled me out and made me even more self-conscious.

It occurred during one of my favourite escapes, the weekly outing to the Saturday matinee. As my sister and I settled happily into the cool darkness of the theatre, I felt a surge of moisture between my legs and thought to my horror that I had wet my pants. Jumping up, I pushed past the other children to get to the toilet and noticed to my horror a spot of blood on my panties. Blood! I waited for several minutes, hastily wiped it away and went back inside the cinema, groping for my seat in the darkness.

'Where the heck have you been?' Maureen hissed at me, but

I sat there, unable to speak, certain that I was going to die. As soon as the movie ended, I rushed to the toilet again, but the blood had reappeared, a pinkish, brownish stain which was spreading in undeniable persistence over my panties.

For several days I told no one and tried unsuccessfully to get rid of it. A worrying verse from the bible kept coming into my mind, the verse about the woman 'with the issue of blood', but I wasn't sure what the strange word 'issue' meant. I simply thought I was doomed, that I would have to put up with this bleeding all my life because Jesus was no longer around.

I was always afraid of dying. The murderous dwarf, the violent nightmares, the operating theatre, the sense of unsafeness were always with me, threatening my life with a sinister and infecting fear. When the blood did not go away, I finally broke down in front of Maureen.

'Oh, Rody!' she gushed, not at all alarmed by my news. 'Let's go tell Mum.'

My mother looked at me in despair, confirming my fears that something terrible had happened. Then she reached into her underwear drawer, pulled out some clean rags and safety pins.

'Oh, no! Oh, goodness me! You've got your 'things' already? Well, you better be careful now,' she said reproachfully. Mother always referred to her period as her 'things', complaining when she felt tired and irritable every month and pointing to her belly in her usual disgust for all the biological aspects of womanhood. She obviously disapproved of my news because now I, too, had the terrible curse.

'You have to be able to do this yourself,' she ordered, stuffing the towel between my legs and pinning it to my panties. 'And throw the dirty ones into the laundry bucket.'

That was all that she said.

I stood there, feeling like a trussed-up goose about to be roasted and worried sick about how I was ever going to hide this ugly paraphernalia from my class mates, especially the primary school boys. None of the girls in my class seemed to be plagued by the same predicament for we were still very young. My sister, on the other hand, seemed quite thrilled with the event and insisted on cooing at me:

'Oh, Rody, you're a woman now.' This assignation, designed to confer status, confused and frightened me. As usual, I felt as if I were in the wrong, that I had prematurely taken Eve's curse upon myself and that I should have had the decency to wait a lot longer before shocking my mother in this way.

I was only eleven years old.

*   *   *

Death continued to stalk us during all these years.

We were horrified to receive the news that one of our most promising cousins, the brown-eyed, curly-haired darling of the town, had died in a car accident after a drinking bout, choking in his own vomit. His inconsolable mother committed suicide shortly afterwards.

We were always conscious of death and I suppose that was why families had a lot of children in those days. Diseases like polio, whooping cough, diphtheria and tuberculosis had not been eradicated and could strike a child at any moment. Any brush with these diseases was considered more or less fatal.

One year the primary school organised for a Mantoux skin test to be administered to all students to detect any signs of tuberculosis. This was an intradermal injection into the inner surface of the forearm producing a palpable raised induration of several millimetres. The reaction was to be read 48–72 hours after the injection and a lump of more than 10 mm meant that there was a serious possibility that the person was infected.

My classmates were very light-hearted and joked about the test, pretending that they were not scared of needles. Nobody had a reaction apart from a tiny blister but, to my horror, my lump began to swell. It was like a golf ball, shiny and bluish, an alien thing growing on my skinny arm. I hid it under my blazer and refused to let anyone see my arm because no other pupil in the whole school had reacted in this way. When the time came for the nurses to check it, I had no choice but to expose my shameful secret and wait for the shocked looks, the vicious gossip and finger-pointing from the other children.

A further test was conducted, then a long wait of eight to ten weeks before a diagnosis was completed.

I lived in terror, convinced that my lungs were rotting away but unable to bear another separation from the family. Images haunted me of an isolated sanatorium in a faraway country like Switzerland with clinical nurses walking briskly along the sterilised corridors and ghoulish patients sitting in deck chairs, staring blankly at the snow as they coughed up blood and mucous.

I rushed to the mailbox every day and lived in fear of seeing an envelope from the Department of Health. It was during this period of intense anxiety that my nightmares unleashed the most horrible acts of violence from the darkest depths of my subconscious. In these brutal dreams, I was trying to stab to death an enemy who would not die, hacking through his medulla oblongata until his head, hanging sideways with his foaming mouth grinning at me, toppled to the ground. It was difficult and dangerous work for a little girl and I wondered if something else, something deliberately sinister and vengeful, had followed my father home from the war.

Every night a new murderer confronted me and one night I physically felt someone lift the covers and slip into my bed next to me. The killings exhausted me and left me little energy to deal with my stuttering in the day. There was no one to comfort or help me and I could do nothing but wait for the adults to come and take me away again.

Finally, the reprieve came. The letter from the Department of Health arrived and I was diagnosed as only having been in contact with somebody with tuberculosis and therefore did not have to leave my family after all.

I had not expected it, a single reprieve after a small life with so much defeat.

*   *   *

Soon it was time to leave Primary School and enrol in High School.

High School. Another school with those dark corners full of snares where students lay in wait, pointed at you and sniggered as you went past. Another school where I would be made painfully aware that I was different and that my difference would expose me again. Another school where I would harbour a hundred bright ideas and fantastic dreams but would never be able to express them to anyone.

But in the end, High School was also my salvation.

Just as we were preparing to leave Grade 6, something miraculous happened which changed everything.

It was one of those days at the end of the school year when the pupils were listless, when they lost interest in anything but making Christmas cards, cutting out angel shapes and dreaming of the long summer holidays ahead. Time seemed suspended and we were all mildly aware that a significant period in our lives had come to an end.

We wondered why we had been asked to assemble outside and sit quietly while the headmistress called out our names in alphabetical order. The elm trees in the school playground were already luxuriant in their spring growth and provided a canopy of shade for the hard, grey planks underneath. She explained that she had received the results from the IQ test we had completed, the Eleven Plus, and would read out the name of the class we had been assigned to in the High School.

High School. It seemed like another country, and I was already imagining the gruelling bicycle ride up a very steep hill to the ominous building on the north of town.

'Rosemary Scherf. 1A.'

The words were announced in an official tone like an attorney reading out a will, dividing up forever what we would inherit from our education and our life as a citizen of Australia. There was no question of contesting the division. The power of academic selection in those days sponsored a very strong community around the notion of being 'chosen', marking us out as intellectually superior and 'special'. I learnt that I was to be in a class with a select number of students, and I would study French and Latin.

It meant saying goodbye to some of my classmates, particularly Lynette. She waited for me outside the school gates as usual but I tried not to look at her as I walked past, for she had been assigned to 1D.

After the first half-yearly exams, I burst into the house and almost exploded with the news.

'Mum,' I shouted. 'Mum, I've come first in French!'

It seems that I had finally found something in which I excelled.

My French teacher was a mousey little woman who was obviously disappointed that her first posting had led her to a small rural town instead of a posh, private girls' school in Sydney. Mum looked at me blankly without understanding why I was so excited. Sitting in the kitchen with the beans in her lap, she simply smiled at me.

My other favourite subject was Latin but the texts required a lot of study. Our fibro house was freezing in winter because the open fire in the lounge room sent all the heat up the chimney and failed to warm the rest of the house. We would stand as close as possible to the fire, burning our legs and taking turns to warm our backside. Trips to the toilet at the back of the house were delayed as long as possible but it was in the toilet where I found my best place for studying.

At 5 am, the alarm would ring. I would force myself to throw off the covers, take my Latin book into the toilet, lock the door behind me and brace myself to sit on the cold seat. My fingers and toes were white, I felt sick and nauseous for lack of food, but I pressed on through the morning light and Caesar's conquest of Gaul.

The headmaster of the school was forced to teach our class because the tiny number of Latin students, particularly in the senior class, did not warrant a full-time teacher. He had tightly crimped grey hair and a swarthy complexion but always looked elegant in his expensive suits with his overcoat draped stylishly over his shoulders.

When it was time for the Latin class, we would wait for a long time outside his office before he finally relented and opened his door. He would invite us, rather ceremoniously, into his private office where we could still smell the lingering aroma of whisky. Sometimes we were fortunate enough to actually receive a Latin lesson but usually he would just send us outside to study.

'Now, you're all good little boys and girls but your old boss is very tired, so go outside and sit in the sun. Oh, and one of you can go over to the corner shop and get your poor, old boss a packet of Bex powders.'

We fell very far behind in the syllabus, but when he was

not suffering from a hangover and mustered up the energy to provide us with a lesson, there was something unbelievably magical about his teaching. Sitting quietly in his office with the open fire warming our bare legs, we were entranced by his recitation of whole verses from Virgil, learnt by heart. In those privileged hours when nothing of the outside world mattered, we re-lived every moment of the barbarian invasion of Rome, our hearts in our throat as those wild, ferocious men stormed the temple, stood momentarily transfixed before the elderly patricians sitting in rows, reached out their hands, stroked their silver beards and caressed their linen garments before slicing off their heads.

The rich intonation of our old headmaster's voice, the proud tilt of his head, the misty, faraway look in his eyes, transported me to another world of learning where knowledge had nothing to do with academic success or a future career but touched the deep recesses of my soul. My starving soul.

The following year, the school received a new deputy headmaster who was given the task of getting us up to scratch in Latin. He was a strict disciplinarian with a lean and hungry look, like Cassius. He took us right back to basics and pounded us with declensions, vocabulary and rote learning of texts.

'Amo, amas, amat,' he would intone, striding around the classroom, waving his arms and bending his knees to the rhythm of each declension, like the conductor of a great orchestra, oblivious to the fact that there were only six students in his class.

School, schoolwork, school sport and school friends consumed our small town lives and became the main frame of reference for our social development. I was surprised at the competitive spirit which was slowly developing inside me, for I was determined to excel in all of these areas. I relished, no craved, the applause I received on Speech Night, standing on the school stage with all my prizes for every year I won several sporting awards and came first in every subject but Maths.

Maths. That was a different story. The one subject I found unfathomable.

'I just can't understand it,' I complained to my older sister for I hated to be beaten in any academic field.

'Well, don't tell me your troubles,' she sighed. 'I could never understand Maths either.'

It ran in the family, a fact our Maths teacher, a former RAAF pilot who knew of our father, could never accept. Every year after the final exams, he would enter the classroom imperiously, relishing the moment when our eyes would dart nervously towards the dreaded bundle of papers under his arm, tied up in twine. Then he would ceremoniously untie the twine, flip open the curled bunch of papers and proceed to hand them out in order, from the highest marks to the lowest.

There was complete silence except for the *thwap* of the papers as they landed on the desks. What was it about Maths that imbued the subject with so much status and reverence? We waited, subdued and terrified.

I was reasonably sure each year that I had answered every question painstakingly, according to the prescribed formulae. Of course I never had enough time to tackle the last question, the problem at the end of the paper, the 'stinker' reserved for the gods of mathematics.

It was congratulations all round for the top students, but as the pile became smaller and smaller and I still didn't have my paper back, my friends turned around and stared at me in gleeful disbelief. There must have been a mistake. No, in a disdainful gesture designed to show his utter contempt, my teacher finally threw my paper onto the desk. I felt as if I had been punched in the stomach as I saw the sickening total, ringed in red, of the third lowest mark in the class. Forty-seven per cent.

Then the Maths teacher would explode, pound the desk in front of me and shout in my face.

'This is disgraceful. You should be ashamed of this mark. Your father was a great pilot and you can't even pass Maths. What's the matter with you? You just didn't try ... you just didn't try. Your father would have been so ashamed of you ... so ashamed!'

Maths.

As difficult as fluent speech.

*　　*　　*

And my father?

Did I forget to remember him?

What became of his memory?

It would have been easier to forget him, for in the uncertain years of growing up there was no father in our home, no father to provide for us, no father to guide us through the difficult decisions we had to make. There was no father to sit down with us when night fell, no father to teach us right from wrong, no father to tell us how proud he was when we won prizes at school, no father to teach us how to drive a car and no father to give us away when we married. The man who was supposed to be our father was absent from everything, from all the small, momentous rituals fathers normally share with their children, from all our birthdays and Christmas celebrations … but it was not possible to forget him.

His absence buzzed around my head.

It is a miraculous thing, the human heart, and who can tell its depths? Father, when the time was right, I came looking for you.

I did not leave you in your ice-bound death.

*   *   *

Adolescence is a time of upheaval, when you gain a greater awareness of others and their judgments, when you endeavour, out of the ferment of your soul, to clarify your ideas of who you are, to choose or reject values, opinions and thoughts, to sort out the past from the present and to label your feelings accurately. Adolescence is also the first crisis in femininity.

I had become a woman too early and this meant that I had to deal with strange, new impulses from a very young age. In my first years of High School, I sensed that an awakening was beginning to take shape and I began to fantasise about breaking away from my small town and finding something larger. Apart from the stuttering, I was a bright, eager student with secret dreams of becoming a High School teacher and this meant re-locating myself within a more dynamic framework. This shift, this peculiar internal disruption, was now compelling me towards something more idealistic, more edgy. More virile.

The father!

So it was that, during those teenage years, my father, even though I hardly knew him, began to reappear, my forceful father with his mysterious past and the huge row of medals on his chest. My mother on the other hand had become an elusive figure, attending to our domestic needs in the background but copping out of her own life long ago. There was something vague about her, something I couldn't get hold of which meant that she had nothing personal to say to me. Her posture of submission, of not making waves, of not asking questions, of not wanting to know, had developed in her a wispy, evanescent quality which made it easier for me to pass her by.

Apart from a few startling revelations, she rarely spoke of my father, his exploits or the circumstances of his death. When I came looking for more information, I had to be content with fragments of conversation and unreliable anecdotes from friends and relatives, even from sentimental drunks in the RSL club. I had some understanding that he had been a war pilot but more than that, he had been a war hero. People always spoke of him in terms of the war and his mythical status remained firmly attached to his war exploits, as if his life and death belonged only to the war. It was disturbing knowledge because I knew that my father did not die in the war. It would have been easier to accept things, to perceive a more normal progression of events if this had been the case.

There were so many questions in my mind but for some reason, I was not allowed to voice them. With each question came the same reply, the same sacred words that shut down all my enquiries and sealed every conversation, like the 'Amen' of a prayer.

'Your father was a great man. You should be proud of him.'

In the face of these walls of silence, I became desperate to know him, to claim him, to live and anchor my being in him. So, with the first heartbeats of love, came confusion and struggle.

Fantasy soon filled in the gaps.

At first, I replaced the blurry image of the man who had lived with us for three years and drove his car at reckless speeds, with a stronger, more idealised father. I pretended that there had been a terrible mistake, that he couldn't possibly be dead, that he was being held captive in some foreign country, like Ulysses, and had to overcome terrible trials before he was able to escape. So strong were these fantasies that they began to fill up the emptiness in my heart and I added more and more outrageous inventions to his expanding profile. One minute, he was a secret spy working on a dangerous mission for the British Government, the next, he was a famous diplomat in a foreign country, maintaining the conditions of the peace treaty. I transformed him into my hero, my guardian angel, my knight in shining armour … and in those dreamy days of childhood when everything seemed possible, I believed he would return to me one day.

There was only one photo of him in the house, a single black-and-white photo of a man in his uniform, staring at us from the mantelpiece in the lounge room. We only used the room on rare, formal occasions so the photo was like a dusty relic, but when the idea of a father started to become important to me, I began to study his features. He was rakishly handsome with a cocky grin, strong aquiline features and the most unusually beautiful hands for a man. In the photograph he was seated on a chair with his slender hands draped over his knees and a faraway look in his eyes.

As teenagers, we were in the habit of developing a crush on certain movie stars like Elvis or James Dean and unconsciously I started to fantasise about my father. His good looks, youth and adventurous exploits so easily fitted that unattainable, seductive image of the Hollywood hero and I suppose I 'fell in love' with my father.

I tried to imagine what he would have expected of me, what things I ought to do to please him, what sort of life I should have chosen that could possibly measure up to his magnificence.

Voices constantly whispered to me, 'You must. You have to. You ought to.' The more I invested into the perfection of his reconstruction, the more I wanted to belong to him, to be like him, to be him.

The daydreaming filled a huge hole in my life but it couldn't go on. Eventually I had to face the truth that the father I now loved was a dead man and the god-like image I had projected onto him was a fantasy. Unfelt emotions locked away and frozen in my heart came rushing to the surface. I had been unable to cry when I first learnt of my father's death but I now became consumed by my longing and my grief. Tears, tears and more tears sprang from somewhere deep within me.

The idea of never knowing him, of never knowing his love became unbearable and I tried to think of different ways to hold onto him. This is when it all started to go wrong for nothing can pierce the perfection of death. The harder I tried, the more he remained aloof, sealed off from me, locked away in some kind of untouchable space, forever beguiling, belonging only to himself.

So, without being conscious of the damage, I set myself a trap from which I could not escape. Too much grief can drive you crazy, especially when you take on an impossible burden, when you forget yourself and become the source of life for a dead man. If I could have continued to fantasise my love, I would have been able to identify with the positive aspects of my father: his courage, his attractive personality, his extraordinary talents, but once the fantasy was crushed, I was not strong enough to sustain myself and I lay crushed in the arms of the 'god' who had turned against me.

So, after years of feeling like an orphan, I finally became my father's daughter, walking a tightrope above an abyss, putting one foot after the other, balancing precariously between not living at all and living in a highly charged spiritual world. Why I continued to do this, I do not know but without a strong bond with my mother, my dead father was all I had. I had created the perfect seed bed for the demon lover.

My demon lover.

I would pay the price for this later on, but not yet. Not yet.

After this, the man in the photo changed. He was no longer the victor returning from the battle but an evasive impostor, smiling enigmatically from the mantelpiece. The roles he now assumed were not heroic but designed to keep me trapped. He was the elegant playboy, the perfect bridegroom, the charming seducer, the arrogant tormenter with a mocking grin like the man in my mother's vision. Desiring and hating him, yet I continued to succumb to him for I had assumed the responsibility of 'keeping him alive'. His 'well-being' became my well-being for unconsciously I had begun to experience myself through him. Better than not to have him at all. His masculine power remained magnetic and, in the end, it made no difference whether I worshipped him or hated him. I was lured into his trap, his elusive trickster quality, enthralled by him, possessed by him, bound to preserving his suave, godlike image.

I did not do what I should have done. In running towards my father, I believed I had been running toward life but the truth is that I was ruining my own chances to grow. My life was unable to find its own channel and I became cut off from my feminine instincts. It was like tossing a precious jewel over a barbed wire fence and trying to get it back.

In my search for a father to love me, I stood alone, a young girl in an empty room staring blankly at the faded photo of a dead man, loneliness meeting loneliness in a debilitating symbiotic bond.

Especially on Anzac Day.

Once a year in April, the townsfolk held this national ceremony in front of the Glen Innes Court House. Everyone assembled in the square with the statue of a soldier standing erect and tall over the crowd and a plaque displaying the names of the faithful servicemen who had died for their country. The townsfolk attended religiously, careful to participate in each stage of the proceedings – the march, the prayers, the speeches, the laying on of the wreath by a visiting military dignitary.

Our mother had dutifully forced myself, my brother and sisters to march as legacy wards in the Anzac parade with two other fatherless children. She did not know how much we hated to be singled out on this day, why we always walked with our heads down, our faces burning with the sting of shame rather than with pride. It was the same sort of feeling when the Legacy man, a well-meaning do-gooder from the Masonic Lodge, visited us with his parcel of charity goods and we were required to put on an act of gratitude while we secretly squirmed with humiliation.

We were a motley little group, unidentifiable and unheralded. We did not have proper uniforms or a colourful banner to announce us like the well organised legatees from the city of Armidale. We straggled along the street, conspicuously out of step with the surviving returned soldiers, and tried not to notice our classmates sniggering and pointing at us.

As the service reached its climax, the bugle played the Last Post and the officer in charge announced the two minutes silence. It was the most silent of any time I can remember in my whole life and it fell across the town like a shroud. All traffic and commercial activity of the town had ceased. Even the random cries of the animals, as if they knew, had faded beneath the bugle notes while the whole community stood at attention.

The spectators, heads bowed, seemed removed, like the souls of the lost at the end of the world, and the sickly, sweet taste of nostalgia coated our throats like treacle.

It was the same every year. Such inexplicable grief and yearning consumed my whole being, threatening to dismantle any defensive ground I might hope to gain. In the sacred silence, the flood gates of my heart would open up and I would release all my longing:

'Oh, father, come back to me. Oh, father, high-flying, crooked grinning, swaggering, free-wheeling father. Bring me your stubbly chin, your arms of a man, your smell of action, your love of speed. Lift me high, laugh with me. Teach me about men. Teach me why their blood runs faster than that of a little girl. Tell me why you loved the sky more than the earth. Help me to understand the hard ways of men.

'Tell me why you left me.'

*　　*　　*

It is amazing how much pain, confusion and unmediated suffering lie beneath an ordinary life. Our outside never matches up with our inside. We learn how to disassociate from the parts of ourselves that are split off, disavowed, unwanted and we exile them to the subterranean worlds of our mind. If we are young and standing on the brink of our lives, we do not want to give time to the rumblings beneath the surface. We are too busy with our careers, new places, new people, new ways of thinking and all the excitement that we are owed as children of the sixties. It is better to ignore the moods, the simmering depression and the sadness of the past.

The trick is to keep going.

I continued through High School, emotionally and mentally fragile but gifted academically, escaping from all my problems into the world of books and learning. While I could not make sense of my life, I could at least make sense of my studies and I would continue to enjoy studying all my life. As the final year of High School approached, I directed all my remaining energy, my hopes and my dreams into gaining an excellent pass in the Leaving Certificate.

At the end of the final year, when it was time to sit for our last exams, my classmates were waiting like an assembled jury at the front gate of the school.

'Did you study last night?' they asked jealously, for there was stiff competition amongst the few students who did not leave school after the Intermediate Certificate.

'No way,' I replied nonchalantly, even though I had been up at dawn and closeted in the toilet with my books. I enjoyed considerable popularity now that I could speak in informal settings and, to gain more attention, I had become the class rebel, whispering to my friends while the teacher was explaining something, passing notes under the desk, giggling about boys and ridiculing the teachers behind their back. Because of my erratic behaviour in class, my teachers were surprised when I gained the highest pass in the Leaving Certificate and won three scholarships to attend university.

When the time came to decide whether to leave my home and

my mother or to stay in Glen Innes, I was suddenly filled with doubt and anxiety. On the one hand, there was something so safe about an orderly life among people who now accepted me, an orderly, ordinary life full of calm routines and usefulness, a life where I could begin to feel sure of myself. On the other hand, I felt frustrated with nothing but a series of partly satisfying experiences to get me out of bed in the morning. Deep in my heart I had to admit I would never be truly happy if I stayed in this small town. For most of my life I had felt like an outsider anyway, suffering from an inner anguish, seeing too far and too deep into everything.

The idea of escape was tempting, but where should I go? It didn't really matter, for what was important was to be somewhere other than here and to be anyone but myself. I simply felt that a well of repressed possibilities existed inside me, that, given the right circumstances, I could finally do and say something. There was also the hope that in the wider world I would find something or someone who would soothingly put things right for me at last.

It was still a hard thing to leave my mother. The thought of her constant care all those years filled me with sadness and guilt; I could not deny that leaving home contained an element of protest, the protest against a home which was not what it should have been. We were a poor, struggling, fatherless family and I had always felt that my mother and I had not shared a really close bond. When I reached adolescence, I just didn't have a very clear idea of who she was and what our relationship was all about. Leaving her, however, seemed like an act of gross indecency but because I was too shy to discuss it with anyone, it remained within me like an inconsolable secret.

There was also something about her behaviour one day which showed me that there was a depth of passion in my mother's heart that I would never have suspected.

We were standing in the garage which she kept scrupulously clean in spite of the dirt floor. Its aromatic dankness rose pleasantly into my nostrils as soon as I opened the door; it reminded me of my grandfather's garage with its pungent, seductive odours. We did not have a car but I liked the garage because it contained things of the earth: good, honest working tools, newly dug potatoes, buckets of scraps for the chickens and winter bulbs waiting secretly in a dark cupboard.

'Mum,' I began nervously. 'I want to take the train to Cooma. I know it's a long way but I've been invited to stay with some friends there. Oh, please say yes. I really want to go and I know I can make the trip myself. Please, Mum.'

My mother stared at me in horror.

'No! No! Rosemary, you can't go. It's too far, I won't let you.'

I could see that my mother was not going to relent so, for the first time in my life, I defied her. She pleaded with me, growing more and more agitated, but I refused to back down. It was to be my first taste of adventure.

All of a sudden, she advanced towards me, her hands outstretched as if she wanted to choke me, her eye wide and flaming like a mad woman, her voice a mixture of shrill commands and strangled sobs. I had actually never seen my mother so overwrought and I ran terrified out of the garage.

There was something in my defiance and independence which had obviously unnerved her and for years after I wondered if she had been going to strike me down or collapse sobbing into my arms.

One Sunday, an answer came to me.

There is a signpost on the crossroads between the street leading to my home and the inland New England highway to Sydney. It is a weathered post onto which were nailed several arrow-shaped pieces of wood with the names of distant towns in NSW in faded black writing.

Wandering aimlessly through the deserted streets of the town on a Sunday afternoon, I would often pause and read the writing on the signpost, sounding out the names of distant towns like Uralla, Moree, Muswellbrook as the semi-trailers rattled by. Perched on a neighbour's fence, I would sit there for a while, wondering what it would be like to see Sydney and dreaming of foreign places even further away, mysterious countries I had read about like France and Russia and America. Bored children in country towns do a lot of daydreaming for there is nothing lonelier than an Australian country town on a Sunday afternoon.

On this afternoon towards dusk, a squadron of wild geese departing from their nesting season flew past. It was one of those early evenings when the autumn sky, instead of retreating into darkness, suddenly turned mauve, heralding an early morning frost. Silhouetted against this backdrop, in perfect V formation, these intrepid travellers slipped through the lavender sky like silk. I watched them, transfixed, because I knew their journey was long and dangerous, across miles of ocean and endless, unfriendly tunnels of space, yet, propelled by an ancient spark of wisdom, they knew their course

They knew their course, for in leaving, they were coming home.

In leaving, they were coming home and I took this as a sign.

My heart knows what the wild goose knows
And I must go where the wild goose goes
Wild goose, brother goose, which is best?
A wandering fool or a heart at rest.

It was decided.

I would attend Armidale University because it was closer to home than Sydney University and I would complete a degree in Modern Languages. I entertained the idea of travelling one day, of joining the Foreign Affairs Department and becoming a diplomat but this kind of employment was not available to women in my time. I was simply grateful to be leaving Glen Innes, my heart in a constant riot as the time for departure drew near. This was my exit plan, my hope and my salvation.

Eventually my mother came around to the idea.

'I don't blame you for wanting a better life, Rosemary. I never had the chance to finish High School so I don't know whether I would have been successful or not. But you are very good at school. You should make something of yourself. Don't end up like me,' she admitted wistfully but I knew she would have preferred that I stay in Glen Innes, find a job in the bank or one of the pharmacies and marry the boy next door.

She stared at me helplessly, aware of her own inadequacy and wasted life yet pricked by a small sensation of pride. I was the first girl in both my parents' families to go to university, and while not being a child prodigy, I was one of the youngest people in Australia to enter a university at the age of sixteen.

I found accommodation in one of the on-campus colleges and before the first term began, I worked in a local toy shop to save up as much money as I could. We were still a poor family so I began to make a wardrobe of clothes for myself, spending hours peddling away on my mother's treadle sewing machine, creating a number of different coloured dresses, all from the one pattern. My secret joy was a pair of shiny, red high-heeled shoes which I saved up for and ordered from a very stylish fashion magazine.

I knew my course.

Soon I would say goodbye to the small town with the small-town people shaping me into their little view of life. I would say goodbye to my dear grandfather, I would say goodbye to the mother who had reared me on her own and to all those friends and people who had either disdained or befriended me. I would say goodbye to the boy I might have married.

I would say goodbye to the girl I might have been.

*   *   *

There was one thing left to do.

I had to go back to Emmaville, to the town where it had all started and where everything had suddenly stopped.

143

A kind aunt who happened to be visiting a friend in Emmaville offered to take me with her. I had not been back to Emmaville or Big Ben since my father's death but now I felt compelled to at least show my face in the town. When the day arrived, I deliberately put on a very sophisticated, figure-hugging banlon dress and my new red shoes. I felt I had to dress in this confronting way because it had something to do with evening up an old, old score.

About eighteen kilometres out of the town, something flickered in my memory and I began to scan the signposts on the entrance gates of the larger properties. My heart lurched as I saw the sign bearing the words 'Big Ben' and caught a blurred glimpse of the homestead at the end of the tree-lined driveway. My aunt stopped the car and squinted curiously through the car window. There was a rumour that a family called Pattinson had purchased Big Ben and that the eldest son had married one of my Scherf cousins, an attractive but silly, young girl who had a habit of giggling excessively whenever she met you in the main street. The fact that the Scherfs had returned in some way to Big Ben seemed to strike a note of triumph in the minds of certain people but I received the news like a slap in the face.

I looked up the long avenue and my heart froze. There was something familiar about the property but I felt like one of the bewildered, forlorn children standing at the top of the Magic Faraway Tree, waiting for a land that had passed by forever.

I sat in the car, staring out the window, conscious only of an acute sense of loss.

'Would you like to go up to the house?' my aunt asked in a

soft, encouraging voice. 'I'm sure they wouldn't mind. I think they would be very pleased to see you.'

'No!' I answered so firmly and abruptly that she started up the car without hesitation. We arrived at the town, I opened the door and placed one red high-heel on the pavement. A glint of sunlight bounced off the shiny shoe like a spark. Immediately I was struck by the inaccessibility of the town, by the sense of its separation from everything to which I had felt entitled as if it guarded a secret to which I was no longer privy. The streets, the houses, the inhabitants seemed to arraign themselves against me and I began my circuit of the town as if I were walking the gauntlet, teetering on my new high-heels.

The local cinema, one of the largest buildings in the main street, was boarded up and one of the emporiums was now a shabby museum with a few old photos and dusty mineral samples. I searched for my family among the faded sepia photos and could find only a few tattered newspaper cuttings about my famous father. It was clear that no effort had been made by the townsfolk to honour his name and in this dilapidated mausoleum, his face stared at me, as pale and uncertain as an apology.

A queasy feeling had begun to form in my stomach and a sharp sense of displacement made me want to flee. I told the volunteer assistant that I was Charles Scherf's daughter and she just shrugged her shoulders. Outside the museum, I saw the dirt road leading to the cemetery and beyond that the dry fields of the Western prairies melting into oblivion. Whirls of dust rose and fell as a few stray cars passed along the road and disappeared into the emptiness.

People who happened to be in the street or pottering in their gardens stared at me in that mistrustful, guarded way country people have when a stranger appears in their midst. It was not the reaction I had anticipated for I had come looking for recognition and, dare I say, admiration. I didn't stop to chat with them because I felt as if the whole town had begun closing ranks against me.

Nobody wanted me here.

It struck me that I had made a big mistake in drawing attention to myself by showing off in my stylish, citified outfit. It only increased the gap between us, making it impossible for them to see me as anything but a 'stuck-up broad'. I did not understand at the time how deeply country folk resented any arrogant show from 'the ones who had got out', 'made good' and come back to rub their betterment in their noses.

The young men hanging around the corner pub whistled as I walked past and I shot them a disdainful glance. My shoes were hurting but I was trying to walk with unaffected poise and maintain a detached demeanour, like a visiting dignitary.

Suddenly a raucous voice burst the midday silence.

'Jesus bloody Christ. Would ya take a look at that! Who in the hell is SHE?'

The woman who had just denounced me so brazenly was none other than the proprietor of the local pub, Lily Gurk, a bawdy, common woman who knew everybody and everything that was going on in the town. She sized me up very quickly, realised what the show was all about and burst into a loud, derisive laugh which undid all my pretensions.

Then a terrible thing happened. The young loiterers outside, taking their lead from Lily and peeved that a posh sheila from a bigger town had looked down her nose at them, began to snigger and point at me. The men in the bar came out to see what the commotion was all about and joined in the laughing and the cat calls. I almost tripped in my new high-heels. The noise of their raucous jeers filled the air like the laughter of those terrible, cackling jokers of the bush, the kookaburras.

My face burned with shame and humiliation and I stumbled over to my aunt's car waiting at the curb. Climbing in, I kicked off my red shoes and collapsed into the wounded silence. They were right, after all. Their laughter, brutally honest in the simple way of country people unimpressed by city slickers, completely unmasked me and I saw myself as I truly was … a pathetic caricature, a ridiculous parody of a squadron leader's daughter, a monstrous upstart who had come here to flaunt her superiority and ended up being the laughing stock of the town.

I slunk down tearfully in the back seat of the car and waited for my aunt to drive away from this blighted place.

'Oh, my dear girl,' she whispered soothingly, but she could not have guessed the real reason for my distress.

Emmaville.

I turned my back on you at last, you, my lovely, savage dream. Big Ben, I do not care if you are sold to strangers and my name no longer holds its claim over your wild hills. You will not hurt me anymore, nor will I cry when some insensitive fool tells me that a witless cousin on the Scherf side has married the son of the new owners and the Scherfs have returned to Big Ben.

For me there will be no return.

*   *   *

I packed my suitcase with my homemade dresses and my red shoes. My mother watched me silently and I tried not to see the anxiety in her eyes. I said a cheerful goodbye to my brother and my little sister, too preoccupied with my own happiness to notice their small, wondering faces. Grandfather was waiting outside in the car, two hours too early as usual, and when I opened the car door he took off before I was properly settled in the front seat. We raced to the railway station and then had to wait a long, long time for the train to draw into the station.

My grandfather, my Poppa.

A wave of nostalgia overcame me and I couldn't help wondering if I might actually be leaving the best part of my life. He lifted my suitcase into the compartment and turned to me with tears in his blue eyes.

'Be a good girl, dear. Remember your little mother who sacrificed everything for you.'

I knew what he meant. I did keep my mother in my mind through all those years of difficult exams and growing up and boys wanting to put their hands up your skirt. I passed every subject with a Distinction and kept myself intact for there was something stronger than personal ambition, something more embedded than duty which I had never expressed to my mother or even acknowledged myself. On the brink of leaving her, I was startled by the wisp of a new sensation, like the first, still, small voice of God in the unbeliever's heart. Then I knew that my mother had not wanted to harm me that day in the garage; she had simply wanted to keep me and hold me close.

For there was love … after all.

My heart soared as the train pulled out of the station. I was wearing my new red shift, my hair was long and straight like the folk singers of the day and my eyes were shining with the excitement of a small town girl on the brink of a grand adventure.

I have won.

I have prevailed.

No more the orphan who couldn't even say her name.

No more the condescending words from charitable relatives, no more the stares and sniggers from school friends, no more the sentimental old men patting me on the back and telling me that my father was a great man.

The lie which stunted my life has been lifted. The murderers have vacated my dreams and I have even taught myself to speak without stuttering. The quicksand of grief could no longer swallow me up and, for the time being, the dead lay securely in their graves.

The stars have offered themselves to me.

I have escaped from shame.

PART TWO

THE FATHER

'I came home from the soaring in which I lost myself'

Rainer Maria Rilke – *The Inner Sky: Poems, Notes, Dreams*

CHAPTER 1

FLYING HIGH

England 1942

Squadron Leader Charles Curnow Scherf DSO DFC and bar, Mosquito Ace pilot was the second highest allied Mosquito Ace of World War Two and the only Australian in the top ten Aces. He was the only British-based Australian fighter pilot to surpass the 1941–42 combat record of the Spitfire Aces, Bluey Truscott DFC of Melbourne and Hugo Armstrong DFC of Perth. Today he is still recognised as the undisputed pioneer of day intruder missions in the European theatre.

Charles was born in Emmaville, New South Wales in 1917, the largest baby recorded at that time in the state, weighing 6 kg. He grew up in Big Ben, a large rural property and the home of the Scherfs, German immigrants who had come to Australia in the 1854 gold rush to make their fortune in mining but had turned to farming instead.

The homestead was large with tennis courts, a nine-hole golf course and river frontage for swimming. Visiting dignitaries to the area were always entertained at Big Ben, the social hub of the small township, and the Scherfs were generally considered to be upper-class snobs. He rode his horse to the local school and received private tuition in musical instruments and singing. Every night he went to sleep to the strains of the great classical composers and in the evening after supper he would charm everyone with his piano recitals of the latest jazz compositions, played by ear.

Charles was a child of great promise from the beginning. Unlike some men who are always clumsy and out of step with life, Charles was born with natural grace, athleticism and incomparable innate dexterity. Every new sport he tackled – golf, tennis or cricket – he played with the style and grace of a professional. He was an excellent rifle shot in the Light Horse Brigade, having joined at the age of seventeen. Many people said that he was born to be a leader for on the football field and in every sport in which he was associated, he was an outstanding personality and the idol of the crowd.

It was generally accepted that Charles Scherf Junior, youngest son of Charles Scherf Senior, would take over the family property one day. The oldest son and natural heir, Henry, had shown no taste for the land and had been allowed to take up engineering studies at the University of Sydney. He now lived in Wollongong with a thin-lipped wife who suffered from migraine headaches. Granville, the second son, had acquired his own land several miles from Big Ben and lived there with his tall, aristocratic wife from North Italy. One of the sisters, Rose, had her own property, Ben Vale, opposite Big Ben, and another Scherf, a cousin of Charles, owned the property next door which they called Little Ben. It was indeed remarkable that the Scherfs owned nearly all the land half-way between Glen Innes and Emmaville.

The two older sons were short, stocky men with rough, fleshy faces, large noses and dark, bristly hair. Charles, on the other hand, had a slim, athletic body and the fine handsome features of his mother's Celtic origins. Born to his mother when she was over forty-five years of age, the finer genes of the mother's Celtic origins had finally taken root in the coarser Germanic stock, for her family had come from Cornwell and were possibly of Huguenot origins. Others noted that since the family had settled in Land's End on the southern reaches of the Cornish coast, there may have been a few sailors from the Spanish Armada who had injected their Hispanic features into the gene pool, because Charles had the smooth, olive skin, high cheek bones, grace and daring manner of a Spanish toreador.

'Too handsome for his own good,' people were later to remark. 'And in his air force uniform, an absolute lady-killer.'

Charles married his country sweetheart, Hope O'Hara, and one year after their first child was born in 1940, he enlisted in the armed forces. Nobody doubted his courage as they all remembered the day he had dived into a turbulent surf as a schoolboy and rescued a man caught in a rip. There was also another incident when Charles noticed a fishing boat that had capsized at the Tweed Heads bar and a man overboard who was being washed towards a rocky point. Charles calmly passed his wristwatch over to his girlfriend and dived into the dangerous sea … shoes, clothes and all.

An onlooker, being interviewed for the local press afterwards, commented:

'It was a peculiar thing to see this boy risk his life to save another, then calmly pick up his hat off a rock, fetch his watch and just walk away. Without seeking any praise or publicity.'

*   *   *

As a member of the Empire Air Training Scheme, he completed his training in Temora accompanied by his wife and young daughter, Maureen, who soon became the darling of the camp. His best friend, L Morrison, described him as a natural, looping and rolling the Tigers while others were still trying to get their landings right. He then went on to Mallala, South Australia, for further training, graduating in 1942 as an 'Above average student' but receiving the comment 'Inattentive to detail' because he refused to tone down his daredevil ways.

The decision to go to war came automatically to him. Like most of the Australian draft, he longed to put his learning into practice as a true fighter pilot so applied for further training in the United Kingdom. The RAF was on the offensive at that time and in desperate need of bomber pilots so Charles was accepted immediately. Before the year had ended, he farewelled his young wife and baby and undertook the long sea journey to England.

It was rather mystifying for the young farmer from the backwoods of Australia to find himself in a foreign country without any idea of the air force branch in which he was supposed to serve. He was taken to the little village of Ford, about 25 miles from Brighton, on the south-east coast of England, where he again found himself at a loose end. Fortunately, he was greeted by a young Canadian who approached him as soon as he heard the Australian accent.

'I always wanted to fly with an Aussie,' he grinned.

So the two teamed up and Charles was posted to the 418 City of Edmonton Squadron under the command of Wing Commander Paul David DFC. Again he had no idea what work he was supposed to do, so ended up volunteering for a special training program which was later to develop into the famous Intruder Squadrons.

A light-hearted, self-sufficient young man with his eyes constantly on the horizon, Charles was at first disdainful of the strict codes of discipline and rigid standards of the English. The comment on his training sheets read 'Good average pilot' but 'Apt to be careless at times.' Not quite the RAF type. A colonial son whom they noticed had not elected to fly with his English peers but had joined up with a Canadian squadron. Yet the AirVice-Marshall of England, the bull-necked Trafford Leigh-Mallory, adamant that the success of the whole war could only be turned by his 'big wings', was desperate to get airmen from anywhere and Charlie Scherf of dubious origins was no less foreign than the last bunch of Czechs who could not even speak English.

'These Aussies are tough. Waggle your wings and they will follow you through hell and high water,' declared the late Wing Commander 'Paddy' Finucane, leader of the Australian Spitfire Squadron in Britain.

*   *   *

It was a rude shock for the new recruits. They had believed in the Hollywood version of England, a misty land of leafy lanes, fields of daffodils and stately country mansions, but grim reality soon set in. The 418 Squadron began life in Debden, Essex, where conditions were crude and austere. Some of the lads were just out of school and still soft with the comfort of their mother's pampering so were disappointed to be accommodated in a chilly, deserted hostel. At first there were no blankets and only one basin for 185 men. The floor was still splattered with the blood of the Royal Airforce men caught in a recent Nazi blitz.

The training was also arduous and carried out against a backdrop of bombings, strafings and fires throughout England. Suitable aircraft were not available at first so they used Bostons and Hurricanes, not an easy choice as great problems of teaching pilots how to take control of the cumbersome machines and how to prepare them for offensive missions had to be overcome. The young men, however, were cocky and confident even though they pranged their long-finned Bostons two or three times a week.

Charles became known as 'Scherf from Down Under', always had a grin for everyone and a humorous quip even in the worst situations. He began a rigorous training program; it took almost two years to reach the high standard necessary to take part in operations from RAF station Ford. This included cross country flights, air-to-air firing practices, single engine flying and night flying. Night flying, that was an achievement to be proud of and Charles never forgot his first solo attempt.

On that night, he had walked too confidently with his Sergeant from the Mess to the hangar. A chink in the blackout of one of the windows shone a thin ray of light on the glistening ground covered in the fairy snow. A dry wind moaned over the bleak field as they crunched their way across the tarmac.

'Well, you couldn't want a better night. Even you shouldn't make a mistake, Charlie, although I bet you'll need three more dual circuits with the instructor before you pass the solo test. Don't make a mess of it. I want to sleep tonight.'

Charles smiled wryly, taking the bet as a challenge. He strode towards the test plane, a squat dark patch against the grey sky, and climbed into the front cockpit after the Sergeant. Settling himself comfortably into the box seat, he glanced over the dimly shining instruments and pulled the stick back into his stomach. The engine burst forth with a stutter and hurled a great roar into the night. He throttled back, waved away the chocks from under the wheels and taxied gently down the flare path. The officer in charge of night flying and a Sergeant with the Aldis lamp sat huddled in their greatcoats like two giant moths at the end of the field.

Charles tapped out his letter on the Morse key and swung the machine into the wind. As he gathered speed and saw the blurred lights of the flare path racing past, he realised he was holding the trigger too tensely. It was the Sergeant who then gave a slight push on the rudder and with a bump they were off the ground.

Charles straightened out at 1,000 ft, pushed the rudder and the stick together and turned slightly to the left. Then he looked down. Below lay the thin, glowing snake of the flare path, ahead lay the silver sea and all around the clear, winter sky, studded with sparkling jewels. A burst of confidence shot through him and he released his clenched hold on the stick. Banking and turning again, he flew into the downwind and released the undercarriage. Approaching the flare path, he baulked at the lights rushing up to meet him and felt himself tensing up again. Reaching the first flare, he started to ease the stick back but the Sergeant quietly cautioned him.

'You're too high. Not yet.'

He had reached the second flare and was still not down when panic set in. Still too fast.

God, I don't think I can make it, he thought.

Suddenly, there was a reassuring bump and the Sergeant was yelling at him.

'Hold her straight man.'

They came to a safe halt, the Sergeant climbed out and muttered to Charles without making any further comment.

'Twice more. And take it up yourself.'

He was back up in the air but when the time came to approach the landing, heavy clouds had blown in and obscured the stars so that he could not make out the flare path. His instruments told him that he was gaining speed and the horrible realisation came to him that he was diving. Enclosed in the claustrophobic space and faced with a thousand bewildering instruments, he experienced a moment of complete paralysis. Panic. He was going to crash! Standing up in his seat, he was consumed by one thought only. He must get out. Damn! Was he even the right way up? Suddenly the flare path burst into sight, he dropped back into his seat and prepared to make the landing, feeling thoroughly ashamed of himself.

Completing a couple more circuits, he relaxed and began to feel what some pilots have described as the joy of flight. To be up there alone, isolated but confident that he was in complete control of the instruments, that the plane would obey his every command, that he was entirely responsible for his own return to earth. That was every man's ambition and for a moment he had nearly lost it.

He completed two more circuits, pulled off two adequate landings and climbed out.

The Sergeant sauntered up to him as he entered the hanger and nonchalantly pronounced the verdict.

'Okay. You'll do.'

When the German offence on England slackened off, there were more intruder operations over France, Holland and Germany. However, apart from close anti-aircraft fire, there was nothing remarkable to note in Charles' logbook. Later, he trained on Lancasters and flew to Germany to escort the famous Dambusters when they dropped 12,000-pound bombs on the Dortmund-Ems Canal. Sometimes the weather was so bad he reported:

'Target not patrolled. 10/10 cloud. Icing at 4,000 ft and St Elmo's Fire on propeller and wingtips.'

From time to time, without warning, a squadron of long-range bombers would drop out of the sky. They would make his station their headquarters, the heavy drone of their engines announcing their return as night fell. Then one day, a Spitfire Squadron dropped in. The trim deceptive frailty of the plane's lines fascinated Charles and he spent some of his spare time climbing onto the wings and inspecting the controls. This was the agile, legendary plane that tipped the balance in favour of the RAF in the Battle of Britain, the plane he hoped to fly one day.

That day finally came and he went off to the field with his trainer, painfully aware that this was a machine in which there was no chance of making a dual circuit as a preliminary, that he had to solo from the very start.

'Don't worry,' scoffed his trainer. 'She's easier to handle than you think.'

Charles climbed into the low cockpit and noted with interest the small field of vision. The voice of his instructor droned on but he scarcely heard his explanation. He was lost in the realisation that he would soon be flying the same plane as Bluey, the fastest machine in the world.

'Have you got all that?' the trainer interrupted his thoughts, sounding a little annoyed. 'Well, off you go. Good luck.'

Charles taxied slowly down the driveway, trying to remember such things as not to push the stick too far forward when taking off and the warning about the brakes on landing. He should have listened more closely because any hard application would result in a somersault and a disgraceful transfer to a shabby, ill-equipped unit.

Suddenly, he was in the air and flying halfway round the circuit without any problems. He came in low for the landing, cut the engine and floated down on all three points. Exhilaration. Three more times he took off and came around for a perfect landing.

You little beauty! He was flying the Spitfire!

After his first solo came an hour of acrobatics and an oxygen climb to 28,000 ft, followed by air-firing exercises and numerous dogfights. The dogfights usually involved a pilot and his instructor who would try to 'shoot' each other down.

On one occasion, Charles took off with his instructor, climbed to 10,000 ft, hurled and spun his plane confidently about the sky as the instructor closed in on his tail. Never had man done such things in a plane, a skill he was later to employ to greater benefit in the Mosquito. Surely he would claim the victory in this dogfight but, coming out of a difficult turn, he was surprised to see the instructor following steadily behind him. Charles tried to get on his tail, pursuing him in smaller and smaller circles but failed each time to get him in his sights. Feeling dizzy and lost, he came to the startling conclusion that the instructor had actually destroyed him a long time ago and was probably laughing himself silly as he calmly headed for home.

Thank God it was only a practice.

It was a hard lesson to learn but the instructor explained

to him later that aerobatics were useless in actual combat. A pilot could easily be tracked while executing a loop and the best method was to pull up and above your opponent, dive down, thinking quickly, fire at once and break away. Another method was to fly above and to the side of the enemy, turn in and let the other plane come through his sights at right angles. In this way he could open fire in front of the enemy's nose and strike him all the way down where he had least protection. Dropping behind, he could then administer another attack from the rear while presenting a very difficult target himself.

He learnt many other things, for example the vital importance of obeying every oral command and gesture of the Squadron Leader, of never following a plane down after hitting it and of always keeping at least in pairs with his fellow pilots. He learnt to only fly in a straight course when you were closing in to 200 yards for an attack, to hold the machine steady in the slipstream of the enemy and to fire in short sharp bursts of two to four seconds.

As for his knowledge of the enemy, he learnt the advantage of height because of the Germans' disinclination to fight with height if outnumbered and of the Messerschmidt's vulnerability when attacked from the rear. He came to understand the German habit of using fighter escorts all around their bombers which gave them the advantage when carrying out pre-arranged strategies but proved ineffective if this order was disturbed in any way. He also learnt that the German mass psychology of grouping together to gain confidence led to a false sense of security which could easily be eroded by an individualist like himself.

In their off duty hours, the pilots would relax in their favourite pub or cluster about the huts, snatch a feed from a recently delivered parcel from Canada or Australia, enjoy a game of cards, bury themselves in letter writing or catch forty winks in an out of the way corner. At these times he would think of his beloved Bunny back in Australia with a new baby on the way. At times the airmen were invited to a country mansion for a small party and the handsome Aussie airman knew, as men know, that there were a few old English girls who would have gladly obliged him with a roll in the cot in one of the back bedrooms but he had his girl and he was faithful to her during the war.

Pay day was a particularly bright occasion, especially if the back pay for those promoted to a higher level piled up. Upon receipt, there was sure to be a party or a 'spot' of leave. For the others, there was often a crap game at one end of the hut and the rolling ivories on a blanket at the other. The losers spent the next fortnight scurrying around for a bit of pin money but the spirit of comradeship among the men meant that there was always a spare 'quid' or two to help out a pal.

These twice monthly occasions were made even brighter when cigarettes and other comforts were distributed by the supervisor of the Knights of Columbus. Cocoa and buns from the Salvation Army provided another welcome treat. In later months, when the Squadron was adopted by the city of Edmonton, there were cigarettes in high quantities and an abundance of delicacies which had the pilots of the 418 eating like kings.

However, Charles would never forget his first Christmas in the Squadron. The winter was severe and there was a shortage of food across England. Instead of the customary roast lamb and goose, golden baked potatoes, Christmas pudding, custard and all the good things of home and family, he ate tinned corned beef and mashed potatoes that were grey and watery.

The fact of war was, however, never far from the airmen's consciousness. Gas drills on Sunday mornings were particularly tiresome but were completed with a certain amount of horseplay. Back up courses were compulsory for all the airmen. Preparedness for action meant that the men had to be physically fit and therefore required to join in all kinds of outdoor activities

In the rugby games, Charles' talent for sport allowed him to fit in perfectly with the sport-loving Canadians. In the local rugby competition, the 418 Squadron acquitted themselves extremely well against the town of Ford, a capable team but no match for the flying Aussie centre. On the tennis court, Charles was the unbeatable champion of the whole Squadron. Handling a rifle was another requirement for the airmen and Charles was an extraordinary rifle shot. Jim Johnson, one of his friends and a good marksman, shot skeet with Charles and admitted:

'His reactions are so bloody fast he can pulverise the bird before I even pull the trigger.'

* * *

So the days went by.

Work, routine, ops, sleep, a bit of play.

Charles' training took almost two years but at last he was deemed ready for operational flying. It was at night that the real work began. The kites would rev up, silhouetted against the early dusk, and roar down the runway into the gathering darkness. Their target was somewhere in occupied Europe, somewhere over an enemy railway, terminal depot or airfield waiting to be destroyed. To Criel, St Andeux, Orleans, Le Crotoy, Javincourt, Dreux, Chartres, Ault, Florennes, Vendeville, Vitry, Laon and other places.

If they were fortunate enough to return, there was ground crew waiting to refuel, rearm and re-bomb with the rapt attention of a mother to a child and a night flying supper of eggs, bacon, chips, baked beans and tea. Sometimes the pilots talked until dawn, their lives blended together in a routine of work, sleep and a few hours of off-duty relaxation in their favourite pub.

As the Bostons kept on hammering and smashing enemy communications, the 418 Squadron started to build a good reputation as a team. However, even though Charles gained valuable experience flying these intruder missions, he did not encounter many Huns himself and thus failed to score. This was to change dramatically in 1943, the year his daughter, Rosemary, was born in Australia. This was the year the Squadron converted from Bostons to the new faster Mosquitoes.

The Mosquito was a masterpiece, and revolutionary from the tip of its rudder to the end of its ailerons. Affectionately known as the 'Mossie', it carried four cannons, four machine guns and a ton of bombs if needed. It was also known as the Timber Terror, the Loping Lumberyard, Freeman's Folly and the Wooden Wonder but was recognised later as 'the plane that saved England'. It was built of laths of birch and balsam wood ply-glued together under pressure, and its wings and fuselage were covered with doped cloth. Two Rolls-Royce Merlin engines propelled the prototype at over 375 miles per hour, and the crew of two, pilot and observer, sat side by side, as in the front seat of a car, enjoying perfect forward vision.

It was not easy at first for de Havilland to convince the Air Ministry that a plane made from pieces of wood and glued together in a moulded wooden bomber was capable of carrying half a ton more bombload than the Boeing B-17 Flying Fortress and flying 50 miles per hour faster. Experts from the RAF advised against it but the de Havilland company decided to construct the revolutionary, clean and graceful bomber at their own expense.

'An ugly plane is sometimes all right, but a graceful-looking plane always flies beautifully,' commented John, Geoffrey de Havilland's brother, who was, ironically, killed in 1943 testing the new plane. Only the Messerschmidt 262 could be compared with it, but the Messerschmidt was more aggressive, coarser, more vicious looking – in a word, more German. On the 21st of September 1941, Geoffrey de Havilland proved his point when he himself successfully carried out a difficult photo-trip in daylight, Brest – La Pallice – Bordeaux – Paris; he was chased by three Messerschmidt 109s but easily out-distanced them at 23,0000 ft.

Hermann Goering, Germany's wartime Aviation Minister,

on hearing about the Mosquito, said the aircraft turned him 'green with envy'.

'It makes me furious when I see the Mosquito. I turn green and yellow with envy,' he announced scathingly to his German officers. 'The British, who can afford aluminium better than we can, knock together a beautiful, wooden aircraft that every piano factory over there is building. They have geniuses and we have nincompoops!'

It was a memorable day, the first time Geoffrey de Havilland Junior, aware of the Squadron's good work, visited their station and showed in a test flight what his company's new plane could do. In a vertical climb, he cut one engine and had his brainchild almost complete a reverse power dive. It was not a circus show designed to entertain the onlookers but a demonstration which showed the men that the Mosquito was the world's best and fastest plane, 19 miles per hour faster than the Spitfire and 50 miles per hour faster than the Hurricane.

The climax to the Mossie's debut came when the men awoke one day to see their runways taped in white. A bevy of aircraft, local and visiting, dotted the aerodrome while planes took off and landed and there stood the Prime Minister himself with the inevitable cigar, accompanied by Sir Trafford Leigh-Mallory, Sir Archibald Sinclair and other dignitaries who had been invited to give the nod to the newcomer. They were accompanied by US general IC Eahker, Admiral Stark and Admiral Boyd who had come to verify what the Allied equipment and men could do, no doubt ensuring that the invasion of the Continent would be more that a haphazard gamble.

In the back of their minds was the master plan.

D-Day.

It was not long before the Mosquitoes began to fulfil more frontline roles than any other plane, being perfectly adapted to daytime tactical bombing, night bombing, pathfinding, intruding and U-Boat hunting. By 1942, there were over a thousand Mosquitoes of various types in service with the RAF, flying regular day flights across the Atlantic over enemy territory as far as the Baltic and nightly raids on Berlin and other targets, regardless of the weather. In spite of all their efforts the Germans never managed to catch them and this kept Berlin in a constant state of alert. In the last six months of 1943, the bomber version flew a thousand sorties over Germany with the loss of only eleven aircrew.

Wing Commander Maxwell was the Station Commanding Officer at Ford at this time and had, himself, shot down thirty-two enemy aircraft. One night as the Mosquitoes were taking off, he gave their pilots a final tribute:

'There go the finest planes and airmen in the world.'

It was perhaps on low-level daylight raids that the Mosquitoes brought off their most sensational feats, in particular the destruction of Gestapo HQs at Oslo and Copenhagen, and the famous Amiens Prison. Hurtling along in pairs at 375 miles per hour, they ambushed German planes deep inside their own country. This individualist way of fighting was the most exciting method of modern warfare and it suited one man in particular: Charles Scherf.

One might wonder at the curious elements which cause some men to suddenly excel in a certain field. Up to this point, Charles had been mainly digesting all that was taught to him. In his modest, self-reliant manner he had waited in the wings, his quiet self-control masking a strong determination. Like most Aussie country men, his eyes were always on the horizon, perpetually scanning the sky. This was to his advantage as the squadron did not use airborne radar in their operations and all victories were achieved by visual combat. He had the right eyes for the task, for the constant observation of detail, for the positioning of three planes travelling at different relative velocities and angles of approach, eyes trained to assess weather patterns with only the moon and stars for reference at night. There was also his love and knowledge of music which had developed his fine sense of timing and balance for synchronisation of the engines and control of the instruments. In those lonely dark hours of night flights, when his instruments were perfectly set, he would lean back in his chair relaxing his mind, recalling the strains of a symphony, and savour once more the profound meditation of flight.

With the introduction of the Mosquito, Charles finally came into his own. He had the right plane to match these abilities, the right plane at the right time for the right man to help alter the course of the war. At last he could show them what he was really made of.

In September 1943 Charles flew an escorting Mosquito for eight Lancaster bombers which attacked the Dortmund-Ems

Canal and was promoted to Flight Lieutenant. On the 27th of January, 1944 he finally got down to business when two formations of Mosquitoes were dispatched to fly a daylight ranger operation over France. Travelling over Bourges, Charles spotted a Focke-Wulf FW200 flying at 150 ft and approaching in his direct path. He attacked from behind, fired a ten-second burst into the port wing and fuselage, then, increasing his deflection, he hit the starboard wing and engine and watched as the FW200 hit the ground, burning furiously.

To avoid flying over Bourges Airport with its flak, he broke hard starboard and spotted another aircraft flying at 1,000 ft. Once more coming in from the stern, he fired a three-second burst and the starboard engine burst into flames. One man bailed out and the big Heinkel spiralled down and exploded. Returning home, he recorded 'Grand Day' in his logbook and, along with other successful pilots from the squadron, enjoyed drinks all round in the Sergeants' Mess. Reflecting on the day, Charles concluded that their success had depended on extremely low flying at high cruising speeds to achieve the necessary degree of surprise and avoid the radar used to detect intruders. This was the germ of a very important discovery.

His next victim was taken out several weeks later. Approaching Florennes in Belgium on his way to Leipzig, Charles noticed a single-engine aircraft heading south and set off in pursuit. He chased the aircraft doggedly for twenty miles and closed in for the attack when it climbed to 7,000 ft and began turning tightly. The enemy dived and Charles, being such an outstanding pilot, pursued the German so relentlessly that he lost control, crashed and burst into flames. It was gleefully noted by his superiors:

'Economy-minded Charlie Scherf. Destroyed his enemy without firing a single shot.'

Five days after his first strike, he destroyed another two enemy planes when he shot down two JU-88s over their own airfields.

With each sortie the germ of the thought about an entirely different way to conduct intruder operations had begun to plague his mind. It was the first time anyone had realised that not only was extreme low flying an important element of their success but that intruder missions conducted in daylight would be much more successful than at night-time. It was a radical thought and the first obstacle was how to convince his superiors. To prove his theory, he would have to fly alone. This would be extremely dangerous work but Charles knew that he was up to the task and began to pester Sir Charles Portal, Marshal of the Royal Airforce.

He was refused three times.

The vital question as to Portal's refusal to not only allow Charles a chance but to later release Mosquitoes for low-level daytime harrying, finally given just six months before D-Day, was seen as leaving a wide area for miscalculation. Perhaps the fires of Dresden were still smouldering in the Commander's eyes. But who can stop the wind? Fortunately, Charles persisted, returning twice more, begging to be given a go. It was Sir Trafford Leigh-Mallory, the man after whom Charles named his only son, who initially allowed him the chance.

This brought a new phase of daylight intrusion sorties into

enemy territory with the pilots flying at treetop level, right under the big guns. The Germans were taken by surprise and the Luftwaffe suffered enormous damage from then on, in particular the destruction of the Gestapo Headquarters at Oslo and at Copenhagen, and the famous Amiens Prison. This technique, pioneered by Charles, was seen by some English historians to link him with Sir Francis Drake, harrier of the Spanish Armada. They claimed that Charlie in his Mossie equated with Drake in the smaller English corsairs whose surprising attacks on the lumbering galleons laid the scene for their final destruction on the cliffs of Cornwell.

Striking with the wicked speed of lightning, he soon increased his tally to seven, running amok among German flying schools in supposedly safe areas, flooring transport aircraft and damaging convoys of moored flying boats. He was appointed to the rank of Squadron Leader and was awarded the DFC.

His mates teased him about his individualistic style, joking that he flew at rooftop level and placed the bombs slap through the windows of his target!

As for D-Day, it would be difficult to estimate his personal contribution to the preparations, bombing ports up and down the coast of France and along the Baltic before the Allied landing. Such courageous feats have remained mysterious, like the inscription on his gravestone recording that he was also part of the British Secret Service, a fact never divulged to his family.

Speaking to his wife on his return to Australia, Charles was reported as saying, 'One day I'll tell you something about the war which I haven't been able to tell anybody. But wait until you're seventy and too old to worry about it.'

What was discovered was that, after D-Day, squadrons found posters on a former Luftwaffe base offering a large reward for any member of Goering's pride who shot down a Mosquito.

One poster advertised a reward of 10,000 DM for the life of Charles Scherf.

*   *   *

Even though Charles was at his best on lone patrols, he sometimes operated with a flying partner. On the 26th of February, 1944, flying with another Mosquito piloted by Howard Cleveland from Canada, he encountered the strangest aircraft he had ever seen. It looked like two twin-engined planes flying side-by-side, joined together by one main plane and fitted with a fifth engine at the join.

'I couldn't believe my eyes … At first, I thought my eyes were playing tricks,' Howie later remarked. 'Then I thought it must be two Fortresses flying wingtip to wingtip.'

It was identified later as a Bi Heinkel glider tug which had five engines, two tails and two crew compartments. It was towing two Gotha gliders in line astern.

Charles and Howard lost no time, each destroying one glider and going on to attack the monstrosity which had a large number of gun positions. Charles attacked first, setting two starboard engines on fire, then the Canadian fired cannon and machine guns, striking the engines on the starboard side. They were amazed at the Heinkel's ability to absorb punishment with three engines burning and bits of wreckage flying everywhere. Charles dealt the final blow when he circled around and attacked the side with machine guns, his cannon all used up, and the monster began a slow spiral to the ground.

They were accredited with half a kill each.

The DFC was awarded to Charles on the 4th of April, 1944 for his 'exceptional courage, keenness and determination'.

Sometimes the enemy was not man. Charles had taken off with Cleveland again, setting a course for North Germany across the Baltic. It was a rainy day but the Mossies, pale grey on top and sky-blue beneath, slid between the sheets of rain falling from the leaden sky like a trout effortlessly making its way upstream. Crossing the German coast at Kubitzer, north of Rostock, they encountered two Junker 87s; Charles immediately turned after one while Cleveland chased the other. His first two bursts, 60 degrees correction, missed because he was turning very tightly but his third was on the mark. As he turned, he saw Cleveland chasing a twin-engined Junker 88, his shells ripping bits out of the enemy who was beginning to smoke. He did not see how the encounter ended because he spotted two Dorniers in a creek. Diving on them, he was pleased to watch the first explode and sink, but to his regret, the second weathered three of his bursts. The flak had started up and he broke, hugging the dunes, but found himself underneath two Junker 88s flying in formation. Upon his attack, the first broke up in the air but as he was striking the second he was hit by a shell which tore out one of his drop-tanks and damaged his rudder. Re-trimming his plane, he set off after the second Junker at full throttle and shot it down.

While all this was happening, he had lost sight of Cleveland

and decided that since the rain had stopped he should set course for home by himself. After twenty minutes of flying, he was relieved when he caught sight of Cleveland flying over the sea but flying with difficulty on one engine which was constantly missing. Over the R/T he told Charles quite matter-of-factly that he had brought down two planes and destroyed a third on the ground. His report came first, his voice from outside sounding muffled through the walls of Charles' plane as from another world but then, in a less audible, shaky voice, he asked Charles to promise to write to his wife, Jeanie, and tell her that he mightn't be able to make it back to England. He'd made up his mind though; rather than be made a prisoner, he was going to have a shot at making it into Sweden.

'Goodbye and good luck, Howie,' was all that Charles could reply, his voice hoarse from the lump in his throat.

As he continued his flight towards home, he passed a German naval convoy and used up the rest of his ammunition on a minesweeper. There was a lot of flak and his observer got hit on the right side. Then a most unusual thing happened. Just as he was crossing the coast north of Heligoland, he was suddenly blinded by the sun and collided with a flock of seagulls. Out of the blue, they rose in a great swarm in front of him, like a barrier of feathers and flapping wings. He did not see them quickly enough as he was turned towards the sun but the result was many holes in his wings and the gruesome sight of mangled carcasses lodged in the radiator. There was blood smeared all over the cockpit and other parts of the aircraft, the aerial was torn off, the port aileron jammed and every forward pane of perspex broken. If the birds had been bigger, it would have been fatal.

Such extraordinary feats by the gallant Aussie soon gained the interest of the British public.

In a broadcast to the BBC, read in his distinctive Aussie accent, Charles described one of his exploits over the Baltic.

'I caught sight of an aircraft flying some miles away so I turned and gave chase at high speed. The German must have seen us coming because black smoke pouring from his aircraft showed us he was giving her full boost. We caught him up with no trouble. Coming in behind, I gave him a short burst and he went down in flames over the sea. Later, beyond Rostock, we saw an aircraft circling. I got into range, fired two bursts at wide deflection but missed. I then got right on his tail and gave him a short burst. He flipped on his back, burst into flames and went straight to the ground.

'South of here, we saw a Heinkel 177 coming over an airfield, so I attacked him from underneath and in front. After a short burst, he caught fire and went straight down into the bay nearby. As I turned, I noticed the other Mosquito chasing a JU 88. Pieces were flying off it but my attention was distracted by an aircraft parked on the field, silhouetted beautifully against the bay, so I came down, gave him a burst and was very satisfied to see him blow up.'

*   *   *

They called him a scientific killer. The younger pilots admired him tremendously, having read so much about Charles

Kingsford Smith and seeing in Charles the same daredevil spirit, competence and killer instinct. The work he did was certainly dangerous but Charles always felt that he was up to the task and needed no admiration. He simply told the youngsters to keep fit and active because he attributed his success to the sharp reflexes he had developed on the rugby field.

At heart, Charles was a modest man but it seemed that in a short time, airforce pilots had become the nation's heroes. It was difficult at first for this average Aussie grazier from nowhere to grasp the concept that he might now belong to a race of men on their own. Through his daily contact with death, however, he had realised, perhaps unconsciously, certain fundamental things, like a flash of insight that matured him beyond his twenty-six years.

It was only in the air, fighting for his life, that he suddenly became aware that he was a man among men, men who had come from so many different backgrounds but who had been assimilated into something larger and higher than themselves. In the air, he had to have a clear mind, his nerves impossibly controlled, his concentration pushed to the limit. But on the ground, Charles would have been the first to admit that he felt very ordinary, content to do only the simplest things, to relax, get out of uniform, drink a little beer, carouse at a local pub, play the radio.

'Coming back to earth' had a double significance for him as for most pilots forced to orientate themselves to a world that seemed so superficial, so blind, so 'out of touch' with what really mattered. When he found himself in social situations among brilliant conversationalists, Charles was only too happy to get back to the Mess, to be among his own kind, to be with men who act and don't talk. In the back of his mind, there was always the longing to be back in his plane, isolated with the wind and the stars, playing his part in the higher cause of man's struggle against the enemy.

One wonders if he ever thought about death. The death of his enemy or even his own.

He remembered the first time he climbed into the cockpit, ready for action, and felt an empty feeling of suspense in the pit of his stomach. That day, it was a question of kill or be killed but strangely enough it never occurred to him that he would be the one to die. For some reason, every pilot had this uncanny sense of immortality, even if he were taking off for the last time.

Sometimes, on the ground, when he was missing his family in Australia, he would think in an abstract way about his own mortality but once in the air, never. He wondered idly what his enemy was like, this man he would kill. Was he a farmer like himself, or a student, or an office worker? Was he young or a veteran of many escapades and would he die with his sweetheart's name on his lips … or the Fuehrer's? Or would he die alone, conscious of himself merely as a man in a machine?

Charles had to admit that once he had destroyed his first plane, his major emotion was one of satisfaction, satisfaction at having completed the job successfully after months of specialised training. At the bottom was a sense of rightness, for he firmly believed that Death had no favourites. It was inevitable that someone had to die in this combat and it could easily have been him; that would have been just as acceptable. In this respect, the fighter pilot was lucky; he had none of the personalised emotions of the soldier handed a rifle and a bayonet and told to charge. The fighter pilot's emotions were those of the duellist – cool, precise, impersonal. It was his privilege to kill well, for if one had to either kill or be killed, it had to be done with dignity.

His opponent deserved that.

*　　*　　*

Ironically, just as Charles was getting into his stride, his tour of duty came to an end and he was given a spell of ground duties at headquarters in the role of Intruder Controller. He found desk work so galling, particularly when news reached him of the Squadron's exploits, that he pestered his commanding officer for one last trip. This was allowed in April 1944, when he returned to his old Squadron and co-opted an Observer, FO Stewart from Toronto, who consented half-heartedly to accompany him.

'This is something you have been threatening to take me on for a long time,' Stewart sighed. 'I guess I had better go along with it and get it over with today.'

Charles plotted out the trip himself and they took off across 1,000 miles of enemy occupied territory in France, flying much of the time so low they could read the time from the clock towers in the villages.

'I've never enjoyed myself so much,' Charles explained later. 'We were flying over enemy occupied country but instead of dark shadows and water, I got a wonderful picture of life in rural France … girls on bicycles, farmers ploughing, German staff cars rolling by. Really ordinary things.'

It was a costly day for the Luftwaffe with Charles destroying two enemy aircraft in the sky and three more left ablaze on the ground. In his logbook he recorded: 'Very brassed off with ADGB, so went on a Day Ranger. Pleasant day.'

For this 'pleasant day', he was awarded the DFC and earned the nickname 'Last Trip Scherf'.

On May 2nd, he made another 'last trip', this time to the Baltic and North Germany with the accompanying aircraft piloted by the Canadian, Johnnie Caine. Charles had seen the sky that morning and couldn't help remarking:

'Now, this is the sort of day when we should be out making the attack.'

The Canadian thought about the proposal a bit then looked at Charles with a mischievous twinkle in his eyes, reading the Aussie's mind and saying just the words Charles wanted to hear.

'Why don't we?'

Both pilots had a field day although Caine's aircraft was badly damaged. The weather was rainy and cloudy, perfect conditions for intruding, so Charles went on alone, destroying one Ju86P in the air and four He-111s on the ground.

It was also a great day for the 418 Squadron for, together with the other pilots, they scored sixteen in twenty-four hours, bringing the total of the Squadron to 103.

On May 16th, after much coaxing and cajoling of his Commanding Officers, 'Last Trip Scherf' was off again on his most spectacular mission. This time, he encountered a He-111 over the sea and immediately sent it down in flames. Over Kubitzer, he chased and destroyed a Ju-86 and not long after, launched an attack on a He-177, shot it down, then strafed two Dorneir 18s moored in a creek. He was chased by flak as he came up under two JU-88s in formation, the first of which broke up in the air as he fired. His plane shuddered as it took a hit from the flak but he pressed on undeterred, pursuing the second JU-88 until it, too, spiralled to the ground.

In the space of fifteen minutes, he had destroyed five in the air and one on the ground.

This trip confirmed him as a legendary Mosquito pilot, verifying the Mosquito's seal to fame and earning him the DSO.

His citation included the following words:

'His successes are a splendid tribute to his great skill, enterprise and fearlessness. This officer has set an example of the highest order.'

His last trip in July 1944, a routine trip in a Spitfire, turned out to be his last mission. Charles recorded these last words in his logbook, 'Last flight in a great country' and, contrary to his first impressions, declared that the British were the finest people he could ever hope to meet.

In newspaper articles of the day, he was described in glorious terms as the true version of the 1944 pilot and undisputed pioneer of day intruding, able to employ a technique absolutely different from the 1942 pilots. In another splendid tribute, he was listed among ten pilots from other countries under the headline: 'England will never forget them'.

During his tours, he flew over 50,000 operational miles and never received a scratch. A farewell dinner in his honour was celebrated at the exclusive Savoy Hotel, attended by senior fighter leaders and Air Chief Marshall, Sir Charles Portal. It was a night to remember for the small-town boy who had risen to such great heights and the farewell tributes from his commanding officers would remain in his heart long after his departure.

Time to call it a day, Charles thought to himself on his last day in London as he prepared to dress, pack his bag and head towards the port. *Perhaps I'll get a chance to have a go at those blasted Japs one day but it's time to go home.*

'Home,' he sighed, trying to picture the hills of straggly shrubs and stringybark trees. 'The other world I used to love … a very long time ago.'

He smiled to himself, feeling weary, alone and more than nostalgic that he was gliding out of this world like a ghost, this world of action and danger that would still be as full today as yesterday. This world where the kites would roll out one more time and head for the coast, without him. He would be gone but his absence would soon lose its shape and the world would continue, perfect in itself, without flaw, without him. As if he had been nothing to the whole enterprise, nothing and yet everything.

He looked out the window at the last view of the great wartime city of London. The traffic was increasing and pedestrians were filling the streets, their heads bent low against the chilly winds. The minutes were calling the minutes, chasing, driving each other forward. He picked up his bag, closed the door and left the hotel.

No turning back.

Go on … go on …

In July 1944, Charles Scherf left England forever and returned to Australia, to Emmaville – where another kind of 'last trip' awaited him.

My father was a toreador.

He had wandered among the stars and danced with death every day, infinitely rich but ultimately condemned. In every moment, when the possibility of death loomed nigh, he had lived in a kind of resurrection, an intoxication of joy as he experienced the sheer gift of life, like a prisoner whose chains have been untied for a moment to allow him to walk outside among the flowers, like a thief who has discovered a chamber of hidden treasures but can't find the way out.

Per ardua ad astra.

CHAPTER 2

BROKEN WINGS

Emmaville 1945

The war ended on the 8th of May, 1945 and millions of servicemen returned to their homes. Nearly 5,000 Australian airmen had lost their lives while 1,854 were missing, 971 were prisoners of war or interned and 2,175 had been wounded. Apart from the destruction of so many millions of lives and homes, the greatest casualty, according to some, was the human mind itself. For the returned soldier, the adjustment to the calmer routines of peacetime and their former lives came more easily to some than others. Not a lot was known in those days about war neurosis, the silent struggle of the returned soldiers to overcome the excitement of military action, the painful memory of the friends who were killed and their own violent part in the destruction of life.

Charles did not follow the direct route home but made a detour to the USA. He sailed across the Atlantic on the *Queen Elizabeth*, arriving in New York after nonchalantly announcing that he was leaving the draft to spend some time with his sister in California.

'She'll be right,' he calmly confided to his fellow Australians. 'I'll hitch a ride to Australia on one of the US military aircraft.'

In San Francisco he was welcomed wherever he went and made quite an impression on the Americans. His glamorous sister was very amused one evening to see her gallant brother jiving on the tabletop of an elegant restaurant with another ex-serviceman. She also remembered another amusing incident.

One night, an unknown diner came over to Charles and slipped two hundred dollars into his hand.

'That's for your sacrifice,' the gentleman smiled and patted Charles' hand. 'We sure appreciate what you boys have done for us.'

'It's all part of our duty,' Charles answered modestly, a little embarrassed by the gesture. 'We wouldn't want that madman, Hitler, to get the upper hand, would we?'

The American wanted to keep talking.

'There's one thing I've always wanted to ask a pilot,' he insisted. 'I've noticed that you boys seem to have acquired some special skills flying those big kites around the skies without radar. How in the heck do you do that?'

Charles grinned and tried to think of the easiest answer, remembering all those long hours of training and discipline but not wanting to disappoint the beaming man beside him with his honest, rather naive enquiry.

'Well, I reckon the main thing is your reflexes. It's so important for soldiers and civilians to keep up their sports training because that's what saves you in combat. A fellow doesn't appreciate the value of athletic training until he's up against the real thing. Then – when it is either your life or the enemy's – it really counts. If I hadn't played football, I can tell you right now that I might not be here today. Certainly, my condition was better, my co-ordination sharper, my reflexes quicker.'

He chuckled to himself, thinking of the strange American football game they called gridiron and all those chaps in heavy, protective gear while the Aussies ran onto the field in nothing but their shorts and a jersey.

The gentleman turned out to be a journalist who wrote up the conversation in an American newspaper article under the heading 'The Lowdown'. It clinched the argument put forward by an esteemed contemporary of the journalist, Cuthbert Gordon, who, since Pearl Harbour, had argued long and hard that those Americans who had a background of sports and athletics made better fighting men than those who were not so energetic.

The journalist had no opinion on the matter until Charles Scherf turned up at the restaurant that night. He concluded the article with the following words:

'Quite a fellow, a hero, no less, and he has the medals to prove it, although we should say that he wears them with all modesty.'

'So there you are, Cuthbert. Your theory about sport is right,' the article ended. 'The Australians say so, too.'

*   *   *

When Charles returned to Australia, he refused a job as a test pilot in the Australian Air Force and resumed his life as a grazier. The head of Pan Am, Juan Trippe, had offered him a job flying transatlantic airlines but his father was ill and needed him on the land. Even the company's beautiful Recruiting Officer, who followed him to Australia, could not persuade him to take up the lucrative offer and the visit had ended badly anyway.

Charles set up his family in a small cottage a short distance from the main homestead and used his war savings to purchase Merino sheep. He had some new ideas about improving the farm and was eager to discuss these with his ailing father.

'I've seen things in England,' he explained. 'I've seen a different type of farming with machines and modern methods. I could really improve things here if you'd just give me a go.'

Charles Senior sniffed, narrowed his eyes and glared at his son.

'As long as I live, I'm still the boss around here,' he replied with that air of ancient authority. The old man did consent to the purchase of a tractor later on, but Charles knew that he would just have to wait. The important thing, then, was to farm the land and to hang on to the things that were promised to him.

He had a wife, two daughters and another baby on the way. Poor Hope. Pregnant so soon after his return. As he rode out over the paddocks, he felt a new surge of life. It was all coming back to him. Stopping to let his horse graze for a moment, he stared at the landscape and felt his inner mind trace out and fill in the sharp contours of the rocks, the jagged rise of the hills and the blurred edges of the shimmering horizon. This was the same land he had dreamt of when fighting in England, when all his hopes were pitched on seeing these hills one more time and when one more dead Jerry meant another step closer to home.

Ah, the earth …

He had read a description in a book once about how much the earth meant to men at war. It was their refuge, their certainty and their mother. When flying on night missions, he had looked down over the dark fields of France and, imagining himself to be the only person awake at this hour, he felt somehow connected to the fields beneath him, almost as if he were cradling this tiny speck of earth in his large, steady pilot's hands. This strange sense of responsibility kept him awake and alert at the controls, like a man guarding a secret treasure. Some of his cobbers had described this experience as poetic, almost spiritual. Others called it bunkum. Other, less sensitive fellows simply called it nothing more than three-dimensional truck driving!

Now, staring at his own piece of earth, he felt the same sacred duty. Yet the countryside here was full of dust and faded, khaki-coloured trees. No more the green dales of England and the chequered fields of France. The brittle scrub stood before him, shallow-rooted and shabby like a child's scribbly drawing. It was a wonder that any tree ever took hold in this parched, wind-swept soil. The gum trees, with their contorted trunks and faded, drooping leaves, gave no apology for their survival and simply continued through the seasons. The rocks, revealed by years of erosion and drying winds, stood scattered across the paddocks in outcrops. The grass was clumps of withered tussocks, thin and listless like the hair of an old woman.

Yet, this land – his land – was alive to him, timeless, holding the secrets of millions of years, enduring, waiting. For the time being, it seemed to provide the answers to all the moral questions which had begun to plague him and standing here, on his own piece of earth, he suddenly felt a resurgence of life and the inner peace that nature brings.

He had plans for the land. Before, he had simply obeyed his father and planted lucerne but now he had ideas for new crops which he had garnered overseas and new methods of farming which he was anxious to try. The way to get the best out of the land was through power farming and he already had his eye on one of those fancy new tractors. The problem was getting past the old man and his dogged insistence on the old ways.

Of course, sheep farming was part of the pioneering experience, and now that the war was over, the price of wool had risen remarkably. He could not deny this. Already they were cleaning out the shearers' quarters and preparing for the shearing season. It would be a hard battle against an intransigent foe but he had to make his own mark somehow.

'I will ride over to the dam,' he thought, breaking out of his reverie, 'and see how much water she still holds. The ewes will be dropping their spring lambs soon.'

*   *   *

The first years of his return were full of promise. The farm was prospering and Australian farmers were reaping the benefits of the wool industry. 'Riding home,' as they would say, 'on the sheep's back.'

Charles was beginning to make his name known in the district. Now, when he was invited to official functions and balls, he was always introduced as Squadron Leader Charles Scherf. On the occasions when his attractive sister was home on holidays, the handsome pair would instantly stand out when they entered a room and remain the centre of attention for the entire evening.

He was overjoyed to find out that his next child was a boy. In true style, he named him Mallory after his best friend, Sir Trafford Leigh-Mallory, Commander of the Battle of Britain. Everyone was delighted; a son for the war hero and heir to all the talent and property his famous father would pass on to him.

There were tennis parties every weekend and Charles would cut a dashing figure in his white shorts and effortless display of talent. The guests would come and go through the large gardens of Big Ben like butterflies. Drinks, sandwiches and cakes would be served throughout the afternoon and the air was alive with chatter and laughter.

By eight o'clock, most of the guests were tipsy and the hilarity had intensified. This was the time when Charles would seat himself at the piano and, to the delight of the boisterous mob assembled around him, bash out the latest tunes which he had heard on the radio. His guests were then entertained by his clever imitation of some of the famous names of his generation, such as Jimmy Durante and Carmen Cavallero.

Yes. Life was optimistic and he was beginning to regain the sense of some new adventure awaiting him in the future. He had always had this feeling, even as a young boy when he would awaken to the corralling of the magpies at dawn, ready for any challenge the day might bring. At night, when he lay in his small iron bed and felt his body growing and hardening, his heart would fill with the most fantastic conceits and he wondered if other men felt the same way, especially the easy-going farmers and the country bumpkins he had to live with.

Of course, this sense of a higher destiny had been fully realised in England with the new race of men arising out of the war. In Australia, Charles had only attended a one-teacher public school, the complete opposite of the British 'public' school, but for the first time there had emerged a harmonious synthesis of the ruling class and the great rest of the Commonwealth, a synthesis of disparate backgrounds, education and upbringing to be seen at its best in the RAF Squadrons. How else could a sheep farmer from Australia have rubbed shoulders with the elite of the RAF?

Now, the glory days were over and he was back at the farm.

Things were going so well that he thought he might indulge himself with a few luxuries. The first was a new car, like the flash models he had seen in America. This came in the form of the latest Oldsmobile which was certainly up to his standard with its eight-cylinder engine, dual horns, vacuum booster pump, sun visors, deluxe steering wheel, clock, chrome wheel trims and cigarette lighter. On many occasions he had tested its speed along the straight strips of road leading to the township, arriving with a screeching of brakes at the local pub. People soon began to recognise the familiar sound as he pushed the car to its limits, descending the steep hill to the town at neck-breaking speed and skilfully managing to negotiate the curve of the road leading into the main street. It was fortunate that nobody seemed to be concerned about drink driving in those days and even the police turned a blind eye to his escapades.

His second wish concerned a horse. Little boys everywhere dream of owning a puppy but Australian country boys desire and treasure a good horse. In fact, the stockman and his faithful steed are a celebrated part of the Australian culture, highly regarded for their skill in all aspects of the care of livestock: feeding, watering, droving, branding, castrating and mating. The early writers of colonial Australia dedicated many stories to the legendary horsemen of the Outback who were chiefly responsible for opening up what one might call the most hostile regions in the world.

As one poet described them: 'They rode with fearless speed, the saddle was their home and the stock whip their heritage.'

If there was anything Charles knew a lot about, it was horses and it seemed right that he should have a classy horse to match his status as heir to Big Ben. His years in the Light Horse had taught him everything about horses, including how to ride difficult horses, to retrain horses which had been badly spoilt, to cure well-defined evil tendencies such as refusing and leading, to ride long distances cross country without becoming fatigued and how to handle a horse in battle.

'I'm going to buy a horse,' he simply announced to his father one day, knowing that the old man could not stand in his way this time because he had earned the money himself. 'I'm tired of riding these old nags around the place.'

Not content to buy a local horse, Charles turned up at the famous William Inglis & Son auction, Riverside Stables, Warwick Farm, Sydney for the Australian Easter Yearling Sales. This auction sold the finest young thoroughbreds in the Southern Hemisphere and attracted buyers from all over the world. Charles felt at home among the high profile, elite gathering and soon won for himself a magnificent red thoroughbred which he named Repshot.

So Repshot, destined initially to be a racehorse, was to spend his days trotting through the dusty fields of Big Ben as a stock horse. It was whispered that the horse cost three thousand pounds and Charles Senior was not pleased.

'Too damn flash to work on a farm. What were you thinking, son?'

His relatives on the neighbouring farms also joined in the mocking. 'Putting on the dog, mate.'

Charles was not deterred. How could they have understood? There was something in this horse, something in his beauty, spirit and strength which represented something very meaningful to Charles. Something that he missed. His lost dream of himself.

The power of flight.

Without wings.

One day, in an outburst of joy, he lifted his young son into the air and sat him on the horse's back. Mallory, terrified by the height of the horse and the rocking sensation of his wide girth as he sauntered into a walk, burst out crying and begged to be placed on firm ground.

'You cannot hurry courage,' his wise, old neighbour admonished him, seeing the fear in the young boy's eyes. 'You just have to let it grow.'

Secretly, Charles was disappointed, remembering his own childish exploits, and from then on, his rides throughout the paddocks were solitary.

*　　*　　*

They called men like him 'returned soldiers' but one might wonder if they ever did 'return' to their homes or what anyone could have done to make their return more 'homely'. Nobody took notice of the little cracks when they started to appear. After the drama of war, time seemed to pass so peacefully and Charles soon fell into the rhythm of life at Big Ben. The seasons dictated his work, the months followed each other in unchanging succession and the land was good to him.

It is hard to tell to what extent his father's obstinacy contributed to the events that followed. When a man has led an exciting but highly dangerous life, it is almost impossible to settle for a mundane existence. Because Charles was not permitted to take over the reins of Big Ben immediately, he was obliged to work the land as a common labourer and not as the rightful owner. He still felt like a young kid when he entered the manor house and somewhat resented the meagre accommodation that had been offered to his growing family. Without a solid anchor, he started to drift, uncertain of his role, the hireling son running around town like some kind of restless playboy.

There was little to distract him among the locals and their everyday conversation and few newcomers to the district.

Until she arrived.

Often on a Sunday, Charles would relax with a game of championship golf in Glen Innes. There was a nine-hole golf course on the property where he could practise, and regular trips were made to Glen Innes with a carload of friends. One of the passengers was the new matron from the local hospital in Emmaville, Joyce Brown, a tall, small-breasted woman with an erect carriage which she accentuated by holding her shoulders very straight like a soldier. She was older than Charles but had an athletic body which asserted itself in deft, vigorous movements on the golf course. Charles thought she must have made an impressive sight on her daily rounds, moving imperiously through the wards in her white uniform and starched veil to the hurried whispers of: 'Quickly. Here comes the Matron!'

She was a guest at Big Ben for the evening meal on many a Sunday evening and was reported to get on very well with Charles' eldest daughter. After the meal, he would offer her a lift back to her quarters in town.

When she was first introduced to Charles at a ball, she appeared to be assessing him with a polite but sceptical gaze.

'So, you're the famous Charles Scherf,' she said in a pleasing but slightly contemptuous manner. 'I've heard so much about you. It's a small town, you know, and people will talk.'

'And you're Matron Brown,' he grinned at her, recognising the immediate attraction.

It was true that women everywhere were drawn to him, and

he was known to flippantly comment: 'If a woman cocks it up to you, what's a man to do?'

He smiled to himself, suddenly recalling the many opportunities in England when the officers were invited to country estates for a party but then he remembered the incident with the American and politely excused himself. He had to admit, however, that he was flattered by the Matron's steady, but slightly contemptuous, gaze throughout the evening.

She had not married because of her career and it was obvious that this backward town was hardly capable of producing a worthy suitor. Besides, she had seen men at their worst and knew they were all basically weak. It was this air of superiority and self-assurance that aroused his desire to pull her down a peg, to show her what a real man could do, like breaking in a proud, little mare. As she was leaving the ballroom on that first night, she gave Charles a quizzical look which meant that she was trying to ascertain his measure.

Then, with a brisk wave, she disappeared into the night.

*   *   *

As far as the local farmers were concerned, Charles had to admit that it was not easy to pick up former friendships. Like most returned servicemen, he found it difficult to talk about the war. In all the reminiscing and kidding and tomfoolery in the pub, he had been unable to explain the exact nature of his work in Intruding. He had also never discussed his great friendship with famous wartime leaders like Sir Rodney Hill, Sir Charles Portal and Sir Trafford Leigh-Mallory, men who knew his worth and respected him as a son. How could he make these simple country men understand the great enterprise they had shared, the dangers and excitement of battle, the camaraderie, the *esprit de corps* which all men at war experience but rarely talk about when they come home. Not even to their wives.

One day, a sudden impulse came to him and he chuckled to himself as he drove to the airport. It was time to give these country bumpkins a practical demonstration, time to show them what his efforts as a war pilot were all about, time to show the flag.

The Mosquito was sitting like a sleek, silver bird on the tarmac. It was a clear day, perfect weather for a jaunt in the old machine. He revved it up and took off, flying in a steady direction towards the sleepy town of Glen Innes. The controls were so familiar to him he could have flown the plane in his sleep, his hands finding the way to the instruments as if by second nature.

He felt confident and relaxed, certain that his motives were sincere and his actions designed only to demonstrate what he could not explain verbally. This was no reckless dare-devil out to impress the locals, but an experienced airman with four years of training under his belt and an impressive war record.

As he settled into the flight, he remembered those immortal words of his dear friend, Sir Charles Portal.

'Charles, when you are in a plane, you seem to be the soul of it.'

He felt elated, liberated, remembering the time he had 'borrowed' a plane from his base in England and gone on his last trip over France. At that time, he was supposed to be taking a rest on ground duties but, on an entirely unauthorised visit, he had secured a plane, flown out over Europe and destroyed five enemy aircraft within a few hours. Whether to court marshall him or decorate him had hung in the balance but, by a nice compromise, he had received on one hand an issue of strife and, on the other, his DSO.

Laughing to himself at the fond memory, he reached the outskirts of the town and prepared to descend. Diving to just a few metres above the main street, he roared through the town barely missing the clock tower in the town hall and skimming the tops of the trees in the park. Completing a circuit over the town, he increased his altitude, turned, picked up speed and descended, roaring across the town at a dangerously low level. Three times he completed the exercise and then disappeared into the skies.

The townsfolk were pouring out of their houses and shops, frightened by the deafening noise and sudden, terrifying rush of air which seemed to drag everything along in its violent passage. Just when they realised what was causing the din, there he came again and there was no time to recover from the shock because he was already turning around. As he roared over the town, the casual shoppers in the main street dived for shelter and the shopkeepers, their hands over their ears, prayed for the safety of their premises.

This was the reality of war they had not experienced in their safe little region, and they were certainly not going to thank him for the demonstration. Feelings of shock, fear and anger hung in the air long after he was gone but were later replaced by the self-righteous indignation of little people forced out of their comfort zone. What right did he have to disturb the peace of their town with such a bloody, stupid prank? Let the war heroes fight in another country but don't bring the war home to us.

Hope, sitting in the hairdresser's shop, waiting for Maureen to have her hair cut, raced outside as soon as she heard the noise. The chill was already in her heart for she knew it could only be him.

'Oh, Charles,' she groaned. 'You've gone too far this time.'

She remembered when he had wanted to show off his plane to her, had taken her to Archerfield and together they had soared into the skies.

'Bet you're the only woman who's ever been in a Mosquito,' he shouted proudly.

She had loved him then and, for a brief moment, had almost understood this driving force within him. Now, she felt nothing but shock and humiliation.

The locals had their blood up, especially the Shire Clerk. At first he had been only too happy to welcome home a local war hero but now he relished the chance to pull the larger man down. Something had been niggling at him for a while now, something about the glory given to enlisted men. Damn it! Hadn't he been just as loyal staying in his country and caring for the ones left at home?

This was his chance at last to even up the score.

There was another reason which would certainly rally the townsfolk to his side. One of the finest trees in the Glen Innes district was the 120-year-old Douglas Fir which grew in front of the courthouse. The virtues of this tree were often extolled by the Shire Clerk, as much attention had been given to its introduction into Australia, its size and historical performance.

'No doubt,' he proclaimed bitterly, 'the tree would have grown taller if it hadn't been swiped by a fighter plane.'

He persuaded the local police to summon Charles to the Police Station immediately. He had a list of complaints from the elderly hospital patients, and some pregnant women who claimed they had gone into labour with the shock of it all. The Principal of the West End Primary School said the children had been frightened out of their wits. Others even swore he had flown under the small park bridge.

Unfortunately, he had dived so low that someone had managed to write down the number on the plane and trace it back to Charles. A call was made to the Emmaville Police but there was no way they were going to divulge his whereabouts to those stuffed shirts in Glen Innes. Charles, now under open arrest, spent two nights hiding out at a friend's house but finally decided to turn himself in.

When he swaggered into the Glen Innes Police Station to answer the charges, he couldn't help smiling to himself. He'd been given the DSO for the same lark in France but now this small town was out to court marshall him.

The Police Sergeant was not in the mood to appreciate the irony.

'What in the hell were you thinking of, Charlie? What's the use of frightening the wits out of everyone? God, someone could have been killed. It was a bloody stupid thing to do.'

Charles could see that he had his back up.

'You're not in the friggin' war now, mate, and just because you won a few medals doesn't mean you can do what you bloody well like! I'm going to have to forward the complaint to Canberra and we'll see how cocky you are then!'

His mother was quick to add her reproach, and this irked him even more than the comments from the Police. She was always following him around, snooping into his affairs, checking up on him. There was no denying that his war record had enhanced their status in the community even more but now he was a family disgrace.

'Oh, Charles,' she implored. 'Whatever got into you? Why couldn't you have used your common sense? Everyone's talking about us now, dragging our name in the mud.'

She grabbed his arm and looked fiercely into his face, becoming more agitated with every word.

'How could you do this to us? To me? To your mother? What will people think of us now?'

The local newspaper, keen to take advantage of such a controversial event, had the final say on the matter. It was clear to Charles from the write-up that nobody was going to support him. Two-thirds of the article were written in honour of the tree which was portrayed as the true hero of the day. As for the noise, the Shire Clerk had even ferreted out an ex-prisoner of war in the town who had been willing to sell the Aussie pilots down the river and was only too happy to denounce the Mosquito in terms of its namesake, an annoying, pesky insect which descended over

Hitler's Germany like a plague and robbed everyone, including the prisoners, of their sleep.

'This,' he complained, enjoying the sudden attention, 'together with the half-hourly reports on the fast planes, made life very difficult for everyone.'

'So much for the plane that saved England,' Charles muttered to himself when he read the article. He remembered wryly how the English schoolboys used to run out of their houses and wave vigorously to the RAF pilots when they flew low over their fields on their return from France, their ruddy cheeks polished by the smarting winds. How could he have ever expected the same reaction from his humourless fellow countrymen, so British in many of their ways in that they valued fair play and the right of everyone to better their circumstances yet who proved all-too-ready to belittle those 'tall poppies' who did manage to push through the ranks.

'And for this I risked my life,' he concluded sadly.

*   *   *

A dark shadow of recognition now appeared in his mind, like ink spilling across a page. There was something about the incident which caused him to withdraw further into himself and the thoughts he had been trying to keep at bay, the murky thoughts which haunt men of action, came bubbling to the surface like mud in a hot pool. There was no denying it any longer; he was out of step with everything and everybody.

It wasn't really their fault. He had lived a privileged time, a time of extraordinary fame and glory, and the people he had left behind, the people he now had to spend his days with, had become strangers. Before the war, they had shared a common background, but now, apart from the boisterous camaraderie of his drinking mates, the gap between them had grown too wide. In this somewhat crazy stunt, flying low over the town, he had tried to reach across the gap, to lift them up, as a father boisterously swings a frightened but gleeful toddler above his head.

How could they have ever understood the sensations he had experienced in his daring daylight intruder missions over France. The thrill of splitting the heavens at 400 miles per hour in the sleek, Merlin-powered Mosquito, the fastest operational aircraft in the sky and acclaimed star of history's greatest air war. An airplane not for the average but for the most skilled and courageous of pilots.

A vehicle for a god. Was that it? Did he think he was a god?

Now, there was this small town out to get him. Now, he had to live with this mundane life and the pain of having mastered flight only to be condemned to the ground. This is what he had come to, shackled to this god-forsaken strip of earth and these small-minded people and nowhere to go and no one to talk to and nothing to do which could ever match the camaraderie he had experienced in that community of men forced to struggle together, forced to go beyond their vulgar lives, committed to the higher cause no matter how unattainable.

A god?

No. Definitely not. It was just his trade, the trade of the war pilot.

The Scherfs were influential people and there was still his war record. His mother wrote to Canberra and instead of a court marshall, the RAAF grounded Charles for one hour a week – on Sundays.

*   *   *

After the incident, things began to unravel slowly and Charles started to drink more heavily. On the surface, the hard work on the land continued, the seasons marked by the lambing, the shearing and the wool sales. It was a predictable routine which kept him sane and there were always the weekend festivities at Big Ben. Nobody said too much about his drinking; a lot of returned servicemen drank heavily, spending their gloomy days in the RSL Clubs, and most of his relatives were hard-drinking men anyway.

Hope was a cheerful, hard-working companion and the three children were growing up. She seemed content just to have him home and she believed, like many wives, that he would be happy to resume their small life, just the two of them in their own safe, little world. She had no idea why he had become so restless and tense and why he had begun to show less interest in the farm. In her practical way of looking at life, she could never have imagined how much the emptiness of the Australian bush was stacking up against his love of the land and how much he missed the excitement of combat.

There were other signs, however, which she could not fail to notice. Suddenly at lunch, he would faint with his head in the soup bowl and the children would stare at him in horror. His terrible nosebleeds became heavier and harder to stop, forcing him to lie in their darkened bedroom for hours. Sometimes, in the middle of the day, he would take the car and disappear into town without telling her he was leaving. He had trouble sleeping and on moonlit nights she could hear the disturbing sound of the tractor starting up.

Hope had never been taught to ask questions of her existence. Her life in a big Irish family of eleven children meant that you just got on with the daily grind and never looked out for a space of your own. Your reward was food on the table, the giant washing gathered and folded before night and a new batch of melon jam ready to pot up.

Every day was the same for her with the never-ending tasks to keep the household running. Country men ate large breakfasts of lamb chops, eggs, grilled tomato, toast with home-made butter, then she had to bake cakes for the morning and afternoon tea. Dinner was the classic meat and three veggies followed by custard and fruit. There were enormous piles of washing each week, a chore which meant boiling up the sheets in an old copper in the laundry room, heaving the sheets out with the aid of a stick, dunking them in a tub of 'blue' and ringing them out by hand. The cottage was old but she kept the linoleum shining in the kitchen and there were always tomatoes from her garden ripening on the windowsill.

If Charles was on one of his jaunts to the pub, she would put his tea on the stove over a simmering dish of hot water and fall into bed, dreading his return if he had drunk too much.

Arriving home, he could be heard crashing into the furniture and she would pretend to be asleep as his heavy body collapsed into the space next to her. She never said anything because all the men drank heavily and none of the wives would have dared to complain. Sometimes, she would ask to go with him to the pub but women were not allowed in the bar so she would either sit in the Ladies Lounge alone or stay in the car with the kids until closing time. As teatime approached, the kids would begin to complain, but still she would have to wait for just one more round with his mates.

By the time he was ready to leave, the kids were jumping all over the back seat.

'Thank goodness,' she would say when he finally appeared, tipsy. 'The kids are hungry. Do you have to stay so long?'

'Oh, I ran into Barney and the boys and I couldn't leave in the middle of a shout.'

His speech was slurred and he was struggling to come up with a good excuse.

'Anyway, you wanted to come, so if you don't like it, don't ask me next time.'

Rebuked, her body fell back and blended into the curve of the car seat. She was silent for the journey home.

'We're hungry, Daddy. We want to go home,' the children whined in chorus as soon as he had taken his space in the driver's seat.

'All right. Shut your whingeing,' he yelled at them. 'I'll take you home alright!'

Feeling annoyed, he took off like a rocket, diffusing his anger into the accelerator. When he was in this mood, the trip home was always precarious. The stones spun under his wheels and he roared the engine until the needle in the speedometer swung dangerously toward the limit. He knew every inch of the road even when he was drunk but the dangerous speed at which he took the curves made the children scream as they were hurled against each other in the back seat. Charles was amused at their fear and laughed as he roared up the driveway to the cottage.

'Told you I'd get you home for tea, you hungry little buggers. Make sure you eat up every mouthful or there'll be trouble.'

Hope had accepted the fact that she could not drive a car herself and that her husband had no intention of ever teaching her. Stranded on the farm, she had to wait for Saturday morning when they would all go to town to get the week's groceries. This was a treat for her, an outing with the other wives who came for supplies that morning, a cup of tea in the Country Women's Association tea rooms and a bag of lollies for the kids.

There was a general store in the town which included a haberdashery where she could buy needles and wool for her knitting, and a drapery selling a few plain clothes. A dusty shop for dusty people. Most of the items had sat there for a long time because the people preferred to shop in Glen Innes.

Hope was not interested in fashion and rarely followed the latest styles. When there was a country ball, she was grateful that her sister-in-law took the trouble to find her a suitable dress. She had the niggling feeling that her in-laws never thought her good enough for their dashing son but when she was dressed up, she was quite pretty and some people even said that she looked like the popular movie star, Bette Davis. When Charles first met her, she had cut a neat, little figure in those fitted jackets with shoulder pads, straight skirts, butterfly clip waves in her hair and a jaunty little hat worn on the side of her head. Yes, she had put on a few pounds, especially after the dramatic ordeal of Rosemary's birth, but she tried to hide her expanding tummy under a pair of very tight corsets.

On the whole, she couldn't say that she was lonely. She had become very good friends with the wife of Charles' cousin who lived on the adjoining property. Hazel was a typical country woman with a heart of gold who could ride like a man, drink like a man and swear like a man. While the washing was drying on the line, Hope would often steal across the paddock for a cup of tea and enjoy Hazel's raucous laughter and exaggerated descriptions of life in the small town. There were always the weekend tennis parties and visitors to Big Ben, even though she felt awkward and shy among some of the guests. At first she would accompany her glamorous husband to Sydney for the wool sales but once again, it was her husband's world. Charles seemed to come alive with the bright lights of the city and would dump her with a friend's wife while he and the husband went out on the town. She tried to put on a bright face, to drink the absurd little glasses of sherry or *crème de menthe* which women drank in those days, but the hours would tick by and there was nothing to do but sit and wait for the men to come home. Eventually, as the number of children grew, she elected to stay at home and he would go off for weeks, returning with a plastic butter dish as a gift.

Yet she remained calm and gentle, contented with her children, the garden, the cooking and a tidy house. The war was over, the grander things of life now seemed compressed into the flow of seasons as she and Charles laboured though the days, bound together by necessity, by the routine flow of domestic life and the hard toil needed to keep the farm going. Together but alone, they appeared a devoted couple on the surface and buried the growing rift between them beneath a polite silence and a capacity to 'grin and bear it'.

Often in the cold evenings, when he came in from the fields, Charles would sit by the fire, brooding in the red light cast by the flames, thinking about the pals he had lost in the war.

One night he noticed his eldest daughter, Maureen, watching him from a distance and sizing up her chances for a bit of fun with her father. She was the most confident of his children and had the knack of making her father smile. Disturbed now, he called her over, his melancholy face transformed by that trickster grin he would adopt when ready to play a lark on his children.

Out of the matchbox on the mantelpiece he took two matches and held them together at the same height between his fingers. Then, like a magician priming the audience for his master act, he held up the perfectly aligned matches and intoned:

'See these two matches. Watch carefully now. The first match is me and the second match is your mother.'

Maureen's face lit up and she reached out to take the matches, but he snatched his hand away. He reached into the fire, picked up a flaming twig and with a flourish ignited the red heads of the two matches. Maureen gave a start at the first blaze of yellow-red light then watched in fascination as the stems started to turn black and curl over.

The father's match burnt first and fell out of his fingers.

'Let's try that again,' he suggested and Maureen thought for a moment that he was going to give her a turn.

'Don't play with fire!' he ordered harshly, pushing her away and reaching inside the box for another two matches. Again, the father's match burnt first and disintegrated in his hand.

'One more time,' he said without any real conviction. 'They say you should always do things in threes or it doesn't count.'

Maureen watched hopefully but the same result ensued. It was a silly thing to believe that two slim, burning matches could determine one's fate but the demonstration was really quite convincing.

'It's always the same thing, no matter how many times I do it. I always die before your mother,' he concluded mournfully and put the matches back on the mantelpiece out of her reach.

'I hate this game,' Maureen protested sulkily and slipped away to find her mother in the kitchen.

*   *   *

Three years.

Had he only been home for three years?

Three years of ploughing and fencing and shearing and wool sales and watching the sky for rain. It hadn't been all bad; there were balls and tennis parties, weekend visits to Glen Innes for golf and trips to Sydney for the wool sales. A son, Mallory. But the doubts and questions, small at first but insistent and deep inside him, were starting to work their way into his daily life.

He had been part of so much death and destruction and it now felt as if the dead were rising up to condemn him. When he was in England, he had regarded warfare as simply 'getting the job done'. It was like putting on a warrior's mask, but away from the heat of the battle, how did one take the mask off again? Safe at home, he could no longer fool himself that the enemy was just an abstract notion; they were real people, they were Germans, the same race as his parents. Christ, he had killed his own people. He had flown so low over enemy territory that he could see their faces and now these faces had begun to haunt him.

A dark patch of blood guilt had formed in his brain and there was this shrill sound in his ears, like the shrieking of a wild bird. The noise was barely audible when it first came to him and he wondered if he had imagined it. Then, as the sound became more perceptible, he began to sense the rustling movement of wings sweeping past his left shoulder. On his lonely trips to check out fences or find a stray sheep, the screeching noise would suddenly begin, followed by the swoop of something sinister flying into the back of his head. Ducking to avoid the impact, he would quickly turn his head but the air was always empty and the scraggy hills lay unperturbed.

At first, he had laughed it off as the vicious strike of a magpie or a plover, guarding their newborn eggs. At some time or other everyone in Australia has been surprised by this feathery attack. How often as a child had he and his brothers run around their father's dam with frenzied plovers, their wings extended, screeching in the air and dive-bombing the intruders. They knew all-too-well the sudden, hostile flurry at the back of their necks, the frantic scramble of claws and beaks to save their eggs.

But this was not a bird.

No, this was like a pair of flashing blades sweeping dangerously close to his body and snipping the air behind his neck. Something was after him.

Payback time.

One night he could not sleep and had climbed out of bed around 2 am, just as the booze was wearing off. Hope sensed that he was leaving the room but drifted back into the thankful sleep of a pregnant mother. The fourth child was heavy inside her and she was not looking forward to the pain of labour so soon after the last one. Better to block it out, try not to understand the torments of her young husband, to escape into the oblivion of sleep.

Charles stumbled outside and sat under the old quince tree in the backyard, staring into the blackness all around him. God, the nights were dark. A growing sense of displacement had begun to seep into his daily life and he had begun to execute his chores like a sleepwalker. As always, there was work to be done, work his ailing father could no longer carry out but now he had to deal with his nightmares and unbalanced mind as well.

What had he come to? Why was it becoming so hard to hang onto the certainty of his war service and the golden memories?

His mind drifted back to his last nights in England. It was

as if he were standing once more outside the Savoy Hotel in London where a farewell dinner was to be given in his honour. He recalled in detail the silver statue of Peter II glimmering from the top of the magnificent art-deco façade and the footmen in all their livery waiting to attend to the guests as they alighted from their cabs. Across the courtyard, the mighty Thames rolled on, oblivious to the prestigious society assembling on its banks, wealthy aristocrats and famous celebrities such as Noel Coward and Oscar Wilde and movie stars like Charlie Chaplin, Lawrence Olivier and Judy Garland who gathered every evening inside the world-famous Thomas Foyer and sipped cocktails under the decadent glass dome.

He had paused for a moment, breathless, wondering what a boy from Emmaville, an unheard-of village in New South Wales, was doing in a posh place like this. It was here that Churchill himself met with his cabinet for dinner and there he was, at the end of his tour of duty, the official guest at a dinner in his honour hosted by senior fighter leaders, HQ Officers and Chief of Air Staff, Air Chief Marshall Sir Charles Portal himself.

He had smiled wryly to himself as he entered the gleaming marble foyer, wondering what they would think of him now, those old chums back in his small hometown in New South Wales. The Savoy Hotel was certainly a far cry from the Emmaville Pub with old Lily Gurk presiding at the bar. He fondly recalled the look of perpetual surprise on the old lady's face and her habit of beginning every sentence with 'Gawd Struth.' When the war was over and he had tried to describe such an occasion to her and the rest of the locals, to tell them about this other world, a world of elegance and prestige, all they could do was look at him in a daft way and say: 'Well, I'll be buggered!'

Of course he knew that he had stumbled into this other world by the great leveller, the war. He knew when his tour of duty had ended that he would probably never see this world again, but he had seen it, had lived it, had triumphed in it. He had the medals to prove it.

That night, on the eve of his departure from England, he firmly believed that English people were the finest of the human race and that night they had gathered to pay homage to their daring Australian friend. What was it that Sir Charles had said to him in a rather uncharacteristic show of emotion?

'Charles, I want you to know that I love you as a son. I admire you as a son and I believe you to be the most outstanding airman I have ever known.'

For a moment, amid the clink of crystal glasses and hovering waiters, he knew that he had reached the heights of a different kind of comradeship. Not the cheap friendship of mates slapping you on the back, bragging and telling jokes in the pub but the brotherhood of men prepared to sacrifice their lives for the greatest cause of all, a world free from oppression. This was what mattered, this was what had made it all worthwhile, this was what he had to hang on to.

But it was getting harder each day.

Now, as he sat under the old quince tree, the jagged edges of the dark hills rose up before him and blocked out the horizon.

He could not see the dark mass of pine trees which led up to the house but their resinous odour filled the night. Ancient, creaking pines standing eternally on guard, like a gauntlet of enemy soldiers, invisible but close. These guards would see him choking with the ice during the long winters and gasping for breath during the hot summer days. They would be the witnesses to his suffocation.

No escape, he thought to himself. *You can't get out of this one, Charlie.*

* * *

So began the darkest of days, the terrible soul-searching which the returned soldier must endure but cannot share with anyone. Withdrawing more and more from other people, Charles would now spend a lot of his time by himself, brooding and depressed. The tremors and the jitters were beginning to take control of his body and he could only find relief in alcohol. Some days it was difficult to tell the difference between reality and the fog which flowed over him, drowning him in a blind, unthinking rage at one minute and an emptiness at the next, a void where communication no longer existed.

Frightening dreams and nightmares had started to awaken him and to occur more frequently. He would wake in a sweat, convinced that there was something pulling at the bedcovers on the end of the bed. Glancing down, he could make out the ghastly faces of the people he had killed, their pale arms, hands and outstretched fingers clutching at the blankets, clambering to climb up onto the bed. *Oh, Christ!* They had followed him from Germany and were walking over his bed at night like an army of ghouls.

Now the questions and doubts were beginning to flood his brain. It had all been so clear in England but now he was ruminating over the vital question. Was he a murderer?

What had he believed in? What had they all believed in? What philosophical sleight of the brain had convinced them that so many deaths could be justified? Was it not just a universal consent to madness? Oh, yes, there was the fight for freedom, the fight so that their children could live free from oppression. Hitler had been a bloody tyrant, there was no doubt about that, and he had had his sights set on conquering the whole world.

Night after night, sitting alone on the dark verandah, Charles struggled to keep his thoughts on track. Oh, what had they talked about in those deep discussions he sometimes had with the officers late at night when the other chaps had fallen asleep? It had all seemed to make sense at that time, for there was something else which pilots understood better than the common foot soldier, something which sustained them in those dark hours of combat. When you took off in your plane and soared into the heavens, you felt removed from everyday life. Flying made you feel as if you belonged to an elite, as if you were privileged, and privileged men are part of some higher goal, something intangible.

This obscure sentiment was something he now needed to go through in his mind, something he desperately needed to sort out before he lost his sanity. What exactly was this higher goal?

Was he aware of such a thing when he was shooting down an enemy plane? He had sensed it, briefly, when he was discussing tactical manoeuvres with his commanding officers, tactics which placed the men's lives at extreme risk. It seems at first that the severity and harsh discipline in the armed forces was excessive, inhumane, but he came to understand that such discipline was necessary because it was not aimed at the men themselves but at eliminating imperfections and avoiding mistakes.

The leaders also placed themselves under the same code; it was no less difficult for them to give the harsh orders than for the pilots to execute them. One of the officers had explained this to him when he was promoted to Squadron Leader.

'Love the men you command,' he had said, 'but don't let them know it.'

Charles never forgot the heroic days leading up to D-Day and how their leaders primed the pilots to take really enormous risks for the enterprise. This deep sense of obligation, this acceptance of a higher call, was always in the back of their minds and it had nothing to do with thrill-seeking or showing off or executing heroic acts in the face of death. Charles, being a modest man at heart, accepted the idea because it was natural for him to go quietly about his business, to play down his bravery to the extent that he sometimes did not even record all his successes in his logbook. But there was something he could not deny; in accepting the call to duty, he had killed a lot of people.

These thoughts began to intrude into his sleep and he would

stagger out to the verandah and sit on the bare boards as the early morning chill crept into his fingers and toes. The stars were cold and silent, their light fading as the watery dawn appeared in the East. This night, feeling weary and dissatisfied, he sighed and went back to the house, thinking he might grab an hour's sleep before it was time to stagger out to the woolshed.

His wife stirred as he fell heavily into the bed beside her.

'Goodness me, Charles. What time is it?' she asked, half asleep yet anxious to know where he had been.

'Go back to sleep,' he muttered. 'It's too early to get up. I'm going to try and grab a bit more shut-eye.'

'But where have you been?' she insisted.

'Nowhere,' he replied in a voice that was hardly audible. 'Bloody nowhere.'

Then he turned his face to the wall.

There was no blessed relief for Charles that night or for most of the nights to follow. Only the innocent sleep in peace.

Listening to his wife breathing heavily beside him, he lay awake for hours, pondering all the events that had brought him to this point, searching, searching for answers to his desperate unhappiness, brooding, brooding over questions he never thought he would have to ask himself.

Once he had once been so sure of his life with his dear Bunny but something had gone wrong. Now, he could not stop himself from wondering: how did Hope fit into the scheme of things? What part had she played in the drama of war? Like most servicemen, he had clung to the idea of his dear wife at home, the source of all he believed to be good and true and the centre of the little world they had created together, but gradually it had dawned on him that his life with her was not as ideal as he had believed.

These doubts would never have come into his mind before the war, for where would a farmer have picked up such ideas? All he had known was land and seasons and crops and animals. It was the late-night discussions with those Cambridge-educated officers, men he would normally never have mixed with, men who had read books he had never heard of, men who loved words and ideas as well as deeds of glory. Domesticity had its limits, they had explained to him, and could not guarantee any certainty. Women could never understand this because their life was based on small illusions of security that kept them happy. All the enlisted men had to sacrifice their personal happiness but they understood something about life which their wives at home would never understand. The danger that they faced with every sortie taught them that life was fragile, whether safe in your own bed at home or risking your life in the war.

Thinking about the routine of his life on the farm, the harsh winters and endless fight against nature, he knew that this was true. The daily grind of a simple life could kill a man as well as a life of risk-taking. Back home, he'd seen many beaten, broken, disappointed men hang their heads in despair. So, it had been the right thing to enlist after all even though he had worried about it at first. Action saved you from this kind of despair.

But what if he were killed? How does the man of action justify a life of danger and imminent death? It seemed as if there was something unique about the air force, something beyond ordinary existence which he had never experienced before, for in the RAF they had found a different reason for living. There he had been surrounded by men of action, all intent on the serious matters of life and death, all fighting not just for a common cause but to *save something in themselves that everyday existence destroys.* That was it. That was the justification for action that he had discovered. It wasn't about heroism or the fight for freedom or even death. There was something more important than human lives, something more durable, and it was to save *this part of man* that the true heroes risked their lives every day.

And where had this *part* of himself gone?

Charles opened his eyes and peered into the darkness. A terrible feeling of loneliness overcame him, and although he wanted to reach out and touch his wife's body, something held him back and he remained rigid and wide awake on his side of the bed. It was all beginning to make sense. So this was why he could no longer relate to the people back home nor to his wife. It wasn't just the war or the destruction of lives; it was the action itself which separated him from ordinary people.

During the war with his fellow pilots, it had all seemed right but now that he was back home, there was nothing to hold on to and the higher vision which united and elevated them had disappeared. This was the deeper truth he had arrived at on this dark night and the truth was bleak. This was the lonely hell in which he was now doomed to live.

Yes, action separated him from other people.

Now it was beginning to separate him from himself.

*   *   *

The good wife, the one who stayed at home and prayed and waited, now watched her husband with growing anxiety and confusion. There was hardly any communication between them, for he refused to discuss his problems and she would not have understood him anyway. She had never been included in serious discussions with men and how could she hope to bridge the wartime years they had spent apart? Better to leave him alone and discuss her worries with another woman.

'I'm so worried about Charles,' Hope confided one day to her neighbour, Hazel. 'He's up prowling around the house half the night and he doesn't get enough sleep.'

'Oh, well,' Hazel replied. 'I guess it's been hard for all the boys. Hard to settle down after the war. Your uncle Tom was like that when he came home. Restless. Couldn't seem to get to sleep. Seemed to be watching and waiting for something to happen.'

'Yes, that's what Charles is like. Can't seem to relax. You're right. It must have been awful for them, for the ones who fought. Guess we'll never know what war was like.' Hope sighed. 'But I thought that Charles would be happy to come home. Safe and sound after so many died. The trouble is he's so touchy and unhappy and he drowns his sorrow in drink. It would be alright if he just had a few beers now and again but he's drinking a lot more these days and what really worries me is his driving. He takes the car out when he can hardly stand up.'

'They all drink, Hope. You know that. You can't say anything. A beer or two at the end of a hard day. Of course, Tom can't drink anymore so I guess I'm lucky. His diabetes.'

'Yes, but when Charles is drunk he does stupid things,' Hope insisted. 'A few weeks ago he nearly backed us all into a mine shaft. I can't talk to him anymore and the kids annoy him. He seems to be lost in a world of his own.'

Tears had started to well up in her eyes and there was a quiver in her voice, as if she were about to blurt out a sacred secret she had promised to keep to herself.

'There's something else, Hazel, something else going on and I don't know what to think. Sometimes I hear his car starting up very late at night after I've gone to bed. God knows where he goes to at that hour! He never tells me. And he doesn't get home until early in the morning. What do you think's going on, Hazel? I'm worried sick and I don't know what to do about it.'

'Oh,' Hazel replied with a deep sigh, the friendly look on her face becoming grim and serious as she stared at the small figure slumped in the chair opposite her. There are things that older women know and see, women who are not fooled by the ways of men, capable women who have taken charge of their households from the beginning and kept their husbands in line. So, the matter was serious.

She had watched her glamorous nephew grow up, seen him racing across the fields after a stray sheep, saw his manly strength on the football field, saw the larrikin grin on his face as he burst into her house for a quick beer, saw the hero in him and the daredevil and wondered what sort of woman would ever be able to pin him down. Yes, there were rumours but now there was this helpless, little woman sitting forlornly beside her and asking for answers with a plea in her eyes and a swollen stomach beneath her apron.

'I think you can leave that sort of thing to the Scherfs,' she spoke decisively, wanting to calm Hope down and deflect the gravity of the conversation. 'They must have noticed anyway. His mother won't let it rest. I'm sure she will sort it out.'

She smiled at Hope and gave her a long hug.

'Come on, Hopey. Cheer up. Have another cuppa. You need to stop worrying and look after yourself now.'

Hazel was right.

Mrs Scherf had started to keep a close watch on her son, her golden boy, especially when she heard his car starting up at all hours of the day and night. No, you couldn't mistake the way he roared down the avenue and took off like a rocket down the highway. They had been so proud of him when he returned from the war and pleased to see how eagerly he threw himself into the hard work of managing the property. Everything had fallen back into place, Big Ben was prospering and their position in the community was again secure. It also added to their status to know that he was the town hero and she was not going to let him throw it all away, especially if he expected to take over the reins of Big Ben one day.

'I don't know what's got into you, Charles,' his mother complained when she couldn't cope with his erratic behaviour any longer. 'You drink too much, son, and people are starting to talk. You hang around with those disreputable friends of yours, that no-good Barney Brennan and his brazen wife, drinking in the bar until all hours. God knows what you get out of it. We would have expected you to show a bit of class, to mix with the right people and respect the family name. For God's sake, son, pull yourself together! You have to think about your future and your poor, old father trying to hold everything together for you. Then there's the children and another one on the way.'

Charles looked begrudgingly at his mother. She was right in a way but she had no idea what was going on inside his head and what he now needed to do to survive.

'I do what Father asks me to do,' he answered defensively, resenting that he suddenly felt like a boy again. 'He couldn't manage without me. I'm here working like a dog for him every day.'

'I know that, Charles. But there is something else and we're all worried. You don't seem to be yourself these days and there's something you can't hide from me any longer. I've seen your car leaving at odd times of the day and coming home very late at night. I insist that you tell me what's going on. Otherwise, I'll find out, Charles. I'll find out if it's the last thing that I do!'

So, that was it. His mother was checking up on him, snooping into his affairs, watching him like a hawk, sizing up every move he made. She'd always been like that and now that he was the town hero, she wasn't going to stand by and let him drag the family name in the mud.

'Where do you go at night?' his mother pressed on. 'I can't believe you need to go to town at those unusual hours. You must be up to something and I won't rest until I find out what it is. I can tell that Hope is very worried but of course she doesn't say anything. You really must watch yourself. We don't need any scandal in this family … it will kill your father.'

Charles glared at his mother, this thin, old woman with the

wispy, greying hair who had given birth to him at the surprising age of forty-seven. He longed to explain his anguish to her for she was an intelligent woman who had published articles in the *Sydney Morning Herald* about wool prices, war, women's needs and the suffering of some of the farmers. Surely she would understand what a soldier must have gone through. Yet there was a hardness in her, a meanness which showed up in her bird-like eyes, her thin, tight-lipped mouth and haughty carriage. Perhaps the vicious gossip was true after all. Rumour had it that when his father had written to England for a bride, she had tampered with the letters, packed her bags in haste and beaten her unsuspecting sister to the ship bound for Australia. A remarkable display of initiative, for sure, but masking a self-seeking and acquisitive nature.

Now she was Mrs Charles Henry Scherf of Big Ben, a leading socialite in the district with her manor house, her maids and her retinue of visiting dignitaries. No one to unburden your dark heart to. Charles turned away from his mother, left the manor house and stumbled back to the cottage.

The road stretched out before him, uncertain and shadowy, and he realised that he would have to travel it alone. His only companions would be the ghosts of the dead and the voices of his comrades. The important thing was to keep moving forward, for if he turned back, the darkness would swallow him. Even if nothing made sense anymore, he would have to keep walking, one heavy foot after the other, like those nightmares when you are trying to escape from something and your legs won't move.

In the end, it seemed like he was taking the same step, over and over.

One night, sitting alone on the verandah and staring into the darkness, he thought he heard the sound of a plane and realised that he was flying in his Mosquito again. It was a cloudless sky and way below, he could clearly see the French countryside, a beautiful picture of yellow sunflowers and purple lavender in the morning sun. Looking down, he spotted a group of German planes flying in a protective circle, a defensive formation hard to break. Peeling off in a power dive and picking out one of the machines, he switched his gun button on to Fire and opened up in a four-second burst. Next minute, he was pulling out so fast he could feel his eyes dropping through his neck.

The sky now seemed to be a mass of individual dog fights. He was coming in for a head-on attack on a Messerschmidt but bullets started appearing along his point wing and he noticed that black smoke was pouring out of his engine. There was an unpleasant smell of escaping glycerol and his windscreen was soon covered in oil. God. He was in big trouble. Sweat was running down his face, a feeling of tiredness overcame him and he began to lose consciousness.

This time he was not going to make it home.

He was going down …

When he woke up, he was lying in a faint on the bare boards of the verandah, his shirt damp with the blood from his bleeding nose.

*   *   *

Quietly, unexpectedly, when Charles felt as if he were losing the war with his own being, Nature also turned against him.

The winter rains had not arrived the year before, which meant he could not plant his spring crops. The summer had been cruel and the worst drought in decades was recorded in the district. Big Ben was severely affected. Everywhere was dust and there was little nutritious pasture left on the property, just brown dirt and tufts of razor grass which the livestock could not eat because it cut their mouth. The lucerne he had planted so laboriously in the winter had withered so there was no supplementary feed for the sheep.

Kangaroos, normally only seen at dawn and dusk, came out of the hills in droves and were in the paddocks eating the last of the grass. Ancient gums on the ridge lines, accustomed to harsh conditions, had started to die, their bark peeling back and hinge-splits appearing in their trunks.

Drinking water for the family had become very scarce and there were no more cups of tea for visitors. The rainwater tanks had become infused with the whiff of mosquito larvae and dead mice, household usage was reduced to a minimum and the family had to take turns to have their weekly bath in the same sluggish, brown water.

Charles had started to daily monitor and identify his weak and sick animals. He was too ashamed to use the whip to move the lean cows staggering pathetically around the parched fields and he just had to abandon them until they dropped. It broke his heart to see the little lambs born in the dust, then lying next to their dead mothers with the crows waiting and watching. Worse was the sight of the starving mothers eaten inside out by their unborn lambs. All the dams were either dry or contained only a few centimetres of muddy water where the sheep, desperate for a drop of moisture, were beginning to get stuck.

One day, as he was doing his rounds, he detected a terrible smell coming from one of the distant dams. As he approached, he noticed that the dam seemed to be covered in brown mud so he rode closer to check if any of the sheep needed to be rescued. To his horror, he saw that the surface was not mud but a layer of the decaying carcasses of dead sheep and kangaroos. Struggling for the last drop of water, they had become entangled, writhing together in a macabre dance of death, too weak to disentangle themselves, the putrid slime of their rotting carcasses gluing them together in a deathly embrace. In all his combat duty, he never experienced such a ghoulish sight.

Everything was dying, and each day the relentless blue skies mocked the blighted earth. There was nothing to it. He had to face the impossible choice and start slaughtering his flock, the flock he had purchased with his war savings. Watching the sheep staggering pathetically around the paddocks, too lean to sell and too weak to survive the drought, he knew it had to be done. Raising the rifle to his shoulder, he began the culling of the flock. It is the worst thing he had ever had to do and as each animal fell with a soft thud, the sound of the shots were like the last fatal raps on the door of his coffin.

*   *   *

Thankfully, autumn came early in 1949 and the dreadful sun mellowed to a warm glow. With the change of seasons, he felt the sense of things coming to an end, not just the end of the tragic struggle against the drought but the end of life itself. He was only thirty-two but already he would not have cared if he died tomorrow. Hope had delivered their fourth child, a little girl whom they called Colleen, but his heart ached for the thought of life in another time, the life he knew before the war, a life of innocence and wonder so easily annihilated by life's spoiling.

Autumn, and he knew with startling clarity that there was no point to human existence and that everything in his life was closing down. The last shrivelled leaf would soon die and fall from the top of the tree and the idea of his own death was as peaceful as drowning. He rode through the fields like a daydreamer, lost in his melancholy, his parched mouth longing for the frothy, stinging taste of the first beer. His faithful dog, Sally, always trotted happily alongside him and often guided the distracted rider and his horse home.

One day, as he was heading home, he realised that Sally was nowhere to be seen. He looked around everywhere, whistled several times but could not see the familiar streak of orange bounding towards him.

'Oh well,' he muttered to himself. 'She knows her way home. Must have sniffed a good trail.'

The dry twigs crackled under the horse's hooves and he let himself be carried, almost motionless, through the dusty afternoon. Another mile and he felt himself drifting off in the saddle when suddenly, out of the corner of his eye, he caught a flash of russet red. That bastard fox. Jolted out of his reverie, he sat bolt upright in the saddle, scanning the bushes for further proof. Yes, another flash of red against the silvery grey leaves of the bush.

'I know where you're heading, mister.' He smiled grimly, remembering the mangled, half-eaten carcasses of the chickens he had found in his yard last week. 'Now, it's my turn.'

He lifted the rifle out of its pouch, hoisted it carefully to his shoulder and aimed it at the spot where the fox had been sighted. His horse, sensing the urgency of the moment, snorted then stood still with every muscle tensed. In just a few seconds, the flash appeared again and Charles fired. A terrible yelp rang through the air followed by a commotion in the bush, then silence.

Charles dismounted, ran over to the spot and stopped dead in his tracks. Oh, God. Oh, dear God. No! There before him lay his beloved dog, blood oozing out of her chest and her flanks heaving. Charles dropped his rifle and knelt down beside her. Her eyes sparked one last flicker of recognition, she struggled to turn her head towards him and faintly lick his hand. Then she fell back dead.

Memories of the past three years flashed in his mind, memories of her tough little body bounding though the paddocks with him, memories of the faithful friend waiting at the door every morning, the gleaming eyes of canine adoration watching his every move, encasing him in her love. His Sally. She lay there, her blood mixing with the dirt and the ants.

He picked her up and walked the rest of the way home, stopping only to bury her under the quince tree near his bedroom window.

All night, he fired that same shot over and over and saw her quivering body and that look of love and submission.

Charles, the scientific killer.

The killer of his own people.

And Sally.

*   *   *

There was nothing left. Nothing and nobody to fight for. Nothing to believe in. Even the children were beginning to get on his nerves and, along with everything else, he felt trapped. To make matters worse, Mallory had succumbed to rheumatic fever and there was no way of telling how the illness would affect him in the future. Trapped. A pregnant wife, a dangerously sick son and two whingeing daughters. Outside, an icy wind was blowing and the children were driving him mad. Trapped.

'Daddy, Daddy. I want to go to the movies. You promised, you said we could go on Saturday. You promised, remember?'

Charles shot them a sullen look. He wanted to get out but he surely didn't want to take the kids.

'Come on, Daddy. There's nothing to do here and we can't go outside. Come on.'

Maureen was not easily deterred; she grabbed hold of his legs and tried to drag him outside but he shouted at her like a mad man and shoved her aside.

'You promised, Daddy,' Maureen insisted, not being the one to back down. The two girls had started to cry, setting up a terrible din which exploded in his brain. How much longer could he keep control of himself? He had to get out.

Grabbing both girls violently, he dragged them outside and flung them into the back seat of the car. The girls were screaming and Hope was trying to intervene, clutching at his arms and yelling at him, terrible howls like a beast in pain.

'No, Charles. No! The roads. The ice. It's too dangerous. Please, Charles, please!'

He pushed his wife aside, slammed the car door and took off for town.

A terrible silence fell over the whole cottage. Luckily, they all survived the night but after that, Hope and Charles only spoke when necessary and the children stepped out of his way, the whole family confined to the dangerous limit they now shared.

What had he become? What had happened to the decent young man who once respected life? When he was shaving, Charles could hardly recognise himself in the mirror anymore. Past and present memories blurred together, the signposts were gone and he couldn't seem to find his way back to himself. Sometimes he felt as if his whole history had been wiped out.

At other times, an old part of himself woke up, an old self with skills and knowledge and habits intact. It was so hard to understand because there were other returned servicemen like his friend, Digger Shields, who had come home and resumed his life without any major hiccoughs. But they had all been killers, hadn't they? How did any of them account for such wilful murder, especially the death of innocent women and children?

He had felt deeply about the casualties at first but he had been forced to let the feeling go, had encouraged it to go, distrusting it. It was a strange feeling because the dead were all around him and he had just shrugged his shoulders, gone on to his next mission, unheeding, suspended, blind. In England, the camaraderie and respect for his courage had eased his conscience but he was back home with a set of strangers and he felt strangely exposed in his present life.

Now he was beginning to fear that what was left of the present person would wilt and shrivel in sadness and unbearable remorse. There was nowhere to turn and the self-hate and guilt were killing him. There was also this new feeling of extreme irritability and agitation as if he were boiling over inside and would explode if he couldn't release the tension. He wanted to seize a gun and fire it, run over somebody, punch somebody in the face, smash every window in his house, smash his car.

A dark stranger was growing inside of him and it was this stranger who followed him around the paddocks and waited for him in the shadows. This self, violent, unfathomable and self-destructive, could not be processed or digested. It did not fit in with any of the feelings he had experienced in the war or afterwards. Even as he went about his work on the farm, trying to regain the things he had loved and enjoyed, this self would rise up and pull him back to the blackest pit.

So this is what he had become – a fragile shell, covering over a more electrical and endangered self. He was reaching the point of no return and the dark man was beginning to consume him.

*   *   *

When you are driving along a country road, you often see a flock of birds picking greedily at a carcass on the ground. The birds are useful and clever, as are all scavengers who wait with patient, beady eyes and swoop down on the stinking remains of the animal as soon as the cars have passed. As your car approaches, you wonder if the birds will rise in time, gain enough leverage and acceleration to avoid the oncoming vehicle.

Most birds escape but sometimes one fails to take off in time. The smell of the roadkill distorts its senses, it flutters for a few seconds like a rag in the wind and then slams into the front of the car.

My father was killed in a car accident on the night of the 13th of July, 1949. His funeral, the biggest ever held in the Church of England, Emmaville, was attended by representatives from nearly all district commercial, rural and citizen organisations. At least one hundred other people, mainly men, waited outside in the churchyard. As the flag-draped casket was carried from the church, ex-servicemen, including three airmen who had served with Charles, formed a guard of honour.

The whole town seemed to have fallen into a state of shock, incredulity and unspeakable defeat. If Charlie could outwit death in the war yet come home and die at such an early age, what hope was there for the rest of them? As the cortege moved off from the courtyard to the wind-swept cemetery on the outskirts of town, two Mustang fighters from Williamstown RAAF station came out of the clouds and circled the cemetery for nearly fifteen minutes. Even the gravestones seemed to stand in reverence as the new tenant took up his occupancy. Then, as the mourners gathered at the graveside, the Mustangs flew over, dipped their wings and continued southward.

Reverend Siddell was completing his funeral liturgy when a strange moaning noise distracted him. It seemed to be coming from a long way off and from high in the heavens. As the noise grew more distinct, the mourners who were deep in contemplation of their immortal souls could just make out the shape of a Mosquito whose engines now roared over the hushed town. It made two or three circles, then, with one of the motors stilled, glided like a silver bird over the assembled crowd and dipped its wings, just as the casket was being lowered into the ground.

Men who had seen similar ceremonies agreed that no tribute was ever more perfectly timed or executed. Even with ground-to-air communication, the timing could not have been better. As the Last Post was being sounded, the faint drone of the Mosquito mingled with the notes of the bugle, then the mystery plane disappeared into the outreaches of the sky, never to be identified.

My father's body was lowered into the ground and the whole world seemed to turn over. The wild ranges around him swallowed the tears of the mourners and the dismal emptiness of the surrounding streets muffled the sound of the departing cars. The cemetery, with its long-forgotten names, closed off its well-guarded secrets and Squadron Leader Charles Curnow Scherf, RAF ace fighter pilot, lay beneath the cold, cold earth, his soul sealed forever in the banality and oblivion of a forsaken Australian town. It was one of the Scherf women who would make the final pronouncement on that dreadful day, 'At least there were some decent cars at the funeral.'

Messages of sympathy and honour to the deceased hero arrived.

The mayor of Glen Innes wrote the following tribute:

Charles Scherf was a man who did not know the meaning of fear. His exploits whilst serving overseas gave ample proof of this, and he played no small part in gaining the ultimate victory which was eventually ours. We as citizens mourn with his family but we must also remember with feelings of pride that this district gave us such a man when the Empire need such men.

Sir Charles Portal concluded his message with these words:

We hope the people of your community where he was reared dedicate a fitting and useful memorial to one of the greatest flyers and heroes who lived on this earth.

The most moving expression of sympathy was to come from his 418 Squadron:

News of Charlie's death was like a punch below the belt. Charlie carried a terrific lot of determination into battle. He fought like a tiger in the air, but on the ground he treated war as a game. For sheer courage and determination we never met his equal, and in our hard and trying times, he had that saving sense of humour.

As time passed and the good citizens of the town moved on to other matters of interest, no monument was ever erected to honour Charles Scherf in the district where he was born.

Regarding his medals, the Australian War Memorial in

Canberra was contacted by the family but were told that they would be stored in a back room and only brought out when certain periods of military history were featured. They were displayed briefly in a glass case in the foyer of the Glen Innes RSL Club but were gradually pushed to the back behind local sporting trophies, forgotten.

The name of Charles Scherf, hero of WWII, has remained unknown and uncelebrated in his country.

It is a sad but true fact that only bushrangers and sporting celebrities achieve legendary status in Australia.

PART THREE

THE ENCOUNTER

'Do not weaken for their grief: do not give in or pardon.
Only through this pain, this black desire, this anger,
Shall you return at last to your lost garden.'

The World and the Child Collected Poems – Judith Wright

CHAPTER 1

THE DUST OF
MANY PLACES

Things have not gone very well for me.

People expected a lot of me and I expected a lot of myself. They thought of me as 'the girl most likely to succeed', for hadn't I won three scholarships to university? I was successful in my studies and my career but underneath I was very disappointed in myself, very disappointed that I had not been able to overcome my insecurities and gain more confidence. Sometimes it felt as if I were living a double life and at other times, there seemed to be no point to life at all.

The unresolved loss of my father continued to exert its influence in all the significant stages of my life and I drifted on, year after year, without closure. There was no father to watch me as I walked across the stage to receive my diploma, no father to walk me down the aisle, no father to advise me on important financial decisions and no father to pick up the pieces when I collapsed.

I only knew only one thing for certain. The living must go on. They continue to live in order to make sense of the dead.

*   *   *

The main problem was philosophical. How did we all make sense of my father's death? What possible reasons could people have given themselves when his youth, vitality and extraordinary courage shouted in our ears? The coroner's report was ambiguous and there was no mention of the other person in the car. No doubt the Scherfs would have covered up any hint of scandal, not wanting to add any more pain to their unbearable grief. The local townsfolk must have come up with their own explanations: mechanical fault, speed, alcohol, war neurosis. Or was it just an accident after all? Strangely enough, my mother never discussed it and kept herself busy.

In my own struggles and questioning, I had to accept that my father did not die a glorious death in some foreign field, forever celebrated by the Anzacs. Instead, he was found all bloodied and broken, his head smashed in, on one of the loneliest backroads of New South Wales. Admittedly, he had belonged to that wilful generation of marauding men, the war heroes. There was no doubting his heroism but in classical literature one might have read that he had too much hubris. His last missions as a fighter pilot were completed with abnormal daring and an unhealthy desire to flaunt death.

Perhaps the furious Immortals were offended and had decreed a suitable retribution. Because he had been so light-hearted, so cheerful and elegant in his sorties, his death would have to be heavy, clumsy, ugly and violent. Because he had pierced the heavens like a gossamer veil, he would collide with the hard rocks and the trees which would not yield to him as the sky had done. The gods would show him he was earth-bound after all.

He would understand that once the blood is spilled, the reaching mind must pay the price.

For me, he had come to represent a vacuum of bewildering forms that sometimes beguiled and sometimes turned malignant. After I grew out of my teenage fantasies, my frozen grief transformed itself into a kind of dance macabre for I had started to carry the secret burden of him, to be absorbed in him and to incorporate his dark force into my adult dreams and ambitions. Every day was the same and I began to struggle with depression as I tried to keep the other parts of my life on track.

It took an enormous amount of energy to keep the contending parties under control. I could not get over the feeling that I had forgotten something or that I should have done something or that I was waiting for something. Waiting for approval. Waiting to live. It was a confusing, dizzying sensation like being on the edge of an abyss.

I thought when I left Glen Innes that it would all stop. I thought my successful career would shore me up against such feelings of insecurity. I had expected to live a new, happy life for I had begun well and forever I would count my days at university as the best days of my life. There I romped freely in the playground of academia, pirouetting up one corridor of knowledge after the other, safe in my ivory tower of literature, foreign languages and the domains of philosophy.

After graduation, I slipped into the optimistic Australian life of the sixties – a career, a youthful marriage to the most handsome boy on campus, our own rented unit and a brand new, red VW Fastback car. The world was my oyster and I began to eat out at foreign restaurants, to sip exotic cocktails from trendy bars in Kings Cross, to buy expensive French perfume from David Jones, to attend the Spring Racing Carnival at Randwick in a white linen suit and a black, broad-brimmed hat.

I loved my career as a high school teacher and was soon placed on the First List for promotion. On the outside, I appeared to be happy and successful but something was brewing inside of me. As my knowledge and insight increased, due to my studies in French existentialism, I became aware that my congeniality was really nothing but a carefully designed act.

Mauvaise foi, the French called it.

It was easy to 'play the game', to slip in and out of the expected roles because, thanks to the example of my popular sister, I was very good at imitating the social transactions of other people, all those supposedly free-flowing conversations with relatives and friends which were not difficult to orchestrate. No one suspected my inner turmoil. If someone asked me a more probing question about myself or my background, I was ready to derail them. I was good at switching directions anyway; my years of stuttering had taught me how to quickly change the conversation so as to deflect any suspicion or shock.

I had suspected this fraudulence for a while but because I

seemed to get away with, I had not tried to develop a more authentic self. It was too tricky. Deep down, my mind was in a constant battle to mediate a mood of panic and dislocation. How could I have allowed my friends, my students, even my husband to see what I was really like? Who would have wanted to live with a distorted, patched up, shabby little girl anyway?

It was a dangerous way to live. Especially when I had to keep an eye on my father as well.

Physical pain relieved my mental torment. Since childhood, I had a habit of biting my fingernails, often down to the quick. Then I developed the habit of stripping the skin from my fingers. I would nibble away at a piece of skin near the nail and ease it away from my finger with my teeth. The longer the strip of skin the more pleasure I derived until it either became too deep and bled or just broke off. If someone noticed my mutilated fingers, I would simply tell them I had been gardening without gloves.

Some days, when driving along a quiet road, I would will myself to go faster and faster. It amazed me how much power could be released by the light, easy pressure of my foot on the accelerator. In a few seconds, I would pass the legal speed limit and the world outside would become a streak of hurtling forms and colours. Reaching a point where I no longer feared an accident or even death, my mind would enter that blissful alternate state where nothing existed but excitation, propulsion, possibility.

This was the dimension where I hoped to find you and repair you, but each time I pulled back because the horrible truth was that I was still alone.

Father, you never helped me. The distance between us

remained unreachable. You stayed in your untouchable space and maintained your image of silence. I could not resuscitate you even though I strayed dangerously close to the outreaches of my mind.

It is so hard for a child to live the unlived life of a parent.

*   *   *

Australia seemed calmer, more coherent and optimistic in the sixties, and we had no trouble finding employment and accommodation wherever we wanted to go. Like Doris and Debbie, I hoped to 'live happily ever after' with my young husband, to save money to afford all the good things available to those born in the 'lucky country' – a home with a large backyard, a couple of kids, two cars and even a second house on the beach. In the 1970s, however, the divorce rate peaked and my husband decided to become part of the statistics.

My divorce came swiftly and violently, like a summer storm. There was nothing abnormal about my husband's inclinations; he liked to think he was different, special, a non-conformist but he turned out to be a typical bloke after all. Seven years of marriage. An unexpected pregnancy. The seven-year itch. It was a shame because he was my childhood sweetheart and we had grown up together, like brother and sister, holding each other's hand, guarding each other's awkwardness as we faced the unknown future together.

It's sad to think how one single thought, one little fox, can slip through the barricade of habit and trust. In the end, it was not the other woman but betrayal itself which became his mistress, the anxious pleasure of sacrilege. There was also something small but deep festering inside him, the need for one-upmanship, for he had failed his final year at university and was forced to take up a Primary School teaching position. I was therefore more qualified and earned more money than he; a recipe for disaster, my Greek hairdresser informed me, as if it were the most obvious explanation in the world. The strike against me was more destructive because I had allowed myself to trustingly enter the domain of love and even abandon myself to it. Now my whole world tilted, the floorboards started to disappear from under my feet and the life I had tried to erect began to collapse before me. My young husband's betrayal was like something physical, like a knife penetrating my heart, violating and vandalising my store of sacred things. I felt like a small kitten that a ferocious dog had dragged in from the rain, shaken and mutilated, dragged out into the rain again and left for the lightning to sizzle and char.

My circumstances were grim. Soon after the affair was discovered, my husband took the car and disappeared, leaving me stranded in an isolated, wind-swept village on the North Coast. That was his advantage, for nobody had taught me how to drive. Funny how we had both chosen this spot because of its untouched wilderness but mostly it was I who loved the solitary walks, wandering through the man-made tracks between the straggly tea tree shrubs to the collapsing sand dunes bracing against the thrashing surf. He preferred the hot, rowdy world of the Tweed Heads Race Track, for gambling on the horses and greyhound dogs ran in his family and every night he would spend hours studying the form guide while I collapsed into bed, exhausted after a day at school contending with the youth of Australia. He disliked going out on social occasions so I spent my weekends alone while he dallied at the racetrack and at the counter of a lady who worked at the TAB.

The days following his departure were some of the strangest in my life. His family appeared to have closed ranks in a conspiracy of silence and would not freely answer the many questions I had. Instead, my sister-in-law, caring just enough about my isolation and lack of provisions, deposited me and my baby in a makeshift bedroom under her house while attending to numerous secret phone calls upstairs. The sound of the phone ringing at all hours of the day and night and the hurried footsteps belonged to a world which had now excluded me. In my loneliness, I felt like a prisoner in solitary confinement, contained and hidden away from the drama unfolding upstairs, punished without reason for a crime I didn't understand. It was only during mealtimes that I was permitted to come upstairs and join in the bright, meaningless conversation while the family secretly plotted my fate.

It was decided that I should return to work as fast as possible. I really had no choice because my husband had no savings and my accouchement leave would eventually cease, so it was merely a question of relocation. My school was situated in the inland town of Murwillumbah, a fair distance from my home, so my sister-in-law found me a cheap flat in the town and was already making enquiries about a babysitter. My heart sank when I was taken to view the small, dingy apartment at the back of an old couple's house where I was supposed to rear my little girl and pick up the remains of my life.

My compliance up to this stage may have seemed reprehensible but I was still weak from giving birth and had not yet recovered from the shock of my husband's adultery. At any rate, when a man replaces his wife there is always an element of guilt and failure in the wife's heart which most women would admit if they were prepared to put aside their moral indignation. Besides, nobody really knows what goes on in the bedroom between a man and a woman and I now knew that a man could have secret longings, desires and proclivities which he might not always control. Like all 'good girls' of my era, I had been innocent when I married and I now felt it had not been to my advantage for never again would I underestimate the power of sex.

It was the sight of the uninviting flat, however, which stirred me to action. I thought of the joys of motherhood I had anticipated in our little cottage near the wild sea, the baby's room with the freshly made gingham curtains, the coffee-coloured lace of the bassinet, the chest of drawers with all the small items of clothing wrapped in tissue paper. There was no way on God's earth that I could settle for these drab rooms in a stranger's house. The robbing had been too extreme, the degradation too unmerited.

I could not wait to contact my only source of escape, the Department of Education, and felt relieved when I could speak to the Inspector who had placed me on the First List for

Promotion. It was fortunate that I had impressed him, for once I explained my circumstances, he answered without hesitation.

'Just tell us where you want to go and we will find a school for you.'

I felt humiliated having to explain the details, but the Inspector was surprisingly sympathetic. Usually, teachers had no say in where they were posted by the Department and expected nothing but grim ordinances from this foreboding Victorian mausoleum in central Sydney, blackened by pollution on the outside and fossilised by bureaucracy on the inside.

'Just send me to Sydney,' I replied gratefully, for my only desire was anonymity, to become a passing shadow in an indifferent crowd of commuters, to disappear under the wave of nameless faces and hold my breath until my heart stopped hurting.

I finally tracked my husband down, sitting at his mother's kitchen table in Tweed Heads with his head in his hands, weeping helplessly when he caught sight of me with the baby in my arms. In this pitiful state, he had become a young boy again and, seeing him like this, I was momentarily overcome by a rush of tenderness for he had been one of the lost, rebellious youths of the sixties and had never really grown up. After his parents divorced, his mother had deposited him in a Catholic boarding school, Woodlawn College, in New South Wales and this may have accounted for his disdainful air and general mistrust of people. Unfortunately, she had also instilled in him the idea that good looks can get you whatever you want in life for he was indeed attractive, classically tall, dark and handsome, resembling a young Clint Eastwood with his supercilious grin and even sporting that famous squint.

My mind flashed back to our secret rendezvous at a train station in Cooma ten years ago and how my heart had lurched when I caught sight of him striding towards me, dressed up awkwardly in his father's jacket which was several sizes too big for him, a boy of seventeen desperately in love and trying to look like a man. I had defied my mother to make the long train journey alone and we had hugged fiercely, so sure of our passion at that time that nothing or nobody could ever part us.

Now I approached him cautiously and spoke to him almost deferentially as if I had no right to ask anything of him for the ties between us, even after ten years, had frayed.

'I'm going away. I've found a job in Sydney. What do you want to do?' I asked in a flat voice for I had already emptied my hurt and rage on him and now all negotiations between us sounded like formalities.

'I don't know,' he sobbed and looked up at me imploringly as if he was waiting for me to give him the answer. 'She's in the hospital. She tried to commit suicide after everyone found out. God, she almost died. Don't you understand? She almost died because of me.'

In that moment, I knew that his mind was not on me. Events had moved him into a different dimension and left me behind. The die was cast, the fruit on the vine had died and I was slipping through the layers of air between us. An image flashed into my mind of those movies where someone has fallen off a cliff and another person has just managed to grab their hand and hold on. Slowly the grip slackens, the gap between the fingers widens and the hand loses its hold on the poor soul hanging desperately over the abyss.

This man I thought I knew so well had formed a full life with another woman and she had been willing to pay the highest price of exchange, her death against his life with me. It should have impressed me but I wondered briefly if he would have been as equally overwhelmed if I had got in first and tried to end my life.

The humidity of a tropical summer was already rising and the air in the kitchen was dripping. I turned my thoughts back to the present situation but could not wait to leave, for a terrible sense of death and finality had grown amongst the moisture and the sweat. There would be no more discussion, for the season between us had passed and it was shocking to think that ten years of living and working together and our first child lying between us now counted as little as chaff in the wind.

I was reeling. The world of rules which I had grown up with had moved on. I turned away from him and started to leave the house but I thought of one thing to say.

'Could you please give me some money?'

He reached into his pocket and drew out $24. That was all he ever gave me and after the divorce hearing, he disappeared and failed to comply with the judge's order to pay maintenance for our daughter.

That night, my sister rang me.

'You've got to get out of there. I can't stand to see you humiliated like this. We're coming to get you. We're coming now.'

'Oh, Mauny. I don't know what to do. I've seen Bob and he's in no state to help anyone. It's a terrible mess. Worse than ever. I just know I can't be involved in this drama any longer. I've told him I'm leaving but I don't know where to start. It's so hard. How can I pack up my home? In one day?'

I was sobbing on the phone, feeling that the loss of my little beach house was the last link.

My sister spoke slowly and deliberately, trying to calm me down and give me some easy, practical directions to follow.

'Just pack a port of clothes and the baby's things. We'll send for a removalist to get the furniture and the rest of the things once you've found a place in Sydney. Just do what you can. Oh, Rody! I know it's hard but you must hang on. Oh, be strong! Be strong! We'll be there tomorrow.'

My sister and her husband arrived from Sydney the next day, driving all night through a cyclone which washed water over the road to my house. The sea, the wind and the rain roared as I packed up a few things and we set out, the baby sleeping next to me in a plastic bathtub. With the world clanging and crashing around me, I suddenly thought about my mother as she drove away from her first home. There was something familiar about this scene … the new baby, the husband gone, the wife stranded in a remote place unable to drive and forced to leave her home. A spark of lucidity, of some deeper insight, flashed across my mind but I did not say a word to my sister who was staring through the rain-swept windscreen, intent on giving frantic directions to her husband. Some people say that the second child is the mother's child and I wondered if my mother had processed her own distressing past through me, for our circumstances were horribly similar.

I knew I was right to get away, for the rift in our marriage had become too wide and there was something else which made any thought of reconciliation absolutely impossible. In the battle between the sexes there is always a winning point, a knockout blow which, in my case, proved more fatal than adultery itself. My husband had crushed me with his betrayal, that was certain, but there was something more sacred which he destroyed, for I have never forgotten the words his mother hurled at me when she first learnt of the affair.

'You'll have to be strong now, my girl. He's got another woman. He was with her the day you had Cybele. He told her, 'Rosemary's had a beautiful baby but I wish it was yours.'

After my father, that was the second death.

* * *

Sydney

Grand old city of impossible beginnings and the start of my wandering.

It was distressing for me to have to wean my baby so soon but I buried my unhappiness in the exhausting process of setting up our new life. There were many things to organise: accommodation, transport to my new school, a babysitter for Cybele. Fortunately, my mother agreed to help me and I found accommodation in the leafy suburb of Wollstonecraft. I managed to do what needed to be done by adopting a cheerful, coping face but underneath, I was still in shock. The numbing pain of the divorce lasted for about two years, two years of waking in a fright, dragging myself out of bed and taking long, hot showers.

Fortunately, my new school was one of the better schools in the region and I soon moved into my favourite role of educating and entertaining a group of eager students. The sophistication and vitality of Sydney entranced me with its promise of a more exiting life than I had ever known. Trundling home on the suburban train, I would sometimes daydream past my stop and find myself in the inner city where I mingled for a brief moment with the happy commuters sipping pre-dinner drinks at one of the trendy new wine bars.

Sydney had always been 'our city', the destination of all wide-eyed country kids, and I started to think I would stay here forever.

At the end of the year, the Principal called me to his office.

I did not like this man as he was one of those pretentious, two-year-trained Manual Arts teachers who had somehow gained promotion to the top and arrogantly referred to his staff as 'disposable books which he could get rid of at any time'. Normally he would do nothing but complain at the staff meetings, haranguing his staff in a strident voice for all their inadequacies and lack of professionalism.

It surprised me when I shyly entered his office that he asked me to sit down in one of the comfortable chairs reserved for parents and serious interviews. In those days, when a teacher was called to the Principal's office, you were usually 'put on the carpet'. I was even more shocked when he started to talk to me in what I would imagine was a very fatherly voice.

'I've been thinking about your situation, Rosemary, and would love to ask you to stay at my school. You are a fine teacher but your circumstances are very difficult. When your mother goes, you will find it very hard to manage your work and a young baby on your own. If you try to stay on in Sydney as a single mother, you will be nothing. Go home, go home, my dear. Go back to the country with your mother and wait until your daughter is a little older.'

I listened to him and realised only too well that there was nothing I could say in my defence. In my dreams I had begun to imagine a glamorous life in Sydney, for I had already made a group of new, interesting friends and I knew where to find the most fashionable hangouts. I now wore the latest fashions, gaucho pants and lace-up boots, and my hair was streaked with blond tips. An attractive young man had begun to visit us regularly and take us for Sunday drives in his little, red MG.

'Thank you, Sir. I will certainly think about it,' I replied politely, tiptoeing out of the room like a student who has been satisfactorily chastened.

I have never forgotten this moment in the Principal's office. The warmth of an early summer was rising in the room, I could hear the faint buzz of the bees nudging the buds on the azalea bushes outside and smell the fresh polish on the Principal's oversize desk. I tried to concentrate on his words but my mind was dizzy and I couldn't stop staring at the Principal's beautiful, matching bookcases and wondering if he had built them himself.

When the school year ended, however, I did take up the Principal's advice. There was something in his manner which touched my heart, something more personal than solicitude, and such a ring of sincerity about his words that I felt compelled to obey.

The impression of that hour has remained as a singular, striking moment in my life because I was suddenly aware that this was probably the way in which loving fathers talked to their daughters.

So, when the azalea bushes were bursting with fully matured blossoms, I decided to go home.

Glen Innes

It was hard to swallow.

Those feelings of shame re-surfaced because I, the girl most likely, the girl who couldn't wait to escape, was back ... and literally holding the baby. I tried to ignore the stares and whispers of people in the main street and to put on a bright face in the staffroom. Lying in my old bedroom at night, I counted the events that had led me back to where I started and I felt like a player in a board game of Snakes and Ladders that landed on the longest snake just when the winning square was in sight. One lucky roll of the dice and I might have made it to the finishing line.

But was it simply a question of luck? Or fate? These questions confused and depressed me because once more I seemed to have lost control of my life. To make things worse, my dear grandfather had passed away and I could no longer seek refuge in his rambling house, see his face light up more brightly than usual when I appeared and hear the familiar greeting: 'Hello, dear.'

I had read somewhere that depression is anger turned inwards. If that was true, then my depression had hidden a great deal of anger and the process of suppression had been going on for a long time. When I was a child, explosive anger or 'temper tantrums' were considered to be a character flaw and in need of strict correction. We were forced to let the anger simmer inside us, to 'keep the peace', never speak back to our dear mother and never question the decision of adults.

In my adolescent years, however, when I was old enough to think for myself, I experienced intense degrees of anger especially when somebody talked about my father or my father's parents. It seemed right that I should be allowed to express my doubts and unanswered questions but my 'impertinent' outbursts were jammed by pious people like my Uncle Reg, the Anglican minister.

'That's a terrible thing to say, Rosemary. You have to forgive people.'

'Why?' I protested. 'Why should I forgive them? They didn't care about me and I don't care about them!'

My uncle was shocked.

'You are a rude, little girl and you should be ashamed of yourself. Your father was a great man. If you keep such hate in your heart, you'll destroy your soul. You must ask God to forgive you.'

It was obvious to me then that anger, especially in a female, was considered an ugly, unfeminine, unchristian emotion. In my mother's generation there were many women who had swallowed their anger for so long that they ended up in middle age with debilitating depression. Then the kindly doctor would give them a prescription for Valium or Serepax. *Mother's little helper*, they called it, and it was heart-breaking to see my own mother eventually succumb to its magic.

On the contrary, I had come to see that anger had a real survival value. It filled me with a new kind of energy. It mobilised thoughts of recovering our lost inheritance one day and of securing justice for my mother. It was revolutionary. It inspired the dream of a glorious reprisal, particularly when we were old enough and our mother told us something about our father that no child wants to hear. From then on, thoughts of my father and his parents took on the pernicious shape of blame and contempt and I looked for ways to show them up. Enrolling in a post graduate degree, I hung on to my anger and pushed myself through two gruelling years of full-time work by day and hard academic research by night.

My old headmaster in Sydney had been right after all.

The two years I spent at home under the gentle care of my mother helped me to consolidate my situation, save some money and watch my daughter grow up in a stable environment. For those two years I was able to breathe more easily, lulled by the slow pace and simple pleasures of country living, face-to-face for the first time in years with something I might have called normality. The memories of this golden time have lingered:

the companionable staffroom which still contained an ancient open fireplace, my brash, unsophisticated country students who obviously had no reason in the world to learn French, my little daughter, ever the tomboy, kicking balls in the backyard until the light faded. At night I would lock myself away with my study notes and be awakened by the sharp thud of the enormous Harrap's French dictionary which I knocked off the table when I fell asleep on top of my books. In my studies I discovered the bliss of solitude I had experienced in my university days and became less and less interested in my poor boyfriend who continued to make the arduous 571 km trip from Sydney to Glen Innes almost every weekend, driving through the long, lonely night, stalwart at the wheel of his little red MG.

Perhaps I should have stayed in Glen Innes but my anger flapped around like a bird in a cage and there was something else I had to prove to myself. I finished my thesis, contacted the Department of Education and waited.

One day, when my mother's red dahlias were just about to bloom, a train pulled into the old colonial railway station at Glen Innes and a man in a topcoat carrying a briefcase alighted. Six weeks later, I was notified that I had been promoted to List 2 and was now eligible to take up a position as Mistress of Modern Languages in a high school of my choice. I ran my eye over the list of prospective schools, imagining my new life in Wollongong or on the outskirts of Sydney, but the name of one school seemed to leap off the page.

Belconnen High School ACT.

Canberra

Canberra, the improbable capital city in inland Australia with all those sprawling, uniform suburbs mutating confidently under the banner of decentralisation. As the capital of Australia, it should have been the final destination of all roads but it lacked conviction and the highways seemed to pass through it and scramble on to secret 'meeting places' in the Outback.

So this is where my ambition had led me.

Even in the worst life there are periods of useful activity, progress and achievement, plans and dreams, and you start to think that you are an ordinary person after all and that, through all the pain and struggle, you can have what others seem to obtain so easily. This period of my life was to last for many years and nobody could have imagined how it was going to end.

It was the 1970s, the era of Gough's dream of a new, fair, multicultural, reconciled Australia snapping us out of the torpor of the Menzies era. His slogan, 'It's time', ran through all our hearts and we felt, not just nationally but individually, that our own 'time' had come. As female teachers we were particularly pleased because it meant that we finally had equal pay. I was swept up in the new wave of change and optimism and felt that my life was beginning to look promising. A new bureaucracy was established, The Commonwealth Teaching Service, supposedly an elite service, but full of the same dull leaders closeted in their offices awaiting retirement and the same loud, ambitious teachers jockeying for promotion. I felt a mixture of guilt and nostalgia defecting from The New South Wales Department of Education which had acted so benevolently towards me and whose policy of external exams and streaming I still favoured. In Belconnen High School we were obliged to adopt the American style semester system, promoted vigorously by the new English Master who was in a race with the other male leaders to move up to the next rung. This meant that in their first year of high school, students could choose their own electives and Foreign Languages had to compete with Jewellery Making and Cooking.

Gough, a visionary leader, had prioritised education with an emphasis on innovation, creativity and the audio-visual technologies so it was exciting to suddenly find a television set in each classroom and a language laboratory next to the new, state-of-the-art library. The teaching profession was revitalised but became a hotchpotch of enthusiasm, innovation and creativity founded mainly on personalities and egos rather than on sound educational theories. Peer assessment meant that more and more charismatic individuals with a cult following of radical, young teachers found themselves in higher positions of responsibility. Of course there was the accompanying degree of sexual energy and as a single mum I was the target of many amorous advances, even from the married men on the staff. The saying that you couldn't hang onto your marriage in Canberra certainly proved to be true.

I was optimistic, however, because as the Mistress of Modern Languages, I found myself co-ordinating the teaching of five languages: French, German, Indonesian, Italian and Latin. It was fortunate that these subjects remained popular in spite of the semester system and received additional support and affirmation from all the relevant foreign Embassies in Canberra. Soon the Language teachers, who were now being challenged about the relevance of their subjects, were mingling with First Secretaries and attending special gala events at the Embassies. As a classical scholar himself, Gough had also funded the new Maison de France which provided a lot of aid and encouragement to French teachers like myself.

It was disappointing that the first day of my new school began badly, a sign of the testing times ahead. I had been asked to do playground duty at recess and, eager to establish my authority, I directed a boy to pick up some trash.

'Fuck off,' the boy growled at me and slouched way.

So this was how it was going to be, so different from my little country school in Glen Innes and the well run school in Sydney. There were 1,300 students in this school, students from the newer suburbs, brash, classless teenagers whose parents were the new, entitled public servants running around in Commonwealth cars. I had never had much difficulty in disciplining students in my own classroom but now I had to set an example for an entire staff.

I chased after the boy and spoke harshly to him.

'How dare you speak to me like that. Do you know who I am? I'm one of the new Heads of Department and you had better pick up that piece of paper or I'll send you to the Principal's office.'

Reluctantly the boy picked up the paper, taking his time to stroll over to the bin and scowling at me as he wandered off into the crowd.

As one of the new Heads I was expected to put on a very convincing display of almost military-style discipline. In fact, being able to control the students in your class had always been one of the main yardsticks of a teacher's competence and failure in this area had caused many brilliant but shy academics to retreat from the profession in despair. I did not subscribe to blind authoritarianism and had always won over my students by friendliness, a genuine desire to help and interesting teaching techniques. This was a different ball game, however, and people were noticing that I was not measuring up.

The Assistant Principal, Alan Scofield, a former Head of Maths and a tough veteran of many of the worst schools in New South Wales, seemed to take a particular interest in my non-authoritarian approach. Whether he had been commissioned by the Principal to confront me or not, he visited my office one day and proceeded to grill me about my views on discipline. Rumour had it that he had suffered a serious injury many years ago and was considered medically unfit to ever walk again. Through sheer bloody-mindedness and a perverse determination to prove the doctors wrong, he had dragged, forced and propelled his poor, wounded limbs along a beach every day until the bones and ligaments miraculously re-formed and he regained the use of his legs.

He had obviously come to my office to sort me out and as he proceeded with his hard-nosed interrogation, I could see him on that beach, gritting his teeth against the pain, the veins in his neck bulging and his face contorted into a hideous grimace. I tried to explain my ideas on a more relational approach between teachers and students but it was obvious that he had never heard of Martin Buber. He left my office dissatisfied but I solved the problem by gaining the friendship of the new Science Master who had worked in a Boys Home and who agreed to cane the worst offenders for me.

There were other problems. I was happy and confident in the classroom but lived in fear of being rostered on assembly because of my dread of stuttering in public. I envied the new female Maths Mistress, a clone of Alan Scofield, who had obviously decided to adopt a masculine style of leadership and put the fear of God into the students. While I desperately avoided the roster, she ran her assemblies with military precision and was feared, even hated, by every student in the school. I retreated to my own little space in the Language Department, was beloved by all my students and continued my friendship with the Science Master.

*　　*　　*

Depression, my old friend, did you finally depart from my life?

Did I feel satisfied with myself at last? Did I finally outgrow the past? Judging from the outside, this could have been one of the most successful periods of my life but underneath I must confess that I was still deeply agitated.

The challenge of being a single mother in a demanding career began to wear me down, especially when my daughter developed whooping cough and I was told by the Principal that he could not allow his senior staff to take any time off. I also had to learn to drive as quickly as possible, to purchase a car on my own and eventually to take the huge step of buying my first home.

I began to flounder under the pressure. The social life of Canberra, the upwardly mobile crowd of aspiring public servants and the weekend cocktail parties in private homes were not sufficiently distracting to take my mind off my problems and I found myself sinking into the pit.

My achievements had not given me the sense of solidity and the higher quality of life which my generation expected from life. I was still alone and my life on the outside had become a treadmill. I had to admit it. On the inside, the morbid apprehension of a destructive and terrifying enemy still lurked in the nether regions of my mind.

Oh, God help me. God help me.

Whatever it was, it was still there.

The bloody thing was still there.

Each night from 2 am onwards I would toss and turn, ruminating about the broken things from the past or devising strategies to arrange and fix the day ahead. There was always this sense of trying to reach an unattainable point like the condemned man in the Greek legend of Sisyphus.

The stigma and pain of my divorce were also more apparent in Canberra. With so many bright, like-minded people thrown together on so many social occasions, you would have thought that I might have met a future partner but preconceived ideas about the 'gay divorcee' prevented me from making any lasting relationships.

Yet there was something worse which the rejection and abandonment had sliced open and exposed. It had shredded my clever facade, my last defence, and exposed the painful self from which I was fleeing. I had to face it. I was heading towards my thirtieth year and my life was nothing but a cover-up. A fake.

I knew it now with startling clarity.

The game was up.

Feelings of being out of step with everyone intensified. My need to please people became more urgent and a chronic sense of guilt spurred me on to more frantic social connections, especially with the men of Canberra. I became more sensitive; one dead animal on the side of the road threw me into alarm. I could not sleep at night because the loud beating of my heart would keep me awake. Each day became a struggle until at 5 pm I could reach for a glass of wine (was that the respectable hour?) and fall into an uneasy truce with the demons of the day. Worse, I could confide in no one. If I had broken my leg or developed cancer, I would have been able to lie down, validated and unquestioned, but it was impossible to talk about or expect anyone to understand. Like an evil trick played upon a sick brain, my depression was so alien to everyday existence, so extreme as to be totally incomprehensible to normal people.

Just like the stuttering.

It was getting harder and harder to keep a grip on reality.

I joined many self-help groups like The Inner Peace Movement and became involved temporarily in transcendental meditation, self-hypnosis and Primal Scream therapies. Never drugs. The doctors wanted me to take medication but I knew the problem was not chemical. I even promised myself that I would only put up with the suffering until I reached the age of forty and then I would end it all. I knew I would never do such a thing to my family but it gave me comfort to imagine a fixed ending to my torment.

I never thought to seek professional help for I had been trained to ignore my needs since childhood. The old adages of my stern and indifferent relatives rang in my ears along with the Protestant emphasis on self-denial and hard work.

Pull yourself together. What will people think of you? You just have to make an effort. God helps those who help themselves. Time heals all wounds.

The Puritan shrinkage of self.

So, every day of the week I would get up and go to work, get up, get dressed and put on my lipstick, put on my red lips of courage, and those critical and perfectionistic commands which I gave myself began to eat me alive from the inside out.

Then the dream came.

I am about to enter a secret building and am standing in front of an elevator. When the doors open, I feel compelled to enter the lift. As the lift descends, I realise I am moving inside a huge skyscraper whose rooms and corridors plunge deep inside the earth. The rooms are deathly cold and contain nothing but tightly packed shelves, in never-ending rows. Rammed inside these shelves are thousands upon thousands of dead, decaying bodies lying as if asleep in their filthy shrouds. There is something both sacred and putrid about this domain, and I know I have trespassed into the very depths of hell's abyss where no man should enter.

I am desperate to press the button and return to the surface and escape but I memorise the location of the building for I am beguiled and plan to return. Something that lured and menaced with incomprehensible evil has taken hold of me and the enormity of my discovery consumes me. I have stumbled upon the greatest hiding place on earth – the storehouse of the dead awaiting judgement.

My curiosity and fascination will not allow me to rest and once more I manage to locate the building and the elevator. I verify my discovery, gaze for a time at the dead bodies and return to the surface, barely able to breathe because of the dank atmosphere and suffocating smell of death. On my third trip I am suddenly gripped by the most violent pang of terror I have ever experienced and I know for certain that if I ever enter the lift again, I will never be able to find my way back.

Something fatal and irreversible will happen to me and I will not only die but face complete extinction.

The warning was clear. The darkness was on the rise.

My father was stirring in his grave but the grave was becoming more mine than his.

*   *   *

How long? How long did I have? How long before the dreadful thing caught up with me? How many decisions and revisions before I broke down completely? I was desperate to get control of my feelings but my brain kept generating sensations that made me feel scared and helpless. Instead of an organ for thought it had become an instrument for registering its own secret pain, minute by minute.

'I think I'm going to have a nervous breakdown,' I explained to my younger sister one day 'It might be a good thing. Then all the struggle and pretence would be over and I could start again. Wobbly but clear and transparent like jelly on a plate.'

'Oh, Rosie, you are a funny girl. Life hasn't been kind to you, that's for sure. I really don't know how you've kept going all these years.'

We had been drinking red wine and listening to the music of Bob Dylan. It was our favourite after-dinner music, then as the night progressed, we'd finish off with Leonard Cohen and sink into a kind of hypnotic state of melancholy.

'I feel like I want to fall off the perch. To let go of everything. To go down.'

'Yes,' she murmured dreamily. 'Go down.'

By the end of the evening, we were both quite depressed but it was not related to anything we had been discussing. It was more a feeling of being amorphous and of floating in mid-air, transported by the ragged, sulphurous voice of the solitary troubadour. There is an understanding between sisters which can never be expressed and I didn't want to break the mood, so we just sat in silence, together. When it was time to go to bed, I looked at her mournfully.

'I'm frightened, Col. I'm really frightened.'

She hugged me without saying anything. Neither of us knew what to say and the helplessness fell between us and flapped against our cheeks, heavy and wet and cold like soggy sheets on a clothesline. I fell asleep quickly, lulled by the alcohol, and woke at 2 am with my head full of pathways, roadblocks, detours, wrong turns and somewhere out there, a point of arrival which kept receding into the darkness.

Sisyphus.

*   *   *

Thankfully I did not 'go down' after all. A remarkable turnabout occurred. A lifesaver in fact.

I married again.

It was a bleak Canberra morning the day we met and I was stranded on the roadside with a broken-down car, a young child who had to be dropped off at daycare and a class of noisy teenagers waiting for someone to mark the roll. He burst through the fog, wearing only a short-sleeved shirt and grinning to himself because his mates in the garage had heckled him about the 'silly sheila up the road who had rung up in such a tizzy.' His ruddy complexion and dark, rollicking eyes gave him the appearance of a bold, saucy knight and I couldn't help noticing his strong chest and broad shoulders. The ice was all around us but we joked and bounced off each other in the way that single men and women do when there is a sudden connection.

A year later, we married. Arthur had migrated to Australia from the Geordie region of North England and he constantly amused me with his distinctive accent and habit of starting his sentences with 'Ee, bah gum' and 'way, aye'. We moved to Queensland in search of the weather he had dreamed about when he was repairing cars in England, a frozen spanner stuck to his chaffed hands. He developed a loving relationship with my daughter and eventually I gave birth to two lovely sons, Paul and Scott. There was a certain peace in my heart each night when I would drift off to sleep in a house full of slumbering children and cuddle up to my husband's strong back. It was a second chance for me, as rejuvenating and forgiving as salvation.

The years passed too quickly, years of birthday parties, first days at school, school uniforms, packed lunches, homework, visits to the dentist, friends, sleepovers, picnics, holidays, adolescent crises, graduations, tears and laughter. I watched with tenderness and pride as my children grew up but I probably needed too much from them. I worried about every stage of their development, their academic results, their friends, the constancy of their relationship with me and I was always on guard, checking for any signs of emotional or psychological harm.

Looking back, it was like diving into the cool sea on a steamy day, encountering a monstrous dumpster wave which sucks up all the water and slams you into the sand before tumbling, shaking and crushing you senseless beneath the massive surge. Desperate for breath you surface amongst the white foam and peer through the strands of seaweed and floating debris to locate your bearings. Dragging your shaking body onto the beach you collapse onto your towel, your head still reeling from the whirlpool, and rest in the warm sunlight. Later, when the sun is setting and the late afternoon strollers paddle in the scum of the receding tide, you head for home. But once you have left the beach, you dream of the cool green depths, of the taste of salt in your mouth and the surge between your legs, and you long to return to the sea, to the toss and tumble of something bigger than yourself.

I tried to emulate the model of a happy family, all nicely

groomed and fitted out, but a nagging uneasiness still followed me through all my days. The external events of my life seemed to flow along more easily but keeping track of what was going on beneath the surface still took up a lot of my energy. It was the family members inside my brain which could not get on together; how do you reconcile success with self-doubt, love with lovelessness, numbing with rage, life with death?

Something was always simmering beneath the surface. At home or at social gatherings I was constantly preoccupied with my inner thoughts and would often disassociate myself from things and people around me. It was a trick I had mastered since childhood, keeping people at bay while I sorted through all the fragments in my mind, phrases from the great European writers and philosophers, a verse from the French and German writers I had studied, lines from modern songs and psychology books – sifting, pondering, trying on one idea after the other, searching for the words and concepts that might reconcile those warring parties inside my head.

'Where's your head now?' my husband would often say to me.

We began to drift from place to place because my husband was involved in many business opportunities, including real estate. I gradually allowed my own ambitions to fade in the wake of his new projects, bright promises and surprising bursts of energy for I realised that the 'quiet, family man' harboured dark, unfulfilled longings, the desperate, last-minute dreams of a working-class man nearing middle age.

We became nomadic, relocating to many promised lands, increasingly separate but together. I lived in many different homes, worked as a teacher in different schools and worried about the children. There was no logical reason for any of our decisions to move, no hidden attraction which favoured one certain location over another besides the green light of opportunity. Movement always offered hope, a kind of suspicious hope that in the next place my husband would finally discover the right 'deal', the lucky gamble, the quick investment which would finally pay off and make him rich. So we submitted ourselves to those forces which dove and swept through the universe, seemingly random but of complex and unknowable patterns of choice.

*   *   *

The years passed and eventually things began to wind down. My children grew up, left home to seek their own fortune, married and settled down to raise their own children. My husband suffered a severe financial crisis, developed a debilitating illness and died several years later. I drove through Glen Innes a few times on my travels but there was no reason to stay after my mother also left the town.

Things were coming to an end.

I retired from teaching and spent my days in the garden. It felt more familiar to be alone again, for was this not the more natural state of mankind, the prime condition and structure of our self-conscious existence? In some ways it was a relief to be able to do what I wanted to, to stay at home and feel depressed without having to pretend. It was almost comforting to think that the world had finished with me and to look forward to growing old with only my cats and books for company, resigned to widowhood like my mother, for in the gamble of love I had already used up two rolls of the dice.

And in all those years my father had not yet said a word.

Sitting on the back steps one afternoon at my favourite time of the day, I was savouring the last rays of the setting sun and the long shadows announcing the turning of the season. A low wind had blown up, the sort of wind that carries secrets, secrets that the true ancestors of our land understood but which rarely revealed themselves to us. I had noticed that this wind often came at dusk, inserting itself mysteriously between the stagnant air of the day and the cool of the evening. It altered the landscape, momentarily stripping back the land to its original, untamed state.

For some reason I began to cry, softly at first but soon great, heaving sobs wracked my body. It was hard to understand the reason for my grief because the love of family had protected me for so many years and wound a golden cloak around my sorrows. I knew it was not the death of my husband which had caused this sudden outburst for during his long illness I had accepted the fact that he would die and was even grateful that his suffering had finally ceased.

No, an older grief was still there, like a stone in a river, unobtrusive, disregarded, but which the water has had to flow over in a different way, simply because the stone was there.

The stone was still there.

My tears were finding their true source and it was like

discovering a well in the desert but a well that has been poisoned. This was the waste dump of all the bad memories and emotions I had suppressed in my period of happiness. Obviously, my loneliness had triggered off some frozen, split-off part in the mosaic of my brain because what I was now experiencing was not just a passing emotional state but a distinct mental system with its old, old history of pain.

I sat on the steps, blinking into the sunset and weeping hot tears, paying homage to the crippling realisation. The dreaded moment I had run from had suddenly, mysteriously arrived and now the floodgate was open. Every memory and emotion that held the hurt came back to me, eclipsing all thoughts of the happiness and security I had scraped together.

So, the part of myself that I had carefully locked away, the part carrying the feeling of being unwanted and ashamed, had begun to announce its return from exile. Trailing after my husband all these years had been a futile task and had offered no real contentment. I now knew for certain that you could live as a stranger in as many locations as possible but the mind could never be sent into exile.

There was something else, something I had been running away from all my life. I could see it now, a black shadow, and inside the shadow was the shape of a child. A wretched, miserable, abandoned child. She was there, lurking in the membranes of my brain, contaminating my existence. The sick rose.

Suddenly I understood everything. There was no escape because she had been there since the death of my father, taking over every possible alternative for my life, blocking every relationship and every attempt at happiness. In trying to protect her, to suppress the parts of her most hurt by the trauma, I had locked up my most creative and lively parts, condemning myself to a dark, joyless life.

It had taken me a lifetime to reach this point of insight and this is why I was sitting on the back steps crying my heart out. I was weeping for myself, for the loss of innocence, for the wonder and magic of childhood so casually annihilated. The child that delighted in all things, the child of adventure and enchantment had died when my father died and when I was forced to leave Big Ben. If she had been able to grow up without the tragedy, she would have known what to do, for in that innocent child lay all the truth, vitality and purpose of my whole life. But I had lost her forever.

The sunset was in its last stages, putting on its most brilliant show as often happens before dusk overtakes it. Soon it would be time to go inside but my body felt heavy and I could not move my legs. Suddenly, out of the bands of colour – pink, orange, gold, red – the sky started to break up and swirl around like the sky in a Van Gogh painting. Some strange inclination, some leading from the past of something given about to happen startled me and I looked up in complete surprise. I watched, dazed, as the colours spun in circles in front of my eyes and the sky began to reform and rearrange. Round and round, moving faster and faster until the whole world seemed to be turning over and I was being sucked into the vortex of streaming elements.

The colours were now inside my brain, flashing and exploding; I was choking and gasping for breath, then the whole world turned black and I fainted.

When I regained consciousness, the universe had recomposed itself, the garden was still there, the house was still there and I could feel the hard, bare timber of the steps against my cold body.

The sun had set, the wind had dropped and the chill of an autumn evening had begun to descend. My body still felt a bit shaky from the fall but my mind was calm and resolved.

The unfinished business had started. The real business of my life.

I knew what to do.

Ballandean

My first instinct was to sell my city home and go back to the land. The move was not too surprising because it had become quite common for retirees in Australia to abandon the city for a few acres of rural property in one of those small country villages of yesterday. This decision was referred to as a 'tree change'.

The 'tree changers' could be found on weekends in tarted-up real estate offices, pouring over photos and mud maps of bushland retreats, looking optimistically at ugly, little corrugated iron sheds which, with a little work, promised to become the perfect getaway.

I began my tree change when I purchased a property boasting one hundred and fifteen acres of pristine bushland in the highlands of Southeast Queensland. This remote tract of land, disowned by most Queenslanders because of the low temperatures, is dissected by deep gorges, wild cypress pines and gigantic granite boulders which rise up out of the earth like hooded hunchbacks. Would anyone really want to live among such an ungodly turbulence of the earth?

I began travelling to my country home every weekend and soon knew the route by heart – the panic to get through the Ipswich Motorway before rush hour, the contours of the land flattening out as I left the city behind, the misty mountains of the Scenic Rim and then the tortuous climb through the roadworks at Cunningham's Gap. Passing through Warwick, I waited anxiously for the spot where the first Cypress pine tree grew then settled into the long road to my cottage – through orchards with flapping hail nets, past old, abandoned fruit stalls, half-finished sound barriers, ramshackle houses and sheds, unpainted buildings with piles of dirty crates and cardboard boxes, fences made of incongruous material, signs with 'Closed' pasted over them, fields full of rusty farming gear – the glorious, random, unfinished, worn-out demeanour of rural Australia.

*   *   *

To reach my place, I turned off the highway and climbed even higher to the rugged peaks of Girraween National Park. A sharp turn through the impenetrable scrub, up a rocky road of decomposed granite and suddenly, like all pioneering ventures of the last century, the miracle of a perfect, little bush shack.

My fibro cottage, with the toilet out the back and the obligatory rusty bathtub filled with stagnant water, was waiting for me, crouched in natural submission beneath the craggy ridge.

As the months passed, I soon became familiar with my new home. Someone had cleared about fifteen acres along the road frontage and planted a fruit orchard which was now extinct. Then followed several acres of young eucalyptus, pungent with fresh growth from the last bushfire. It was in this forest where I loved to immerse myself, feeling I was in the right place at last, pinned down by the happy silence.

Behind the tract of flat land rose the silhouette of the mountain, the horizon's utmost boundary. The mountain was black with power and I could always sense its brooding presence. Granite boulders larger than towers stood in vast files up and down the mountainside, greyly mysterious, eternal guards like the entombed warriors of ancient China. I plunged amongst them, trying to reach the summit, scratching my arms and legs on the spindly shrubs. Huge gums with their flailing limbs had fallen who knows how many years ago, stripped bark lay in curls on the ground, *boronia granitica* and wild rosemary bushes struggled against each other.

As the months passed by, I also became more aware of the sky. Those of us who have travelled know only too well the unique tumble, sweep and reformation of Australian clouds. I hardly noticed them in the city but now they became the background to all my activities as they moved at the wind's command in never-ending patterns across the sky. At night, the brilliant panorama of the stars, undiluted by city lights, turned on its most glorious show. Looking up, I would feel myself flattened out and spinning in the infinite reaches of space, nine-tenths sky and one-tenth earth. In these moments, I was transported back to my home in Big Ben and to that night when I was suddenly aware of the presence of God.

How mysterious is the link between people and places, how magical the way in which physical places are ultimately transformed into psychological landscapes?

I knew exactly what to do. I had the blueprint in my mind after all.

There were non-negotiable elements. First, there was the manor house, then the long avenue bordered by pines, then the gardens, the tennis court and a fenced paddock for some sheep. It was back-breaking work but I toiled at a feverish pitch, my heart in a riot at night as I planned the next stage. With the mountain at the back and the cottage at the side of the manor house, it formed an exact replica of Big Ben.

I couldn't wait to bring my mother to my new home, hoping that it would strike a nostalgic note in her ageing heart.

'Why would anybody ever come here?' she exclaimed almost fearfully. 'Where are the street lights? It's so isolated. Whatever possessed you to buy a place so far away from everyone? I really don't know what has got into you.'

It was then that I realised that my mother had never loved the land and had only put up with country life for my father's sake. My new property was clearly no consolation prize for her. I, on the other hand, loved getting my hands into the dirt, to fuse a part of myself with the land. It lifted my depression and helped me to keep my mind on the present. Every morning was a cheerful invitation to link my life with the earth, with the friend that would never betray me.

Months later, I was very pleased with the result. The house was completed, the gardens were set out and I enjoyed sitting on the verandah in the evening when the air was all blue and silver. Everything was ready and I just had to wait. Some strange compulsion, however, had made me want to empty out my bedroom and sleep on a bare mattress, whereas the rest of the rooms were decorated with substantial antique furniture like the houses of my aunts. The stark simplicity of the cold, pared-down room was soothing and it made me happy just to lie there, alone and gently shivering, huddling an old grief to myself.

Father, I remember you. Father, I'm coming back.
Father, I would say your name again.
Father, I would lie in a field of stones with you.

One day, however, the strangest things started to happen. A sense of disquiet crept into my mind and I felt the beginning of a new but contradictory outworking of all my plans. Just when I thought everything was going right, something odd was brewing.

Out of the corner of my eye I glimpsed a dark shape fleeing past the window. It appeared again on numerous occasions but I did not pay too much attention to it. It was too quick for me to be able to identify if it was a person and I thought it could well have been a passing shadow or a trick of the light. A few weeks later, I noticed that one of the large rocks seemed to have shifted its position. It would have been impossible to move such a heavy mass but now a bush I had planted dead centre in front of the rock was growing to the side without any signs of having been shifted. At night, I heard footsteps on the verandah and once I thought I saw a face in the window.

Superstition was something I tried to avoid, having conquered my fear of the dark when I first came to this land, but suddenly I was afraid of going outside at night if the fire needed another log. If I did have to step out into the dark, I was dismayed to discover that the land I loved had now become an alien territory full of snares. There was a bunyip behind every tree, a murderer crouching behind every rock and every twig I stepped on turned into a brown snake. I slept fitfully and thought I heard the door rattling.

A terrible unease began to develop in my spirit and I kept glancing over my shoulder. Someone was watching me, someone was following me around the yard ready to jump me from behind. A sense of disillusion, futility and collapse invaded my thoughts and for the first time I began to doubt the instincts which had led me here.

Was this the landscape of the living or the dead?

It was all coming to a head. Something loose and incomplete had been dragging along behind me all this time and now the strands were tightening into a complete entity.

Something was about to announce itself.

Then, the dream came.

I finally met him at last, after years of trying to keep him out. I have run down a hundred corridors trying to escape him while all my history was following me. I knew he was getting closer because the doors were becoming harder to secure and the time between his penetrating my life and my just barely managing to slam the locks was growing dangerously thin.

Tonight he is stalking me one more time and I stand breathlessly before the cellar door. I have just run through the whole house bolting every entrance securely. I congratulate myself on racing to the cellar before he can get in, then the most horrible realisation overcomes me. Oh, no! I have forgotten the laundry chute, that little tunnel which leads from the upstairs bathroom into the laundry. He could easily have gotten in that way. Quickly!

I'm gripped with terror as I try to rush up the stairs but my legs are heavy and I feel as if I am wading through deep water. Reaching the bathroom, my heart sinks as I see that the laundry chute is open. I recoil in fear and I try to run out of the room but I sense that the embodiment of my fear is standing right behind me. It has beaten me.

I turn to face it, expecting to see the most terrifying incarnation of pure evil. Instead, I see the figure of a beautiful man, slim, clean-cut, dressed in a tailor-made suit. His expression is one of total sang-froid. I look into his cool, calm face with an obvious question in my eyes, the question that has haunted me since childhood.

He has read my thoughts and he surprises me by speaking. His voice is detached, assured and he speaks like a murderer who explains in detail what he is going do to his victim.

'I've come to take your mind.'

I did not expect this response, so could think of nothing to reply because there was something so deliberate and inevitable in his manner — like the dwarf.

I know I cannot change his intention, but I want desperately to defend myself.

'That's not ethical,' I stumble over my reply, speaking from a world of clear behavioural rules but thinking immediately that my words would be powerless.

'There are no ethics,' he smiles mockingly and, satisfied that he can now proceed with his worst intentions, disappears with a snigger.

I woke in the most terrible fright. It was the worst dream I had ever had because it told me I had been tricked.

My demon lover.

The trap had been set in my grandmother's house many years ago when I was forced to sleep outside of the house. So this was how it was all going to end, not in physical annihilation but in madness. You should never leave a child alone in the dark for monsters to come and dig in the frightened, little mind. For the strong man will come later, without effort or obstruction, and complete the job.

So this is what had been coming for me all those years ago and now it seemed that all my attempts to survive and restore my life had failed.

Something must have gone terribly wrong. I must have misread the signs on the verandah that afternoon or perhaps the signs had pointed in the wrong direction? I was so sure I had been on the right track but I must have taken a wrong turn or taken too long to get to where I should have been. The demon lover had waited.

Could I believe this dream, this nightmare that seemed more

like a visitation? What if I were to really lose control? What if one day I would go crazy. What if tomorrow were that day? What if …? The thoughts exploded in my head.

My life would be over. I would be institutionalised in an asylum like the people with rotting lungs. My mind would be full of puss and mucous and cobwebs, my red-laced eyes would be rolling around in my head and I would hear myself screaming and screaming and screaming.

I saw myself locked up, fastened into a straitjacket, dragged into the hospital and wheeled on a trolley through those forbidden doors of the operating room. Was this why I had always avoided this room in our childhood dares? Then a team of beefy nurses would come and strap me down to a gurney while other medical officers placed electrodes on either side of my head and passed a quick jolt of electricity between them. I saw myself thrashing uncontrollably, foaming at the mouth and lapsing into a stupor.

Madness. The word that drops in the mind like an axe, mentally disembowelling the brain.

Madness. The terrible trick played on the diseased mind by its inhabiting psyche. Madness. The word that stuns and imprisons, like a dungeon of twisted thoughts listening to the terror through the walls.

Madness. I could smell it, as fetid as damp, mouldy feathers, a decaying carcass or an unwashed menstrual towel. I could see it, the ghastly wart-covered toad that lies under a cold stone, the writhing, half-formed glutinous insects under the rotting log, the squirming snail dying in its bubbling slime.

Madness. I could hear it, the banging and clanging in my brain like the unfastened door of a tin shack.

I staggered into the kitchen, desperate for a glass of cool water, but the scream was beginning and I couldn't hold it back. I heard it coming from a depth far away, like the howl of an arctic wolf in a frozen wilderness which nobody sees. It escaped through my chest and came out of my mouth like an anguished wail. The ice turned to fire inside me and burned hot. Something worse than fear was rising — a raw, undifferentiated emotion which unlocked the door to my rage. I was boiling over.

I picked up a number of crystal glasses from a shelf and began smashing them one by one onto the brittle tiles. Sparkling fragments flew everywhere and the noise of the shattering glasses was as sharp and clear as the snapping of two fingers together. The broken pieces rolled all over the floor creating a carpet of twinkling fragments which I kicked and stamped on, trying to extinguish their heat as if they were hot coals which had fallen out of a fire box onto the carpet.

I was on a rampage and it was all going to come out. I would end it now, one way or the other.

The fire inside me burned white-hot as I continued smashing the glasses, then died down to blood-red embers. I became silent, standing among the debris.

My rage simmered.

A smouldering fury.

I remembered that point in my life when everything changed and split apart. The green ladies had wept for me but who else had been there? Who had jumped me from behind?

A solid plain of hot ash had begun to form between me and the people I knew and thought I could trust. To get to this unholy distance from where they once existed in my heart meant only one thing … somebody had turned traitor. Now somebody would have to be called out. Now somebody would have to face me and listen to what I had to say. The unspoken words would finally be spoken and somebody would have to pay the price.

I would not wait for heaven.

You see, nothing really dies. There is a place in the universe where all things are hidden and stored. I would retrieve what death had stolen and tried to hide from me. The laws of the universe say it is impossible but I already knew where to find the way.

The elevator.

It would be a perilous journey. They say there are things in the universe that you shouldn't disturb. The doctors had warned me but my rage made me careless and I was ready to risk all.

A rift in the universe had appeared.

It was bright on the other side.

CHAPTER 2

THE RECKONING

She seemed to be spinning in space.

There was a great pressure in her head. Distorted thoughts and memories, each one so painful, came into her mind then shattered into pieces, like an explosion of energy within. Her stomach twisted; her heart raced in shock as the whole world began to crumble around her. She wanted to scream but her mouth was full of clouds and bits of flotsam, and she had begun to shake uncontrollably.

Then she blacked out.

When she regained consciousness, she couldn't remember where she was. At times she could detect the sound of hushed voices and quick footsteps. She could also hear doors opening and closing. Figures in white loomed up before her like blown-up paper cut-outs, then disappeared. She tried to move but was pinned to the bed.

It was dark for a long time.

One morning, she suddenly awoke to find herself back in her home. Everything seemed so bright and sharply outlined as if she had woken up in a foreign land under a new, dazzling sun but it was all still there, the familiar paths and gardens, the tennis court and the homestead. There was an eerie stillness as if all the objects had been frozen in time like the stage sets in an empty theatre. Yet there was a calmness in her heart which she had not felt for a long time and she fell quickly into the routines of her old life.

*   *   *

It was during her morning walk in the bush when the stranger appeared. He looked like a man who had suddenly fallen from the sky into the tangle of the harsh Australian bush. His clothes were torn and there was a raw gash with congealed blood on his head. He didn't seem to notice her at first and started to walk straight past but she grabbed him by the arm.

'Hello. You're hurt and you seem to be lost,' she said gently, reassuringly. 'It's getting dark and I think you had better come with me. I know how to get out of this wilderness and my house is not far away.'

She pointed to a side path amongst the scrub but he hesitated as if he had hardly heard her words. Then, putting his hand to his gaping wound, he lurched forward in the direction in which he was heading.

'I've come a long way and I'm very tired,' he said, pausing to catch his breath. 'I think I should keep going. This path must lead somewhere.'

'No,' she insisted. 'You will have to come with me. We'll rest here for a while, but then we'll have to hurry before it gets too dark. You can't trust the bush in Australia. After a while, big tracks and little tracks all look the same. You think you've found the way out but you just go round and round in circles.'

'Where am I?' he asked, still a little dazed to find himself wandering aimlessly in an unfamiliar tract of bushland.

'You're in a national park,' she replied. 'You must have been hiking with some tourists but you've lost track of your group. You've also fallen and injured your head. Don't worry. My property backs onto the park. We just have to go over this hill and we'll be home. I'll ring the park ranger in the morning. Do you think you can walk a bit further?'

It seemed a reasonable explanation and he now felt he had no alternative. Reluctantly, he began to follow her along the small bush track and began to push his way through the scrub of wattle trees and eucalyptus saplings which criss-crossed their path and tore his bare arms with their spidery limbs. The track gradually disappeared and the terrain became more and more uneven. Suddenly, great boulders like walls of metal rose up before him. Clambering and losing his foothold on the slippery granite, he soon began to regret his compliance. He also felt a little foolish at having put his trust in this unknown woman.

The sky was a blur of ultraviolet light and the roar of the cicadas in the afternoon heat was deafening. He had forgotten how loud the Australian bush was, how everything crashed and vibrated like cymbals in the midday heat. It occurred to him that he had been away a long time. It really stood out, this raucous, theatrical cacophony of birds and insects compared to the quiet, misty fields of England.

A wave of nausea came over him and he wanted to be rid of her, to escape from the monotony of the heat, the flies, the ants, the granite rocks, the gum trees but suddenly she turned off and headed down a clear track between the rocks.

Pausing to catch his breath again, he called out to his guide to rest for a minute.

'What were you doing up there?' he gasped.

'I go there all the time and wait,' she replied in a rather off-hand manner.

He did not have time to pursue the details because she had taken off again. Suddenly they arrived in a sort of clearing and he could see the corrugated iron roof of a house glinting between the gum leaves. He looked at her more closely and studied her face, taking in the long brown hair tinged with grey, the narrow cheeks, the slightly snub nose and the large, expressive eyes. They broke free of the scrub and came out into a clearing where the grass had been mowed. Before him stretched an avenue of Cypress pines leading up to a large country home with a bull-nosed verandah, gardens and veggie patches, a tennis court, a chook yard, flower beds of roses, clumps of lavender with more formal gardens of clipped buxus and gravel paths.

He was amazed that someone could have created such a civilised place in such a wilderness.

'How did you ever get this all together?' he asked, obviously impressed.

'I've been about my father's business,' she replied, fixing him with her gaze.

'I'm so tired,' he sighed, glad to be inside the house at last.

'Of course,' she said. 'I'll give you something to eat and bandage that gash, then you can go straight to bed. You seem a little dazed. You can contact the park ranger in the morning. He should be able to help you.'

He ate gratefully and she showed him to his room where he collapsed.

The stranger woke early but she was already in the kitchen, boiling water for the morning cup of tea. Outside, the mist had started to rise off the frost and he could just make out the distorted shapes of the trees.

'I've rung the park ranger,' she announced as though they were in court and she had been called to give evidence. 'He's gone away for several weeks. You see,' she added quickly, 'he has the dual job of thinning out the population of kangaroos in the outlying farms. He's actually one of the few qualified rangers who is registered to shoot kangaroos from a helicopter.'

The stranger seemed very impressed by this explanation and she could see him mentally working out how such an operation might take place. The faraway, lost look in his eyes made her feel that, for an instant, he would have much preferred to be up in the sky with the ranger instead of being confined to the land with her.

He seemed very restless for the remainder of the day and

spent the afternoon sleeping and wandering around the gardens. The next day, he enquired about the ranger but was tactfully dismissed. This daily enquiry went on for a week. At the end of the week, he politely brought up the subject again but made it seem as if he were simply musing aloud and not pestering her with the same question.

'I wonder if the ranger is back yet,' he said almost to himself but she pretended not to hear him and walked outside.

After two weeks, he felt rather reluctant to bring up the topic in case it annoyed her but the insistent quality of his voice made her realise that he really did need to know when he would be able to leave. She seemed happy to provide him with more information but was still unable to give him a definite date for his departure.

'Oh, sometimes he has to go away to do a refresher course. It can take up to several weeks. Once he even went to South Africa to train. Perhaps he has gone there again and who knows how long that will take.'

There was a tone of finality in her voice.

The man went to his bedroom, shut the door and lay on the bed, staring at the ceiling. It dawned on him that there was no ranger, that he was stuck in this house with this looney woman and there was no way out. Oh well, he had been in worse pickles. He would just have to wait it out and see what transpired.

He must have been suffering from amnesia because he could not remember what had happened to him or even where he had come from. When he was fully recovered, he would start to do a little investigating. In the meantime, he knew he needed to stay on the good side of his hostess because she was providing him with food and shelter after all. So, at 6 pm, when she knocked on his door for tea, he made an effort to be particularly chatty and bright during the meal and he never bothered her with questions about the ranger again.

The days passed and they fell into a kind of uncertain routine. She seemed to be waiting for something, lost in her own world, almost oblivious to his presence. What bothered him was that as the night closed in on them, the features of her face began to change and she became more remote, her face hardening with more than a hint of menace. After that, he did not sleep well and lay awake for hours, wondering how he was going to escape.

One day, he noticed that she had left her bedroom door slightly ajar, and he peeked inside. The bare mattress on the floor of an empty room hit him like a slap in the face because he had expected to see an antique bedroom suite and pretty floral curtains. He began to wonder about the other rooms in the house and the room with the door that was always locked. Of course she had the right to keep it shut and it was none of his business anyway. It intrigued him, however, and a strong instinctive feeling suggested to him that it might reveal some of the mystery. He watched where she casually hid the key, almost as if she wanted him to find it.

One night, when he was sure that she was asleep, he sneaked down the hallway. It was filled with the bluish light of the full moon and he couldn't help smiling to himself. A good night for mad men and mad women. He hesitated before the door but suddenly felt compelled to go inside, like a parent who sneaks into a child's bedroom when the child is away and reads the secret diary.

He turned the knob of the door. It stuck at first but he pushed against it and it jerked open. In the moonlight he could make out rows of bookcases, a filing cabinet, stacks of old papers and letters, photo albums, manila folders full of typed notes. He closed the door, drew the curtains and switched on the desk lamp to get a closer look at the room.

On the wall facing the door there were two photographs – one of a young girl in her graduation cap and gown, the other of a handsome man in uniform. The girl was beautiful with large eyes, her long brown hair falling from beneath her mortar board and gathered into a thick ringlet over her shoulder. Underneath her academic robes she wore a white formal dress and carried a scroll in her gloved hand.

The man was half-seated on a side table with his unusually fine, elegant hands draped over his knee. His face was handsome, long and thin with well-defined cheek bones and a confident grin. He wore his pilot's hat at a rakish angle and seemed completely unaware of the serious row of medals on his right shoulder.

The stranger was at first mesmerised by the sight of two such good-looking people. He noticed that they resembled each other, for they both possessed the same unusual eyes – large, grey-green eyes that were not focused on the camera but appeared to be looking far away into the distance. The photos were mounted in thick black frames, edged with gold. In contrast to the disarray and clutter of the room, they had been carefully positioned on the wall, exactly measured to sit together like twins. Children of destiny, he thought, their moment of promise captured and preserved forever in two black-and-white portraits.

He turned to the bookcases and browsed through the shelves of classical literature in four languages – French, Latin, German, English. A rich storehouse of old Europe, he thought, surprised. In the boxes lay masses of university notes and a thesis written in French, contained in a bound cover.

What sort of woman was she? This farm girl who pushed a battered hat over her face each day and trod out into the fields. He made up his mind to ask more questions about her life because the incongruities were mounting.

She seemed quite charitable the next evening as she laid out a nicer than usual meal and a rich, creamy dessert. He seized his chance.

'What did you do before you retired to the land?' he asked politely.

For the first time since his arrival, she seemed quite willing to engage him in conversation. She poured herself a glass of wine and began to muse over the details of her past.

'Oh, I really wanted to be a diplomat but they did not train women for such positions in those days. I had the right degree in foreign languages but I was the wrong sex.'

'Why the interest in foreign languages?'

'Yes, it is a bit strange,' she conceded. 'It is of no relevance to most people in Australia now but foreign languages were once compulsory in high school if you wanted to go to university. I also think I was obeying the call of my ancestors who were all piled up inside me, all trying to get out, all trying to establish their fading world in someone's skin before they disappeared in the war. I learnt a lot about the world by studying foreign literature, things I could never have learnt in Australia.'

'I'm sure you can't learn much about the world in Australia,' he agreed, looking rather bemused. Then he added, with a wink, 'Of course, we didn't have much time for such things in my day. Too busy clearing the land and doing what country lads know best.'

'Oh, I don't know,' she replied. 'There were always some migrants with a piano who brought their love of Mozart, Beethoven, Schubert to the Australian bush. My German grandfather used to play the violin and his family would listen to recordings of classical music every evening after dinner.'

Something familiar flickered across his mind, the sound of a musical piece, but he couldn't remember the name.

'Anyway,' she concluded. 'I love my old books. They're my friends. Whenever I'm lonely I sit in the study and browse through them. They will become more important to me as I grow old and face the final journey. It's good to go out with the Greats.'

He was silent for a long time, thinking that he had never had time for books but remembering that he once knew educated men who would quote from famous authors all the time.

'I was a high school teacher after all,' she continued. 'English and Modern Languages.'

'A high school teacher? Whew, that must have been tough.'

'Yes, sometimes. But you could never let your students know. It was important to love them and believe in their potential.

Besides, it was a profession you could always return to so I was able to stay in the same career all my life. I had the same holidays as my children, the same working hours but I spent every Sunday afternoon with a pile of marking on the kitchen table and on Sunday night the anxiety and anticipation would start to build up inside me.'

The unease in her eyes saddened him and he imagined the years she had spent, planning, correcting, explaining, striving with reluctant young minds. As their discussions came to an end, he asked her to recite a few lines from her favourite poets because he liked the cadence of the rhymes and the old-fashioned words from another world. It became a nightly ritual and sometimes she would finish off by singing a charming little French folksong or her favourite German folksong, *Die Lorelei*. She explained that the song referred to the legend of an evil fairy who would bewitch unsuspecting sailors and lure them to their death on a nasty reef in the Rhine River. He didn't like the explanation, but he loved the music and, remembering all of a sudden that he could play the piano, he wished that there had been piano in the house.

The days and weeks passed in gentle harmony and in the evening, he began to look forward to her performances. At night, when she was asleep, he would sneak into the study, stare at the photos and browse among the paraphernalia. He saw her then, understood her hopes and her faith, believed in her magic and wished he could have sat in her classroom, even if he had just sat in the back row with the cheeky louts and pretended not to listen.

*   *   *

Suddenly the time of camaraderie was over. He didn't know how or why it happened but the hospitality and the growing friendship between them were suddenly replaced by a cold aloofness in her expression and she seemed completely preoccupied with her own thoughts. During the day, they continued with their work but she hardly spoke to him. She was shutting him out. The blinds were closed, her face took on a surly expression and she barely spoke to him after dinner.

He began to retire early, lying on his bed, staring at the ceiling and wondering how he was ever going to get out of the place. A few nights later, he woke very early after midnight and felt a strong compulsion to go to the study. The whole atmosphere in the house seemed to have changed and he felt the sense of things, whatever they had been, had come to an end. A melancholic mood had settled upon his heart, like the inexplicable sadness which always accompanies the end of summer … or was it something else? He didn't know why but he suddenly thought of the wretched sailor in the song.

'*Ich weiss nicht was soll es bedeuten*

Dass ich so traurig bin'

He opened his door and crept out into the hallway. Checking that the woman was still asleep, he found the key and sneaked into the study. The shafts of light from the rising sun made him feel as if he were passing though the translucent curtains of a diorama. The furniture and the dusty books seemed to stick out at odd angles and he felt as if someone were watching him through a peephole. The office seemed unusually cramped and stuffy and he began to search frantically through the piles of books, folders and cardboard boxes even though he had no idea what he hoped to find. Suddenly his gaze fell on a plastic box full of papers which he had not noticed before, wedged behind a heap of cardboard boxes and old paintings. Inside, he discovered a mass of faded newspaper cuttings, some of which had been pasted into scrapbooks, a tin of old photos and a bundle of letters tied up with a ribbon. The newspaper cuttings told about the exploits of a famous World War II pilot and there were photos of a home, a home that he had seen somewhere before.

As the man sorted through all the papers, a sickening nausea began to rise in his stomach and he had to clutch the edge of the desk to stop himself from falling. For a moment, he could not tell the difference between himself and the objects in the room but a terrible coming-to-consciousness had started to creep into the back of his mind, like a beast which has waited in its filthy den to be released. A kaleidoscope of images began to bleed into the blank edges of his brain, then a rush of events from his past life started to flash before him, faster and faster, in a motion of spiralling energy. With each memory he felt himself sliding into the funnel of a vortex and he could hear the swishing sound of sliding doors, opening and closing. He saw his home, his mother, faces from his childhood, the small face of his wife, his war plane and his comrades. Faster and faster. There was a terrible pressure in his head and blood had started to pour out of his nose, running down his neck and soaking his pyjama shirt.

Then he fainted.

When he regained consciousness, there was a stale taste in his mouth and he could feel the congealed blood around his throat and chest. He staggered to his feet, left the study, locked the door and went to wash his face and chest. Discarding his soiled shirt, he crept back to his bedroom, scrambled through the drawers in the wardrobe, found the clothes that he had been wearing when he first came to the house and quickly dressed. Now there were no more riddles to solve, no more questions to ask, no more searching in the study for answers because his mind was made up, ranger or no ranger. The time had come to get away as soon as possible.

She was waiting for him in the kitchen. His Lorelei.

'You were in the study,' she said flatly while she continued to prepare the breakfast things.

Damn, he thought. She must have heard him fall. He tried to think of something pleasant to say, something to restore the trust between them, something that would allow him a chance to stall her and get away without any interference. It was difficult because the atmosphere in the house had changed and he felt that something ominous was about to happen.

'Yes, I couldn't sleep,' he replied, thinking very quickly in spite of his befuddled brain. 'I thought you might have something I could read.'

The look on her face told him she didn't believe his

explanation and he realised that the former civility between them had completely disappeared. He thought he may as well confess, glad to have the thing out in the open at last, glad to end the bloody charade for once and for all. Now it was time to turn the tables on her when he'd had to tiptoe around her for the past weeks, now it was time to blurt out the truth and get out as fast as he could.

He faced her squarely.

'My God, girl. What have you done? I know who you are now but you've gone too far, you and this colossal replication.'

'Yes,' she answered quietly. 'It wasn't easy. I worked so hard to get this together. I risked everything for this chance. Now, it's here … at last.'

He felt the tension in the room rising and, anxious to avoid a nasty confrontation, turned to leave but she grabbed him forcefully by the arm and asked him to sit down in a chair.

'You can't go,' she persisted. 'You're not getting out of this one. I've waited a long time for this day, this moment.'

'For what?' he asked, unable to hide the impatience in his voice.

'For this showdown with you,' she announced with the gravity of a Clerk of the court opening a murder trial. Then, looking him straight in the eye, she continued, 'Almost like a showdown with God. For the blighted life I did not ask to have.'

'You're mad,' he protested, his head reeling with astonishment. 'Mad. No good will come of it. It's damnation, I tell you, infernal damnation.'

She did not back down because she knew the time was right.

A sort of resolution had formed in her voice and the floodgate of so many stifled thoughts was opened.

'I don't care,' she replied sullenly. 'I want you to hear what I have to say so you will understand at last. We lost everything after you died – our home, our land, our life. You left us behind and you didn't care. You and your great adventures. You always did what you wanted to do. You disappeared into some place where we could not reach you and there was this untouched space around you that drove me crazy. Can you imagine what it was like for me? For our family? You got away with it while I had to be silent and worst of all … forgiving.'

He was stunned.

Her breathing had become heavier and she fixed him with a terrible, piercing stare, as if she were trying to read something in his face. She started speaking again and the words were out, the question was out. Oh, yes, the question that had dangled over her for her whole life.

'Why DID you leave?'

He thought for a while, trying to think of something to calm her down, trying to remember the things that had motivated his actions, things that had only seemed important to him at the time.

'I had a job to do. I was fighting a war for my family, for my country. For you,' he responded earnestly, thinking that this would end the conversation, but then felt he had to add, 'It was a good war.'

'I wasn't talking about the war. But, in my opinion, many people died trying to prove it was a good war. You lot should have found something else to do with your aggression. You should have found another way a long time ago.'

'How could you have understood?' he replied, annoyed at her easy dismissal of his patriotism. 'How could you have ever understood what war was like?'

'On the contrary, you placed your war inside me. Inside my brain. All those nightmares. The raw fear of kill-or-be-killed. It travelled across the oceans and seeped into our brains.'

She paused, recovering her thoughts from those dreadful nights while he stared at her incredulously.

'Didn't you think about all those mothers who lost their sons, all those dead children, all those widows and orphans? The womb has its own kind of vengeance.'

'I sacrificed myself as well. I suffered too,' he retorted angrily but suddenly became silent, remembering for a moment the children clambering over his bed. 'I put my life on the line every time I took off for a mission. Did you ever think about that? You should have been proud of me.'

'I had to fight, too,' she continued. 'In fact, my whole life has been a battle against chaos, a battle to stop myself from collapsing, a battle to stay alive and sane.'

'What in the hell are you talking about? Crikey, girl, I don't understand you. I don't understand a damn thing you're saying,' he admitted, shocked and taken aback.

He ran his hands through his hair, looking at her dumbly as if he were seeing her for the first time.

'I came home after the war, I took you back to my home, I

worked hard on the land. I … I … looked after you and your mother and the other children, didn't I?'

It was hard trying to think of the right words; his head was reeling from the loss of blood the night before. Besides, he was beginning to be exasperated at having to justify himself to this girl.

'Yes, but it was not as simple as that. The problem was that you did not die in the war. Your lucky escape should have brought you back to us but there was a part of you that never did return. You were never my father or my sisters' father or my brother's father or even my mother's husband. Our short life with you was like a roller-coaster ride. And what did you leave us with? Your fame, your exploits, your reputation constantly held over us, drowning our questions, drawing us into your image. We never learned how to be ourselves. We were nothing but a reflection of a dead hero.'

Too taken aback to move, he remained frozen to the seat of the chair. The drama in the room was building and he wondered how long he was going to have to sit there and put up with her accusations. He had always been able to talk himself out of a tricky situation with a grin but to have his past dissected and disassembled in this way was unbearable.

'A public hero but a private shambles,' she concluded and the words were as heavy as a judge's gavel at the final sentencing.

The shock and effrontery of her words hit him like a slap on the face. He stared at her, dumbfounded, too distressed to speak, then turned his face away and was grateful for the long silence that ensued as it gave him time to recover himself.

Gazing mournfully through the window, he could only think of terminating this conversation as quickly as possible and escaping from this mad person. The morning light outside was rising and he wanted more than ever to be on the road.

For a few moments, she seemed to be lost in the pain of her thoughts, sitting quietly across the table from him and fidgeting with her fingers, but then she resumed the discussion as calmly as if she were uttering an afterthought.

'If you had died in the war it would have been easy to accept your death, for death changes nothing in a war. In fact, it is an essential and natural part that fits into the scheme of things and nobody is surprised. But you did not die in the war and for me, it was your death here that changed everything. After your death you became so … so … tricky. You took on many disguises as a hero and it was hard trying to keep up with you. Hard to pin you down, to live my own life and not be absorbed by you.'

She smiled wryly and he noticed that her face was hardening again.

'You insisted on remaining at the back of my mind as I grew up and I was obliged to keep you alive in my thoughts. We had a cunning pact, you and I, but it was a lopsided one and now the game is over.'

The words were piercing. They were beginning to undo something in him, stripping him bare, removing all his reference points. It was all too confusing. He either did not understand her meaning or else understood it too well and so could not reply.

Sensing her opportunity, she continued relentlessly, piling up the accusations.

'Don't you know what it is like to have a hero for a father?' she explained in a voice that was becoming more strident, more urgent. 'I endowed you with such idealism and perfection that I was too exhausted to live my own life. Your masculine power stood like a wall between me and my life. I could not become a person because that would have meant letting go of you, and letting go of you would have meant falling into the abyss.'

'What do you mean? You were never on your own. Even after I left, you always had someone to look after you. You had your own life to lead, you did well and I …'

His words were beginning to lose their conviction. A terrible confusion had begun to seep into the edges of his former certainty. How far would he have to go with her? Was he really going to let this woman drag him down and reshape his whole history?

'Yes, you did return. Sort of. But life on the farm was never good enough for you. I was never good enough for you, so I found it hard to accept myself. It's a shame. If you had stayed, you might have liked me. Instead, I was always seeking your approval as if you were still alive. I lived a kind of … provisional life.'

The words were stirring a deeper response in his heart. He never dreamed he would have to account for himself like this. He was trapped and all he could do was let her finish.

'Did you EVER think about what your death would mean to us? It wasn't just that we would miss you or that your children would grow up without a father. The worst thing about your death was that it took away our right to a trial with you. And that's the trouble with the dead. They rob us of a trial, they rob us of a chance of justice. They drive us insane. How long can anyone live without justice?'

He stared at her, helpless, then tried to say something in his defence.

'How was I expected to know that your life would turn out this way? You were just a little girl. It happened a long time ago and you grew up alright. You obviously did well for yourself.'

'I grew up in a dark sun. I don't think I ever achieved what I was capable of. You stole my life in a way. I never had enough time for myself. Your unlived life was always buzzing around me. My life task was in, in … resuscitating you!'

The man turned away from her, unable to go any further with the implication of her words. A stifled sob was about to break through her composure and she was struggling to control herself, to muster up her courage to speak the final, unspeakable things.

'Did you think your death would take you away from me? It was the yearning and the love … the love I was stamped with from birth and which held me in suspense all my life. I shaped everything around it. But you did not love me. It was not your love but your absence which filled up my life.'

He looked at her face, pale and trembling like the moon in water. How had he not noticed it before? There was something unformed about her features, something straggly and unfinished.

'In the end, I did not miss you but I became attached to the gap of your absence. I became addicted to it. It was the hole at the centre of my life. When I tried to recover what was lost, to build myself from the inside out, there was too much guilt, too much sorrow, too much betrayal to finish the task.'

The man had heard enough. Now he could feel his male anger rising. A child, no matter what, should never have spoken to her father in this way; the old laws endorsed that. He recalled the medals he had won, the speeches in his honour, the acclamations, the light-hearted approval of his peers each time he returned from a successful mission. Abruptly, he stood up and headed toward the door. The whole thing was a rotten stunt. How dare she? He was not going to hang around this madhouse and listen to this crazy woman anymore.

But the ugly thing was growing in the room, as old as the original sin. She crossed the room and grabbed him by both arms. She seemed to be searching inside herself, searching for something deeper, searching for the words that would allow her to unburden the pain at last.

'There is something worse which I have to explain to you.'

She spoke deliberately, imploringly because the tears were starting to distort her words.

'Because you were always inside me, I had to find the part of me where you lived. There was a space around you which I couldn't get into. But when I searched, I did find it. And I found the shape you took.'

He stared at her wearily, holding her at arm's length, tired of her insistence, her introspection, her accusations and her surprises but forced to be surprised again … by the final revelation.

'I found the place where you dwelled and it was the darkness. It was the dark hole which cracked open when my first marriage collapsed. It was the nausea, the getting through the day with the vomit pushing against my throat. It was the biting of my fingernails down to the quick. It was the stuttering and the stammering. It was the grinding of teeth at night until my cheek was lacerated and my tongue full of blisters. It was the keeping watch because I never felt safe. And the not knowing, and the ignorance and unhelpfulness of everyone, and the blame and guilt and the insomnia. And the waking with a fright and the fear of going insane. Oh God, what a strength of will to hide it and pretend to be normal in front of everyone. But always the loneliness, the depression, the sense of doom. A life of eternal night. And a heart broken for eternity.'

She was sobbing loudly now.

'This is the place inside me where you lived. This is where I have known you. In the dark, dank hell of a decayed mind.'

His face had turned white. He stared at her, the stare of the infernally damned and a groan came out of him, the groan of the soul without redemption, the groan that finally recognises that there was a price to pay after all.

She wanted to stop him, the final question – the vital question – still hanging between them, but it was too late. In silence, she watched him run down the long avenue of poplars, frantic at first but slowing down as if walking against a force, his silhouette becoming smaller and smaller in the fading sky. Then, it appeared to her as if he was bobbing like a cork in a river, his gait becoming more and more unsteady as he struggled to hold himself upright.

Something broke inside of her and she tried to run after him, the dust of the road rising in billows and swirling inside her brain. The question of the other woman still burned in her mind but when she finally caught sight of him, she noticed in horror that his neck was dangling to the side of his head and he was floundering, wading in a pool of blood.

She turned and staggered back home. The trees in the avenue were rustling but there was no wind in the air. Something was forming in the gap between the trees, something shadowy and sinister. A glint of steel flashed in the darkness.

Then, she heard the sound of a car revving.

CHAPTER 3

THE DARKNESS REVEALED

Emmaville, 13th July 1949

Winter had come early that year. The long, green grass had turned into thin, creamy feathers and the deciduous trees, having dropped their leaves, were already bracing themselves against the frosty air. In the morning, the plants, black with frost, crinkled under his feet.

The rocks under the pale moon had become grotesquely alive and seemed to writhe in the earth. Outside, he could hear the moaning of the terrible pine trees as the wind blew up and, beyond that, the creaking of the darkened earth as the ice began to harden in the cracks. The wind blew over the earth as it had done for millions of years, carrying the secrets from other lands but here, in this isolated continent, you felt like a prisoner.

Australia, Charles thought. It was his home, but on winter nights when you had to go outside to the loo, it was a hellish landscape. A good place for tormented spirits in search of a guilty heart.

Guilty? Nothing made sense to him anymore. He could not get the doubts out of his head and he had begun to ask himself the same question over and over: who were the innocent and who were the guilty in times of war? He was no longer sure and he no longer believed in the pure morality of action. Everything was mixed up in his head. Was it wrong to kill and still survive the war? To come home when so many of his cobbers had died? Shouldn't he have done the decent thing and died in the war with them?

Trapped inside the house, he grew more and more restless. When he tried to distract himself, he heard the click like a rabbit trap shutting and *bang!* he was inside the den one more time. Once inside, the sickness inside his head was so dark it was beginning to consume all his thoughts. It scared him to death.

The children had begun to stare at him warily, for when he was in this mood, he would lie down on the floor of the lounge room, slightly tipsy, and grab for their legs as they tried to get past him. He staggered to his feet, desperate for air, opened the door and stumbled out onto the back verandah. The silhouette of the dark hills filled his heart with melancholy. Like a ghost forced to haunt an abandoned place, he no longer felt connected to the physical world around him. Everything seemed to be suspended in time and place and he realised he was nothing more than an aimless fugitive.

Charles went back inside, trying to escape his thoughts. The kerosene lamp flickered in the gloom and he kicked the log on the fire to stir up the heat. He badly needed a drink, something to calm him down and distract him from his thoughts but there was only the sound of the radio and the voice of his wife putting the children to bed.

An overwhelming urge to escape stirred his adrenaline, even though he knew that the roads would be icy and dangerous. When Hope came into the room, he flatly announced that he was going to town. He was starting to feel light-headed and careless about his absences and he no longer took his wife's feelings into account. Any sentiment of guilt and remorse had long since left him and he uttered the words as casually as if he were instructing one of the farmhands.

'What? You can't!' she protested in disbelief. 'It's not safe. What if something happens to you? Oh, please, Charles, not tonight!'

He ignored her pleas and brushed past her into the bedroom. Along with the dark man, he had discovered the cruelty inside him.

Hope stared at him in shock, then sighed in resignation because she had learnt to hold her tongue when she could see that red fleck in his eye. Hope, the docile wife with the acquiescing nature whose flimsy presence stood no chance against her husband's blatant indifference, for his neglect had opened her up and eaten away a little more of her capacity to stand up for herself. Deceit and deviousness were something she had never had to deal with, so she bore her husband's worsening treatment of her with silent patience. It was so much easier to blame it on the war.

However, tonight was different, the climax to many

things which had been building up and which demanded an explanation. For months, Charles had been driving into town more frequently and coming home later and later. She would wake up with a fright, check that the baby was still sleeping in the cot and look at the time. It would often be 1 o'clock or 2 o'clock in the morning and still he had not come home. The pot she customarily left bubbling on the wooden stove to keep his dinner warm had boiled dry, and she had stopped bothering to refill it. The stew on the plate had looked grey and sluggish and a slime of stale gravy had formed around the edges. The fire had gone out in the lounge room and the first draughts of winter had stolen through the gaping boards of the cottage.

She knew that something was drastically wrong. So did the baby. Little Colleen would cry for hours every night, demanding to be rocked to sleep even after being fed and settled in her cot. On many a night, Hope would struggle alone with the baby, jerking the cot back and forth until the frustration would boil over and spill onto the bare floorboards. Then she would push the cot into the spare room, close the door and collapse on her bed with a pillow over her ears

Things were starting to add up. For example, all her husband's trips to Sydney and Brisbane at unusual times of the year. Were they really just to sell the wool? Then there was the cheap, little plastic butter dish he had bought her as a gift when she had seen the receipt for the fancy hotel he had stayed in. What about the way in which he always took off, playing golf every weekend while she stayed at home with the children? And that strange affair with the American woman which she had never forgotten?

It was getting harder for Hope to let things slide. His heavy drinking and restlessness were getting worse and then there was the sound of the Oldsmobile leaving, always leaving – leaving early in the afternoon when he should have been ploughing, returning later and later at night, shouting at her for questioning him, rebuffing the accusing look which was growing in her eyes.

Tonight, when he announced that he was going into town, she was ready.

'I think you had better stay here and listen to me, Charles. For the first time, I want you to listen to me.'

'Even a worm will turn' is an old saying and I suppose that was what happened to my gentle mother that night. A trusting nature can only take so much and there is a breaking point for every down-trodden creature. Even the most subservient animal can suddenly become enraged after years of mild neglect, such things as forgetting to bring him inside on a freezing night or forgetting to change the water in his drinking bowl and letting the slime grow. Small things that do not kill but add up over time, and too much time had already passed for Hope. Besides, she had a solid reason to confront him this time.

A slip of paper, as fragile as a feather, had fallen out of his coat pocket while she was brushing it. Careless to leave it there to be discovered, she thought, but hadn't he become very distracted lately? It was a hotel bill for a double room in Glen Innes when he told her he had been in Sydney. The booking clearly stated 'Mr and Mrs Scherf'. There was no other name but she would find out. She had intended to wait until morning but his sudden announcement had brought the matter to a head. He could not deny the evidence this time and she would not wait until the next day.

Her blood was up and she stood before him but seeing his angry face, she suddenly did not know how to begin.

'I've found this, Charles,' she blurted out tremulously, holding the piece of paper out to him. 'I've suspected it for a long time but now I know I was right. Who is she, Charles?'

He turned away and refused to answer.

Her whole body shook as she mustered up the strength for the final strike.

'I will find out who she is. I will, I will find out.'

He snatched the piece of paper and stared at it in dismay. Damn! If he hadn't been drunk the night he came home, he would have gotten rid of it but there it was, and standing there with the incriminating evidence between them, he was suddenly aware of the disgusting banality of the thing. A hotel receipt. Such a small thing to show up the pretentious sham of his life and turn his grand affair into a vulgar cliché.

'Where did you get this?' he demanded angrily, shocked and more than slightly rattled.

'I found it in your shirt pocket,' she confessed.

'Snooping around in my things, eh?' he retorted, seizing on a reason to deflect his guilt.

'No. I was getting the washing ready ... and it fell out,' she stammered, feeling a little less sure of herself.

'I wish you would leave my things alone,' he roared in her face. 'Leave my bloody things alone.'

The sudden pain in her eyes should have stopped him but he

had discovered his advantage.

'I think you were deliberately trying to snoop. It was a private bill and you had no right to read it. No right, do you understand?' He glared at her defiantly, feeling the old male dominance returning.

Hope hated to argue with him and now her confidence was flagging. She knew she would have to fight harder but her tender heart was not trained for such a confrontation.

'Anyway, it's not just me,' she spluttered. 'Your mother knows, too. I showed her the note and she was furious. She's been watching you for some time, Charles. She thought you had another woman, and now she knows. Now we both know.'

Suddenly she was breaking down, sobbing and pleading.

'Oh, Charles, how could you do this to me? How could you?'

So, the game was up. The two women had spied on him and had now joined forces. He hated his mother at that moment, hated her prying ways, snooping around and spying on his every move. And he hated his wife, hated her goodness, the self-righteous indignation hardening the features of her face, the judgmental face of the goody-goody. He had finally seen through her and now believed that her long-suffering and self-effacement sprang not from a sense of innate goodness but from a moral superiority bordering on smugness.

'Leave me alone.' He pushed her away. 'I'm sick of you, sick of you both. You're always trying to run my life, complaining and talking about me behind my back. Can't you see? I'm fed up with you and your smug, little face. Fed up with you and the whingeing kids. Fed up with my snooping mother. Fed up with my whole bloody life here.'

A look like murder passed over his face and she knew she had gone too far. Hope was no fighter after all; her resolve was collapsing and there was a hysterical sob in her throat. Her whole being had begun to shudder and she staggered towards him with her arms outstretched. He stepped back, shocked at the depth of her emotion and not knowing whether she was going to hit him or collapse at his feet.

'I've got to get out of here,' he growled, pushing her away and lurching towards the car.

Funny how he had lived and fought with men but now it would be the women's turn and he could not endure it.

He reached the car and began frantically working on the crank. Hope had followed him into the dark night, sobbing and clutching her cardigan around her. He pushed her away with one arm and yelled at her to go back into the house. The rift between them was opening now, like a shaft that the whole family would fall into.

The shock of the cold night air almost took her breath away, but he could hear her final threats as he jumped into the car and slammed the door shut in her face.

'I'll find out, Charles. I'll find out if it's the last thing I ever do.'

She couldn't do anything once he was in the car and speeding away from her. That was his advantage. That had always been his advantage.

Hope watched him tear down the avenue and saw his lights disappearing along the main road. She staggered back inside and went straight to check on the children. Silence, thankfully, but a silence that had to be negotiated because this was the silence of a very unfamiliar world.

With her husband gone, she felt she no longer lived in this house and everything had become a blur, like the time when she had almost drowned in a creek. In the yellow-grey stillness of the world under the water, she had experienced the same eerie sensation, the feeling that time and space had ceased to exist, that all her memories were being wiped out as she sank to the bottom and the muddy blackness began to turn off her brain. She realised with a shiver that this was the same world, a world where so many familiar things had disappeared and where each breath felt like it could be her last.

Yet, she had not died in the drowning incident and on this night, she would have to find a way to stay alive again. Hope slumped into an old armchair near the fire and stared into the flickering ashes. Nobody would ever have been able to imagine her thoughts that night and the stumbling, half-blind journey to the turning point where love became hate.

As the panic inside her began to subside, she found she could think more clearly about the terrible argument and the awful secret of her husband's betrayal. Her thoughts came in short, sharp bursts like the blasts from a trumpet. So it was true, after all. She had caught him out. He had not denied it. There was another woman. Oh, God, it was true. He was seeing another woman.

The turmoil inside was now being replaced by a deep, simmering anger and she did not regret the words she had spoken in the argument.

'I'm glad I said something,' she spoke aloud. 'I'm glad I bloody said something at last!'

It was all beginning to add up and, for the first time, she saw the shame of her wasted life, her foolish habit of giving in to everybody as if there had been some reward in being complaisant. What good did it do? What good had it ever done? To let him come and go whenever he wanted, to say nothing, to sacrifice herself, to give in to him all the time, to put up with what he did to her, even when he was drunk, and to lie there when the dreadful thing was over, terrified of getting pregnant again.

And all the time …

It was her own nature that she blamed, for it had allowed him – had allowed everybody – to treat her like a child. For that is all she was, a silly little girl. Now, a terrible certainty had begun to replace her naive trust in the world, and the certainty was poison.

She glared at the last embers in the fire, feeling that she had aged in a single night. The intensity of the anger building inside alarmed her but there was nothing that could hold back her fury now. She would take the cup of staggering, the water from the pool of Marah, and drink it all, drain every last drop until the blood in her tender heart had turned to gall.

Hope was glad that he had gone. She would lie down now and try to get some sleep before the children woke up. She knew how to survive, her old habit of lying quietly, taking the pain inside herself and waiting for it to subside.

In the years to come, people would comment on my mother's courage and will to survive after our father died. They would ask themselves how the lonely, young widow had found the strength to carry on after that miserable night and to raise four children on her own. They should have realised that hatred and bitterness can mobilise a woman as much as love, especially if the woman has been scorned.

They did not also know that my gentle mother was born under the sign of the scorpion.

*   *   *

Speeding along, Charles hit the straight section where he knew he could press the accelerator to the floor. The speed and the adrenaline made him dizzy, for he was still enervated after the terrible argument with Hope. Faster and faster he drove, wiping out his wife's words and the look on her face which he had never seen before.

Suddenly, he was in his plane again, peeling off from his squadron in a power dive. He felt the old excitement of intruder flying, that strange gap between shock and release of tension which should have been fear but translated into exhilaration. Levelling out, he sensed that he was wandering among a sea of stars, lost in a dimension of space which he alone inhabited. He clutched the steering wheel tightly as if he were holding the weight of the universe in his hands, hurtling desperately from star to star, his life like a useless treasure which he would soon have to return.

With a shock, he realised he had reached Emmaville.

Emmaville, the unholy place where all the accounts would be balanced.

He skidded the car up against the path of the pub, and almost fell inside, knocking over a bar stool. Old Lily Gurk turned around to see the cause of the commotion and came over to him straightaway.

'Gawd Struth, Charlie, you look awful. What in the hell have you been up to?'

'Just give me a drink,' he ordered, impatient for the frothy booze to calm his nerves and blot out the click in his head. He drained the glass in one gulp. 'Give me another one.'

She set the glass in front of him, but cautiously. A publican can tell when a man can't handle his drink anymore, so she refused his demand for a third.

God, he thought. That piece of paper. His wife. And worse, his mother. For this was the time when scandal in great dynasties was still to be taken very seriously. His mother would never forgive him, and though she hadn't approved of Hope in the first place, divorce was completely out of the question.

He glanced through the doorway and could just make out the familiar silhouette in the passenger seat of the car. His stomach turned over. So, there she was again. It had begun to irk him that she took the liberty of just turning up whenever she heard his car drive into town. She knew the sound of his engine and the thrust of the throttle. Who didn't?

He did not say a word to her but climbed into the driver's seat and drove out to a dark street on the outskirts of town. He parked the car and sat staring ahead with the muscles around his mouth twitching.

She saw the cold look on his face and the bloodshot flecks in his eyes. Something was really wrong, she thought. Something was really, really wrong. She lit a cigarette, drew deeply on the smoke and settled back in the seat. The red glow of the cigarette in the dark was lurid. She tossed her head back as she inhaled, then released the smoke ever so slowly through her half-parted lips, the sophisticated action of the modern woman. He used to love that action but tonight he thought it looked sinister.

'Are you going to tell me what's the matter?' she asked.

'Why do you just turn up like this?' he snapped at her. 'Just turn up and get in my car as though you owned it? You never ask!'

'Oh, is that all?' she replied rather matter-of-factly. 'It never bothered you before.'

He seemed more agitated by her curt reply so she knew she would have to come up with a better explanation. Damn it, she thought, with increasing annoyance. He had no right to speak to her this way. It wasn't the first time she had waited like this in his car outside the pub. They had known each other for months now and she was no floozy.

'Remember the times you used to wait for me outside the hospital? Remember the times you couldn't wait to pick me up? The dates you used to arrange with Barney and his wife? The trip to Glen for golf … and the drive home?'

The strangeness between them was something new and unexpected. Normally he couldn't wait to tear off her clothes and jam his hard cock into her with the force of something like desperation. Now, he was sitting fixedly on his side of the car, arguing and staring into the blackness. Something was wrong, something was terribly wrong.

'For God's sake, Charles. You look terrible. You have to tell me.'

He could see that her composure was beginning to slip. So, she could be rattled after all, the standoffish, tight-lipped matron. Well, and he was beginning to relish the perversity of his thoughts, let's see what she does with this bit of information.

'It's Hope. She knows I'm with another woman.' He almost spat the words at her. The winning argument, after all.

'God, Charles, how did she find out?'

'Don't be stupid!' he yelled. 'She's not a complete fool, you know. All those nights of getting home late, those weekends away. It was getting harder and harder to make up an excuse.'

'She's never complained before.'

She began to build her case carefully because she knew that she would need every point on her side now.

'She can't possibly suspect me. I've always been welcome in your home. She cooked some nice meals for me, had them waiting on the stove when we came in. And she always liked the presents I bought for the kids. She seemed to think that we were all just friends.'

'It's more than that,' he groaned. 'She found the receipt for the hotel in Glen in my coat pocket. Now my mother knows as well. Oh, God.'

He let his face fall into his hands and slumped onto the steering wheel.

She wanted to say, 'You bloody fool. How could you have been so careless?' But when he finally looked up at her, she could have cried. His once handsome face had become pale and blotchy, the daredevil grin was a twisted gash of pain. She thought of the newspaper cuttings she had seen of him while he was away at the war, a young man of adventure with the dashing looks of a hero. When he came home, his eyes had lost their faraway look and he bore the battle-weary mask of the soldier. A secret anguish seemed to hang around his slender frame, and at thirty-two, he looked as if he were shouldering the weight of the whole world.

Tonight, his whole body seemed to be collapsing. It was freezing cold outside but beads of sweat had broken out on his face. His hands were shaking and his breath was coming out in short gasps.

She had heard about soldiers who returned from war wounded but not in the physical sense; instead, their symptoms were similar to those previously associated with hysterical women. What did they call it? A strange French phrase. *Crise de nerfs.* She personally agreed that this kind of collapse in a man was really some sort of weakness, a sign of poor morale or defective training but it couldn't possibly apply to Charles because Charles was one of the bravest men she had ever met. At any rate, the studies were only new – and French, to boot. She believed more readily in self-discipline and control; after all, he'd been a squadron leader in charge of other men. Surely he could control himself now. One just had to make the effort.

'Come on, Charles. Pull yourself together, for Christ's sake.' She spoke to him as if she were giving an order to a sick man. She was the matron of the hospital, after all, and she hadn't reached this position by going soft every time a patient complained of pain.

'Look,' she continued, 'you have to calm down. Just go home and tell Hope not to worry. Say you're sorry. Tell her you had trouble with the car that weekend and we had to stay in Glen until it was fixed. She will get over it in a few days and everything will be alright. Hope doesn't like a fuss.'

Charles stared into the darkness, like a man in a fog searching desperately for some way to get back on track.

'I'm lost,' he murmured and a terrible groan escaped from his mouth.

She tried to touch him but he pushed her away.

'Don't you understand? It's gone too far! I've made a mess of everything.'

He was floundering now, tripping and stumbling on a course he could no longer correct. How had he come to this? He had been faithful to his wife at first but what he had seen and done in the war had destroyed his moral compass and now there was nothing to measure himself against. Since his return, every act he committed, good or bad, had seemed equal and one form of love had become as good as another.

What the heck, he had thought when they first crossed the line, and hadn't she teased and egged him on from the very beginning, leaning close and touching his arm when she laughed and looking boldly, scornfully into his eyes when he lit her cigarette? Well, he had grown tired of her taunting him and had finally showed her what a man could do, ramming his cock into her over and over until she lay in his arms without speaking. After that night, they met quite frequently, taking more and more risks and planning weekends away together. Now she had become a nuisance and he was beginning to hate the very thing he needed from her and the hold she thought she had over him.

The dreadful argument with his wife had jolted him into a prior reality, a state of innocence where meaning and faith and ethics once existed. She had forced him to face the truth and his mind was reeling with the memories he had once cherished, a picture of the young girl he had married, the flush on her face when he first came to her house and caught her with her hands inside a dead chicken, drifts of feathers clinging to her face and arms, blood oozing between her fingers. He remembered, before the children arrived, the vivacious, small, windswept figure as she rode her pony full-pelt across the paddocks to collect the mail. How could he forget the time they had lain together under a tree in the afternoon light and he had stolen what he should have waited for?

What had happened to the little world they had once created? What had happened to his family and his dear wife, his Bunny? Suddenly they seemed to be the only thing that mattered and this woman beside him was a cheap hussy.

There was nothing magnificent or special about their sordid little affair. He'd behaved like a savage child, doing what he wanted to, chasing the next thrill, grasping the forbidden pleasure. Yes, he'd taken her, this other woman, taken her over and over, taken her brutally, shoving into her his disappointment and his broken wings. Now the thought of losing his wife filled him with panic and the worst thing was to realise that he had wasted his time on a path of no value.

A desperate hope formed in his heart. He looked across at Joyce and she saw the plea in his face.

'We've got to end it now. Hope won't rest until she finds out who the other woman is. I can't be involved in the scandal. It will kill my mother.'

Joyce sat next to him, shocked at the finality of his words, and felt the cold seep into her bones. The set look on his face disturbed her and she felt the bonds between them unravelling. She did not know this new Charles and she was not prepared for this rejection. Night after night she had listened for his car and rushed out to meet him as soon as he reached the town. Even in the afternoon, when he was still in his work clothes, she would feel his hard, sweaty body against her, urging her to break every rule for their pleasure. She relished every instance of their betrayal, taking more and more risks to please him until she had closed the gap on the wife, and in the end she had loved him.

'Well, really, darling,' she retorted, 'it's not as simple as all that. I've put my reputation on the line for you as well. You can't just walk away. Besides, I love you.'

He turned away and stared grimly out into the frosty night. She blew out a mouthful of smoke and stared at him, coldly studying his features. He was just a boy, after all, a wild, uncouth boy. She was the older one, the one in charge. She could easily take him in hand again.

'Look here, Charles. I think that you're letting things get out of hand. Hope will calm down. Just go back home and say you're sorry. Act normal and in a few days, she'll be over it. I know Hope. She'll do anything to keep the peace.'

Joyce stared at him determinedly, hoping to bring some order into the pit he was digging for both of them. She had handled crazy men before, men who had been rushed to hospital after a gruesome farm accident, demented men with a desperate plea for life in their wild eyes. She knew how to settle them down with her calm, precise commands, her starched promise of a reprieve from their agony if they did exactly what she ordered. Deep down, she despised them because they were all weak underneath and blubbered like a baby when they were hurt. She just needed to take control of the situation again.

Confidently, she placed her cool hand on his forehead as if to test his temperature. His face was terrible and he knocked her hand away, every muscle in his body working to shut her out now. He looked at her as if seeing her for the first time, the old spinster with the thin face, hard body and cropped black hair. The stuck-up old sheila the guys in the bar used to laugh at behind his back, her professional demeanour, her high and mighty air covering a mean and covetous nature, an avid go-getter who wanted a hard, working man's cock in the back seat of a car as much as any bitch on heat. It was exciting at first, but he grew to resent her and now she was here, in his car, telling him how to run his life.

In that moment, he loathed her.

'I don't want to see you anymore. I'm going back to my dear wife and there's not a damn thing you can do about it.'

There was a finality in his voice which told her he meant it.

So, the showdown had begun. She knew now that she would have to fight with different weapons. It wasn't easy to stack up against the good wife, four children and the Scherf name in the district. She knew that it would come to this one day and she knew that the course she had steered him upon had damned her own soul as well. He was not going to get away with it.

'You won't walk away so easily,' she hurled the words at him. 'I'll go to Hope. I'll tell her everything. I'll tell her about those weekends, how you lied and sneaked away with me while she was stuck at home with the kids. I'll tell her about all those weeks when you said you were at the wool sales. And I'll even tell her about the sleeping tablets I slipped her after Colleen was born so that she wouldn't hear your car!'

'You wouldn't!' he screamed back at her. 'You wouldn't dare tell her that.'

'Well, you better think again about getting rid of me,' she threatened, 'because I'll never let you go. I love you too, you know. Oh, God help me, Charles. I love you, too.'

She was fighting him now, flinging her tense body at him, clawing at his face and his chest, moaning like an animal.

This was the last straw. He could feel her foul woman's desire all over him and the smell was suffocating, dragging him down and consuming him. Repulsed, he pushed her away, ramming his hand into her face, groping for the car door and trying to shove her outside. They writhed in the passion of their hate, shoving and punching each other, clinging together like two exhausted boxers in the final round. His head was bursting and he could not contain the images in his mind any longer, the clicking noise and something else driving him on towards a final act.

Outside, the trees had begun to sway and moan. In the spaces between them, three vile shadows were forming and the abhorred shears were glistening in the night. An ancient order had begun to establish itself and for those who had come under its sway, there was no escape.

The three sisters assembled now to take up their appointed positions; Clotho with her dreaded spindle and Lachesis with her thread, then Atropos, the smallest of the trio but the one who can never be turned away. She lifted her razor-sharp shears and in a second, cut the thread.

He felt the stab in his heart. Unable to breathe, he struggled to put down the window and take in a few gasps of cold air. Exhausted, she sat there trembling in the cold while his breathing became more regular. When he turned to face her, it was the dark stranger who spoke with the sharp thrill of triumph. There were no more questions to ask himself and nothing more to say to her; he had found the perfect solution.

'I'll kill myself and kill you, too!' he screamed and revved the car engine.

The car took off with a full throttle blast, wheels spinning, stones splattering. He kept his foot jammed on the accelerator and relished the surge of power as they roared down the road into the tunnel of darkness. He belonged to the machine now, his hands glued to the wheel, his shoulders moulded to the curve of the seat, his mind at one with the only thing that mattered: speed. All he had to do was to keep his foot on the pedal and it would soon be all over.

'You'll do,' he thought he heard his old Sergeant saying.

She lurched all over the speeding car, grabbing at his hands on the wheel and screaming at the top of her voice. Suddenly her foot knocked against something lying on the floor of the car.

Yes. Quickly. She must try to stop him. Stop him. Oh, Charles.

Everything was moving so fast. She managed to grab the spanner and swing it blindly in the direction of his head, bashing it desperately into his skull as the car failed to take a sharp bend, skidded off the road and headed towards a tree. The tree absorbed the shattering collision for a moment, stood erect in the dark, then in one agonising shudder, split completely in half. The bolts, valves, tubes, wires, metal pieces, all the apparatus of motion had come to a steaming halt.

A neighbour, who had heard the screams and the car accelerating, rushed out to the scene of carnage and managed to drag open the smashed door. He reeled at the sight of the mangled bodies and almost fainted with shock when he recognised Charles. He caught sight of the blood-stained spanner and, in the moment of horror, all he could think of was to quickly dispose of it before the police arrived.

The woman was unconscious but alive. In the following weeks she recovered sufficiently to receive a visit from Hope Scherf, then she disappeared from Emmaville forever.

Parts of the shattered metal had penetrated Charles' body and there were deep gashes in his skull, bones protruding from his right arm and blood pouring from wounds all over his body.

He was rushed to hospital but his injuries were too severe to save him.

There was no police investigation into the accident.

337

CHAPTER 4

THE AFTERMATH

The war ended in 1945 with so much destruction of lives and land. The warriors came home but for some, there was no return.

Where are the true fathers of the land?

They have all gone now – all those great, wild men who lived so extravagantly and died so ignominiously. It would seem that there is some kind of symmetry of divine intent, some fascinating, confounding principle of contraries which see men, whose prowess has enabled them to win great victories in life, die inglorious deaths.

Sir Charles Portal Marshal of the Royal Airforce was created Baron Portal of Hungerford in 1945 and then 1st Viscount Portal of Hungerford in 1946. His only son died at birth and, as there were no male heirs, the viscountcy died with him. His elder daughter, Rosemary, succeeded in the barony according to a special remainder but as Rosemary remained unmarried and without issue, the baronetcy became extinct in 1990.

Sir Trafford Leigh-Mallory, Air Chief Marshall, Battle of Britain and Allied Invasion of Normandy was killed in 1944 in a plane crash in a remote area of the French Alps. A court of enquiry found the accident to be a consequence of bad weather and Leigh-Mallory's insistence that the flight proceed in such poor conditions, against the advice of his crew. All members aboard were killed, including his wife. The bodies were found by a peasant seven months later and were buried on a remote hillside near the crash site. On a small backroad near the tiny village of Allermont, there is a dusty shop with a small front window displaying a fragment of a plane and a faded article about the great English war leader who died obscurely in the frozen French crevasses.

Squadron Leader Charles Curnow Scherf, Ace Fighter Pilot WWII, was killed in a car accident in a remote town of NSW that nobody knows. His medals, logbook and incidental items were auctioned off to a collector of Second World War memorabilia, a stranger who lives in Sydney and has remained anonymous. There is no monument to his deeds and he has passed into Australian history unknown and unrecognised.

We, the children of his enormous recklessness, were disinherited and left to fend for ourselves, to wander in the ashes of the empty treasure house like a miner whose claim has been stolen.

I, his daughter, have lived so long without him that over the years his memory has faded. All the narratives and ways of looking at people and human personality have also changed but I try to remember some of the fine sentiments and good old stories which used to keep him alive in my mind. Unfortunately, the words have been lost in this new world and they can no longer sing him back to me. He has become a lost moment of origin which I have endlessly tried to retrieve but never recovered.

A ghostly archive.

A distance without remedy.

If you are passing through Emmaville and happen to strike up a conversation with a few old codgers in a pub, they will probably tell you that their grandfathers sometimes spoke about the great Charlie Scherf who flew his plane sideways up the avenue of Big Ben. They will chuckle when they tell you that he had a mistress but they will look at you curiously if you talk about me, for there was never a mention of any children.

History is a jealous god who has a way of selecting his own favourites, eliminating certain details and privileging others. My father has emerged in the folklore of the district as the solitary, romantic hero and my separation from him is now complete.

Big Ben, the family estate of the Scherfs, was eventually sold to a mining company, the great pines were cut down and made into pencils, the cottage was burnt down, the manor house sold, re-shaped and re-sold. I think of the house, but when I say house, I say father and when I say father, I say house. Big Ben. House of the lovely, pale memories of my childhood. It was here that I started to grow and form my dreams but it was the place that belonged to my father and when he died, his death excluded me from this house forever. I have tried to find other places but all the roads I have ever chosen have only led me back to the graveyard of my past, unable to repair the lost foundation but trapped forever inside its longing.

And I? I am an old woman now, old enough to be the mother of my father who will remain young forever. It is a strange thought. Years have passed since my breakdown and I have settled into a kind of uneasy peace. I think about my struggles, trying to connect the life of the past that existed with my father to the life of the present when he slipped away. It was an absorbing task and since I could never make the connection, I have never arrived at my own life. I have lived in an interminable act of self-finding.

It is hard to talk about the higher road, that unruly yet divine path that can lead us to forgive our fathers, those fugitive figures so yearned after, yet so often characterised by absence. In this journey towards forgiveness, I have remained inert and silent but my stillness is not a sensation of loss when time is frozen and language recedes. My stillness is not emptiness; it is a feeling that is waiting, waiting for the right words to be created.

And there is something else which madness and rage could not efface.

For there was love ... after all.

The End

There is a small church and a medical building on the outskirts of Uganda. It is run by a brave African minister who has pledged his life to helping the victims of witch doctors. The children's skulls are slashed with a machete and a small piece of their brain removed without killing them. They are left paralysed and disabled. The clinic assists these children to get medical assistance in Uganda and Australia.

There is a plaque on the wall which pays tribute to a man whose medals, sold at auction for a very large price, paid for the clinic to be finished. The money from the sale was donated to the children of Uganda by his daughter, Rosemary.

The inscription reads:

In memory of Squadron Leader Charles Curnow Scherf D.S.O., D.F.C. and bar GM. RAAF RAF RCAF

'He fought, he died that the children of the world may live'